A PENGUIN MYSTERY

AMBROSE BIERCE AND THE DEATH OF KINGS

Oakley Hall is the author of more than twenty works of fiction, including *The Downhill Racers, Warlock, Separations,* and his highly acclaimed *Ambrose Bierce and the Queen of Spades.* Director of the Programs in Writing at the University of California at Irvine for more than twenty years, Hall is also the General Director of the Squaw Valley Community of Writers. In 1998, he received a Pen Center USA West Award of Honor for a lifetime of literary achievement. He lives in San Francisco.

AMBROSE BIERCE
AND THE
DEATH OF KINGS

OAKLEY HALL

PENGUIN BOOKS

PENGUIN BOOKS
Published by the Penguin Group
Penguin Putnam Inc., 375 Hudson Street,
New York, New York 10014, U.S.A.
Penguin Books Ltd, 80 Strand,
London WC2R 0RL, England
Penguin Books Australia Ltd, 250 Camberwell Road,
Camberwell, Victoria 3124, Australia
Penguin Books Canada Ltd, 10 Alcorn Avenue,
Toronto, Ontario, Canada M4V 3B2
Penguin Books India (P) Ltd, 11 Community Centre,
Panchsheel Park, New Delhi–110 017, India
Penguin Books (N.Z.) Ltd, Cnr Rosedale and Airborne Roads,
Albany, Auckland, New Zealand
Penguin Books (South Africa) (Pty) Ltd, 24 Sturdee Avenue,
Rosebank, Johannesburg 2196, South Africa

Penguin Books Ltd, Registered Offices:
Harmondsworth, Middlesex, England

First published in the United States of America by Viking Penguin,
a member of Penguin Putnam Inc. 2001
Published in Penguin Books 2002

10 9 8 7 6 5 4 3 2 1

THE LIBRARY OF CONGRESS HAS CATALOGED
THE HARDCOVER EDITION AS FOLLOWS:
Hall, Oakley M.
Ambrose Bierce and the death of kings / Oakley Hall.
p.   cm.
ISBN 0-670-03007-4 (hc.)
ISBN 0 14 20.0133 3 (pbk.)
1. Bierce, Ambrose, 1842–1914?—Fiction.
2. Journalists—Fiction. 3. Hawaii—Fiction. I. Title.
PS3558.A373 A8   2001
813'.54—dc21   2001017990

Printed in the United States of America
Set in Granjon with OPTI Lagoon Light
Designed by Carla Bolte

CHAPTER 1

BELLADONNA, n. In Italian a beautiful lady; in English a deadly poison.
A striking example of the essential identity of the two tongues.
— *The Devil's Dictionary*

DECEMBER, 1890

Ambrose Bierce was at the height of his powers and influence at the time of the tragic Hawaiian affair, with his weekly newspaper column and his nationally admired short stories of supernatural events and the Civil War. He was a prince of San Francisco. Headwaiters sprang to his attention, bartenders bustled to prepare his favorite restorative, Pacific Heights matrons and pretty young poetesses vied for his favors. In his dealings with the opposite gender his motto was When falling into a woman's arms be careful not to fall into her hands.

He was described by Gertrude Atherton at about this time as "a tall man, very thin and closely knit, with sandy graying hair, a bristling mustache, beetling brows over frowning eyes, good features and beautiful hands." Atherton had had an unhappy meeting with him. A successful young California novelist with a good figure and a magnificent head of blond hair, she had come to visit the famous man in Sunol, where he was rusticating because of an attack of asthma.

He told her that the covers of her last novel were too far apart, and that the genre was an inferior literary form. She responded that story writers were simply incapable of writing novels, and laughed triumphantly when she rebuffed his attempt to kiss her beside a pigsty. He grumbled that she had ruined his day.

That was Bad Bierce.

Good Bierce was her correspondent for twenty years, loyally praising her work in print and proffering professional advice. He also got her a job as a feminist columnist on the *Examiner.*

Bad Bierce was noisily scornful of the opposite sex: "Intellectually woman is as inferior to man as she is physically . . . she hasn't any thinker." But Good Bierce spent hours editing and emendating the verse his flock of not very talented young poetesses brought him.

———

He was the most brilliant satirist in the country, maybe in the world, maybe since Voltaire, but at this particular time he had no enemies worthy of his steel. In the past, civic and state corruption, especially the Southern Pacific Railroad and Collis B. Huntington, had challenged his indignations. When his resources were not fully engaged his column was reduced to scolding poets and evangelical ministers, "stretching butterflies on the rack," as was said of him.

He was, just now, in a low ebb of outrage.

I was employed by the *Chronicle*, which was more respectable than Willie Hearst's *Examiner*, where Bierce's "Prattle" appeared in the Sunday edition.

He had been my journalistic mentor, and he did not hesitate to criticize my published work. For instance, he disapproved of a piece on the Chinese slave girls that I had published in the *Atlantic*: "Your writing is meritorious, Tom, but I perceive that your motives are wrong," he told me. "You should write for the love of art rather than the purpose of helping repair God's botchwork world."

I was less interested in success in "art" than I was in helping to liberate the slave girls.

We had not seen as much of each other lately as we had when we were a team of detectives solving the infamous San Francisco playing-card murders. Bierce was separated from his wife and family, and his eldest son Day was a suicide in a love triangle so banal I knew the lack of common dignity must have struck Bierce almost as hard as the personal loss. I had offered him condolences over his tragedy, and he returned the favor over my own.

———

Before the princess disappeared, before the royal counsellor was murdered and the king died at the Palace Hotel, I met my true love, the Hawaiian beauty Miss Haunani Brown.

I was writing a magazine piece on San Francisco poets, especially Edward Berowne, who was being honored just then, and had called on him at his fussily fancy little house on Telegraph Hill that gazed north toward Alcatraz Island and the Marin hills. I did not know that his niece was visiting from Hawaii.

Berowne was a fancy form of Brown, as the poet would be the first to laughingly tell you. His poetry and stories were published in the *California Monthly*, of which he was the editor.

Seated on his veranda, we were served tea by his houseboy, Chang.

Berowne's thinning hair was so neatly brushed, the part looked like a chalk line. He had a large curved nose and profile, so that his face, framed by bushy burnsides, resembled that of a benevolent tortoise. He gleamed top and bottom, pomaded hair and shiny boots.

"The British have honored our P-p-poet of the Sierras, Joaquin Miller!" he said, waving his hands, palms up, as though presenting a prize. He went on, speaking at some length about Charles Warren Stoddard, whom he claimed to love dearly but clearly didn't like. His comments on his fellow poets always contained a barb.

"You must meet my niece, Thomas," he said, in a change of subject. "She arrived from the Islands two days ago. This handsome young lady must b-b-be p-p-provided with p-p-proper admirers. Young men of style and fortune!" He had a slight stammer which I had come to realize he employed to capture the attention of his auditors.

"Well, that is not me, I'm afraid."

"Ha, ha!" he said. "She is half Hawaiian, you understand, *alii*, of course."

I didn't yet know what the word "alii" meant.

"It refers to Hawaiian nobility, Thomas. The Hawaiians had a caste system the B-b-british understood full well! The *alii* were—are—the chiefs, chiefesses, and minor chieftans. There are p-p-princes and p-p-princesses as well. The nobles are larger in size, handsomer, and more intelligent than the lower classes of natives." He offered up his hands.

I saw a woman standing in the interior shadows. She came out onto the veranda, a tall figure proudly erect, a large young lady with a noble head of brown hair which she wore swept up as though to make herself appear even taller. Her gray silk gown was much embroidered and befrogged. She bowed her head to kiss her uncle's cheek while he beamed at her.

Startlingly blue eyes in a golden-brown complexion examined me as I rose to greet her. Her face was at once tense, amused, and bold. Her color made her look as though she were illuminated from within.

Introductions were made. This was Miss Haunani Brown.

She had an impressive figure, deep-breasted, narrow-waisted, full-hipped. She must have stood six feet tall! One eyebrow was cocked a quarter-inch higher than the other in what seemed to me to be a mocking of her role in her uncle's house, in San Francisco.

I asked if she would change her name to Berowne to conform with her uncle's.

"Uncle hopes it will be changed to something else entirely, Mr. Redmond," she said. She had a warm contralto voice.

"That is simply not true, my dear. I ab-b-bsolutely decline the role of matchmaker!"

He winked at me.

He brought up the subject of the Hawaiian king, who was presently traveling in southern California.

"David Kalakaua is fond of travel," Miss Brown said. She had seated herself with one arm lying along the railing. Her tan hand with its tapered fingers and shiny nails was so perfectly formed it made the backs of my legs ache.

"And are you fond of travel, Miss Brown?"

"I am very new at it," she said.

Her uncle gazed at her as though he found her appearance fascinating. I found her fascinating also, with her golden skin, her lighter hair, her still lighter eyes with their expression of mischief.

"And you are a journalist, Mr. Redmond?"

I responded that I was a journalist.

"And I am to look for your writings in the *Chronicle* newspaper?"

That was also correct. "Has your uncle been exposing you to the sights of our city?" I asked.

"Yes, he has," Miss Brown said, with an arrogant cock of her head. "But he would be pleased if others would relieve his responsibilities."

And so it was arranged that I would escort Miss Brown to the Cliff House for luncheon on Saturday.

———

When I returned to my rooms Signora Sotopietro was singing. She had been a famous diva, who now, fat and infirm, was living out her life in quarters adjoining mine. Her voice was still the voice of an angel, until it splintered into coughing.

After my wife's death I had moved from our cottage in Oakland to these rooms in San Francisco. When my neighbor's voice singing "Caro Nome" from *Rigoletto* sounded through the thin walls, sometimes I would go out, and sometimes stay in and sob over my loss.

I ate most of my dinners, alone, in Papa Franco's Italian Restaurant around the corner. There I could wind a yard of tagliarini around my fork while drinking red wine and reading a novel propped against the bottle. Tonight I stayed in, gripping my arms around my chest and luxuriating in grief while that angelic voice accompanied by her piano filled my heart.

The coughing fit inevitably came, and the song ceased, with a few notes more on the piano before silence.

———

On a sunny Saturday morning I transported Miss Brown to the Cliff House in a rented rig. There were many fine turnouts in the park, buggies and carriages moving slowly through congested crossroads. Miss Brown, who became Haunani to my Tom, was amazed at this traffic, the splendid matched pairs, the fancily dressed gentlemen and women in the buggies and carriages, the horsemen, the bicyclists by the dozen, the pedestrians in twosomes and groups. The sun flashed off glossy equine haunches and varnished wood. Tree shadows striped the tan earth of the roadway.

Haunani was outfitted in a jacket and skirt of changeable silk, and a white jabot that set off her complexion spectacularly.

She was an inch taller than I even without her feathered hat. I understood that she carried her head high not in arrogance but because of the rude stares at her size and exotic coloring. At lunch we gazed out at the seals on their wave-slashed rocks.

She was unimpressed by the gray slice of ocean beyond the rocks. Hawaii's Pacific was blue.

She could be one moment prickly and the next physically friendly, squeezing my arm when she was amused, or hitting my shoulder with her brown fist. She pushed aside my hand that had been held up to assist her to a seat for the ride back to the City.

In the buggy she sat upright and queenly, gloved hands clasped together at her waist.

"You must not be sensitive to people's stares," I told her. "You are a beautiful young woman."

She muttered something in the Hawaiian language. Then she smiled at me brilliantly. "Thank you!"

I enquired about her impressions of the young bachelors of San Francisco who had been provided by her uncle. I was able to joke with her about Berowne's role as matchmaker.

"These society swells are a flimsy lot," she said.

"Flimsy?"

"No muscle. You have some muscle," she added.

I attended a gymnasium on Kearny Street where I performed exercises with Indian clubs and belabored a striking bag.

"I do not admire young gentlemen that I could take down in a wrestle," she said, chin raised scornfully.

"You are very strong?" I asked, although it was clear that she was.

She grinned at me and made muscle-flexing gestures. "Strong and beautiful," she said, adding in pidgin, "You no mess wid me, *haole*!"

I said I wouldn't dare to mess with her.

"Unless I tell you to," she said.

Driving slowly homeward through the park, she told me something of herself. Her Hawaiian mother had died when she was a baby; she had been raised by her father, William Brown, and her uncle—then still plain Edward Brown—who were descended from a proud Virginia family. They had owned a plantation on the Island of Maui. When she was eleven her father's illness caused him to sell the plantation and move to Honolulu, where the two of them had been taken in by the sugar magnate Silas Underwood in his mansion.

She was sent to boarding school with other *alii* children, where she had been one of the *hapahaoles*.

As such she had been scorned by certain blood Hawaiians who played a role at the court, and, I came to understand, was sensitive about her color because some of the European and American society scorned Hawaiians.

"I know my dear uncle worries about my color," she said. "I know he loves me, but after all I am brown not white. He tells a story of a black person who was uppity with him, and how he put that person in his place. He does not remember that I am a brown-skin person when he tells me that story."

"I think every Southern man has such a story to tell," I said.

"He worries that his grand friends will scorn me."

I said when she married the son of a Comstock or railroad millionaire in the grandest wedding San Francisco had ever seen, no one would dare scorn her.

She gave me her self-deprecating, malicious grin.

Back in the City she wanted to see where I lived.

———

Fortunately Mrs. Gray had cleaned and straightened my rooms on Friday. Haunani stood gazing out the bay window down Sacramento Street. Then with a dramatic motion she swung around, stripped off her hat and almost flung herself down on the sofa, where one side of her face caught the dusty sunlight coming through the net curtains while her other cheek was in shadow. Like the two races of her own self, I thought.

Gazing at me with her brilliant eyes, she said, "Uncle tells me your wife has recently passed away."

Just the word made my throat constrict. I seated myself facing her. "That is true."

"Tell me about it, please." It was as though since she had told her story, I must repay with my own.

"Our child was stillborn," I said. "She was unable to recover from the tragedy."

"I am so sorry," Haunani said. "It is the curse on the Hawaiian race also. The stillborn children. So many stillborn *keikes*!"

I heard the first notes of "Caro Nome" from the piano next door.

"She became very wild," I heard myself say. "She cursed everything, although she hardly knew how to curse. She— flung herself about. It became clear that she would not recover. There was a decline of some months before she died."

"I believe that is how my mother died," Haunani said, looking at her hands knitted together on her knee. "What was her name, please?"

"Catherine."

"What a pretty name."

"Yes."

Signora Sotopietro began to sing, her voice low at first, then more loudly. "What is that?" Haunani wanted to know.

"It is Signora Sotopietro next door."

"What a lovely voice!"

"Yes," I said.

"You are a Catholic by religion, Uncle says."

"Yes."

"In my religion it is already decided who will go to heaven and who will not," Haunani said in a hard voice. "It is no matter whether you are good or bad! *Maikai!* I will not go to heaven."

"Why?" I said.

"Heaven is for *haoles*."

"That is not true, my dear Haunani."

"That is my belief, my dear Tom."

I had not looked up at her for some time because my eyes had misted from the music that pervaded the room, filled it, overflowed. When I glanced at Haunani again she had removed her jacket. Her arms were round and golden.

"You are weeping," she whispered. "Come!"

I rose with difficulty and went to kneel before her. She took my face in her two hands and pressed it to her bosom. *"Aloha waiu,"* she whispered.

Signora Sotopietro's voice ceased in coughing, with those last few sad notes from the piano.

———

Later Haunani announced that she was hungry, and I went out to the little stand on Powell Street for roasted chestnuts and opened a bottle of Veuve Cliquot. It was something that Catherine and I had done when celebration was called for.

———

The next day I encountered my neighbor on the stairs, where, panting, she rested her weight on the railing. The yellowish locks of her wig were piled on her head, her face was tragically rouged and powdered, with raccoon patches beneath her eyes that could not be concealed by powder. Her bulk was hidden beneath a fine black scarf embroidered with roses, with which she had wrapped her bosom and shoulders. A hand crowded with sparkling rings clutched the stair rail.

"Good evening, Signora," I said.

"Good evening, young sir," she replied in her good English, for she could not remember my name.

I told her that I had very much enjoyed her singing last night, and she thanked me graciously.

———

In January King Kalakaua was stricken ill in Santa Barbara and transported to San Francisco, it appeared, to die.

He lay in the Royal Suite of the Palace Hotel, attended by aides, courtiers, counsellors, petitioners, creditors, and the finest San Francisco doctors. He had suffered a stroke, had been diagnosed with Bright's disease, and his kidneys were failing. On his deathbed he had not yet named his successor.

———

"David Kalakaua has many faults," Haunani said, reclining in my easy chair on one of her visits to me. "But he is loved by his subjects. Liliuokalani—his sister—is not loved so much."

"Is she his heir?"

"Unless he names someone else."

"Can he do that?"

"He is the king," Haunani said. "The Mainland was bad for him. Hawaiians should remain in Hawaii."

"You didn't."

"I have good reason, my dear Tom."

I thought then that her good reason might not be merely the announced one of finding an appropriate husband.

The San Francisco newspapers followed the Merrie Monarch's decline. There was some interest in his little kingdom of half a dozen islands in the Pacific Ocean. I myself had become more interested in Hawaiian affairs.

Fortunes were being made by the owners and proprietors of the sugar plantations there. The most powerful of these was a descendant of the missionaries named Silas Underwood, who was often referred to as "Uncle Sugar." A cartoon in the satirical newspaper, the *Wasp*, depicted him as an octopus spreading its arms over islands in a blue sea with tentacles grasping fasces of sugarcane. Uncle Sugar was known to have supported the spendthrift and debt-ridden monarchy out of his own pocket for years.

Haunani referred to him as Uncle Silas, for she had been raised to young womanhood in his mansion in Honolulu called *Hale Nuuanu*.

CHAPTER 2

MONDAY, JANUARY 12, 1891

With what must be the most sensitive ears in the state, my father had heard in Sacramento that his son was squiring a young Hawaiian lady in San Francisco.

We were having our bimonthly dinner at Malvolio's, on Kearny Street.

The Gent was an authority on the Kingdom of Hawaii, as with all things connected with the Southern Pacific Railroad, whose faithful servant he was. He had spent time in the Islands tending to seaborn SP business. The railroad monopoly encompassed everything to do with transportation and the State of California.

"Those poor people," he said, leaning on the gleaming white tablecloth and shaking his big head sadly. "Died off by the thousands from white-man disease. Consumption, syphilis, measles. Just about the worst disease they had was missionaries from New England. Protestants! You see photographs of these birds, and their ladies, too. They have got no-lip mouths. Not a lip among 'em! Puritans from New England. Before they came Hawaiians had had an easygoing good time of it, tended their taro patch, raised a pig or two, danced, drank their native popskull.

"Imagine those first whalers sailing into Lahaina Roads, tacking past the beautiful wahines riding their surfboards, hair streaming out, naked as snakes!"

He frowned at me. "I've admired some of those big girls myself, son. This lady's *hapahaole*, you say?"

"You were talking about the missionaries."

Nodding, he said, "Shiploads of Calvinist joy-killers. They say those missionaries coming out of Salem were constipated the whole time it took around the horn to Hawaii. And when they struck land they took it out on the poor Kanak.

"Going to end up taking their pretty islands right away from them, too."

"Will they?"

"They surely will. Those missionaries turned into business-men, sugarcane planters, factors, merchants. Those birds won't rest a minute until they've seen Hawaii annexed to the U. S. of A."

Steaming platters of clams, oysters, and mussels arrived, and my father stuffed a corner of his napkin into his collar and arrayed the rest over his lap. "Dig in, my boy."

We dug in.

"Coolies!" my father said in a lull in the ingestion, shaking his head. "Hawaiian natives wouldn't do that hard low-pay canefield work, so the sugar planters brought in coolies to work the fields. By the thousand. The Chinese disease came with 'em. Leprosy! Kalaupapa!"

"What's Kalaupapa?" I asked.

"It's a peninsula off the Island of Molokai that's cut off

from the rest of the island by a mountain wall. Where they dump the lepers. Like a garbage dump.

"Missionaries say leprosy's a disease like syphilis," my father continued. "That comes from fornication which the missionaries told the natives they was hellfire-bound because of it. Others think leprosy's just another disease the Hawaiians never had before so it went through them like piss through a funnel."

"Those would be Hawaiian field workers shipped off to Molokai to die," I said. "Not the *alii.*"

"Doesn't matter if you are nobles or not, how much money you have, what connections. Lepers go to the Kalaupapa hell-pit sure as certain. There was a Prince Peter died on Kalaupapa! And let me tell you who it is on Molokai caring for those poor damned lepers. It is not Protestants, it is RC!"

And he went on to enquire about my religious duties like a parent enquiring about the state of a child's bowels.

"What's 'preterition'?" I asked. It was a word Haunani had used.

"Means passed over. There's the elect that's headed for heaven, and the reprobate that ain't. And preterition is the separation into sheep and goats."

I shook my head.

"If ever," my father said, "a man was to worry about some theological nonsense in the Roman Catholic Church, he has only to look in on the Protestants."

Was preterition a matter Protestant children talked over among themselves? How did you know? Some check mark of yes or no in letters of fire on your forehead?

And on top of the eternal punishment of having the missionaries, there were also Pele and the evil *kahunas*, whom Haunani had described to me in terms of awe.

The Gent had ordered a second bottle of red. He began to

tell me about the beautiful hula girl with whom he had become acquainted on Oahu. There was some embarrassing description. He caught himself, fell silent and bent to his repast again.

"It is like railroad funds, you see," he said when he surfaced.

"What is, Pa?"

"Preterition. Whether you receive the heavenly grace of the SP dollar or not."

"Well, sir, you do," I said.

"Elect!" my father said. His cheeks had reddened with some emotion. "Chosen! My boy," he said, leaning conspiratorially forward toward me. "I parcel out the railroad dollar in the legislature. Mr. Collis B. Huntington has put it most clearly, you see. He wishes to reward those who agree with him, and not reward those that don't. Anything wrong with that reasoning, my boy?"

"Only with the practice," I said.

His laugh cocked the heads of the feeders at the nearby tables. He said loudly, "There is nothing cheaper to buy than a politician!"

It seemed to me that he should not talk this way in public. The Railroad had ears. He should not even be thinking this way, even though any change of heart on his part was to the good.

He grasped a fork in one hand, a knife in the other, and held them upright before him like the guardians at the gate. I knew what he was going to recite. I had heard him recite it before, red-faced and inebriate, and loud:

I'VE LABORED LONG AND HARD FOR BREAD,
FOR HONOR AND FOR RICHES,
BUT ON MY CORNS TOO LONG YOU'VE TREAD,
YOU FINE-HAIRED SONS OF BITCHES!

People near us turned to glare. Malvolio himself was moving toward us, stern-faced, napkin held between his hands as though to stifle my father with it. But the Gent subsided, and took another sip of wine; the incident was over.

He asked about my friend Ambrose Bierce, Bitter Bierce, of whom he heartily disapproved, and seemed pleased when I said I hadn't seen Bierce for some weeks.

———

I hadn't been home in the early dark more than fifteen minutes when there was a knock on my door, and Miss Haunani Brown paraded inside in her finery, snatched off her hat and sailed it onto the table, and flung herself into my arms. She had spent the afternoon with a Nob Hill fellow, and had had a dreary time of it. The young blades of San Francisco, mobilized by her uncle, entertained her during the days, but many nights it was Tom Redmond she turned to.

———

The most exotic woman I had ever known lay in my bed beside me, smiling, showing a line of gleaming teeth like pearls, while my breathing recovered from the conclusion of what she called *panipani*. She was a lovely dark golden color from head to toes against the white sheets, her coloring a little paler over her breasts, as though the fabric of her pigment stretched thinner where there was more flesh. The aureoles of her nipples were darker, the bush of the juncture of her thighs darker still. In the tan flesh of her face her eyes were a cool blue, her hair pale brown where it swept across her forehead. Her size was monumental.

I understood that she had had considerable experience in *panipani* at the Alii School in Honolulu, where, among the young Hawaiians of noble blood, such intimacies were not considered sinful despite the preachings of the missionaries.

I lay with my eyes closed, filled with an awareness of

sinfulness, of the fragility of these moments, and a gladness in the sweet flesh that rested beside me.

She prodded me with her elbow.

"I'm hungry, Tom!"

———

We went to Brady's Seafood House on Montgomery Street for an oyster loaf, which was half a loaf of French bread hollowed out and filled with a dozen oysters, all baked in the oven and served blessedly hot.

Haunani murmured with pleasure when the loaf was set before us. She loved to eat. She seemed to feel no guilt or shame fulfilling her appetites. This was a revelation to me, who had always found guilt to be the penance of pleasure.

We were sitting at the window with dregs of coffee in the cups before us, reluctant to bid each other good night, when a familiar figure paced past outside in the bright pool laid down by the light standard there. Moments later Ambrose Bierce appeared inside, handed his hat to a waiter, and joined us.

There was always fuss over Bierce in restaurants, as he was a famous figure in the City, and a chair was brought with some fanfare. I introduced him to Miss Brown.

I was proud of her. It was impossible not to be impressed by her physical presence, her generous bosom and the silken flesh of her shoulders in her magnificent striped and fringed dress, her thick light hair done up like a helmet. With a jingle of beads and bracelets, she extended her brown hand to Bierce. He kissed it formally.

"How do you do, Mr. Bierce?" she said. "I have heard so much about you from my uncle and from Tom."

"And I have heard much about the beautiful niece of my friend Edward Berowne."

He said to me, "I have exercised my powers of deduction to find you here, Tom."

That should have been a clue to me that he was engaged in detective business.

The champagne that he had ordered was brought to us.

"I understand you are a friend of the Hawaiian princess Leileiha, Miss Brown," Bierce said.

"Leilei and I were in school together." Haunani sat straight-backed facing him with her chin raised.

"The princess has disappeared," Bierce said. "She is a member of the king's entourage," he told me. "The managers of the situation are fearful of public attention to what may have been her reasons. I have been asked to look into the matter." He frowned warningly. "I must request that secrecy be maintained."

"Do they think she is in danger?" I asked.

"It is possible."

"How long has she been gone?"

"This is the third day."

Haunani sat holding her champagne glass six inches above the table.

"There is no evident reason why she should have vanished," Bierce said, looking into Haunani's face.

She widened her eyes at him.

"It seems that she and her consort Alexander Honomoku are rather closely related," he said.

"They are related on his mother's side, and her step-father was also his father—it can be very complicated." She smiled her hard-lipped smile that I knew meant she was ill-at-ease.

"Would that complicate Alexander Honomoku's claim to the throne?"

"It would for *haoles*."

Bierce said carefully, "Do you think, Miss Brown, that that complication could be the motive for Princess Leileiha's disappearance?"

When Haunani shook her head her silver earrings flickered with light.

Bierce pursued the point and she looked increasingly irritated. "Mr. Bierce," she said, "unfortunately I am neither Hawaiian enough to know what Hawaiians are thinking, nor *haole* enough to know what *haoles* think. My uncle thinks I am too Hawaiian for his plans for me, and others would say I am poisoned by *haole* blood. So you see." She spread her hands.

"I see a charming young person who has chosen to adopt a disarming pose," Bierce said.

I knew that pose of Haunani's well.

A pair of carriages and a hackney passed by at a swift trot on Montgomery Street, lights gleaming, a wheel striking sparks off the paving stones.

"What can you tell me about Alexander Honomoku, Miss Brown? Apparently there is some feeling that he should succeed the king rather than the king's sister."

"*Haoles* would prefer him," Haunani said. "Liliuokalani would overthrow the Bayonet Constitution. Only natives could vote. There would be no land leases to foreign nations."

I had heard Haunani speak of the Bayonet Constitution before, which the *haoles* had imposed upon King Kalakaua by the threat of force.

"Alexander would try to please everybody," Haunani continued. "Big but hollow is a thing we say in Hawaii. Alexander Honomoku is big but hollow."

"I was told he has taken the disappearance of the princess Leileiha very hard," Bierce said.

"He loves her," Haunani said.

"And she him?"

She shrugged and nodded simultaneously.

"How is it?" I asked. "That Alexander who is not a prince is in the line of succession, but Princess Leileiha is not?"

"He is of the Keawe line and she is of the Kawananakoa."

"There is something that always occurs to me," Bierce said to her. "It is the issue of why something happens at all, and why it happens at a particular time. Can you think of any reason why the princess would choose this particular time to disappear?"

Haunani shook her head.

"When King Kalakaua dies his remains will be returned to Hawaii on a naval cruiser," Bierce said. "Alexander Honomoku and the princess would have accompanied him. Could it be that the princess does not wish to return to Hawaii?"

"Yes," Haunani said.

"Why?"

She shrugged. "Some *pilikia*."

"Trouble," I translated.

"Because she and an almost-brother are lovers?"

She made a shocked face.

"Something political?"

"I don't know these things, Mr. Bierce." There was an opaque quality to Haunani's features as she gazed back at him, as though she had decided to dislike him.

She rose, and said to me, "You must take me home now, Tom."

Bierce and I hurried to our feet as she swept off toward the door. The waiter bowed as she passed him. Her wrap was produced, and she shrugged her shoulders into it.

Bierce said to me, "Will you accompany me on a mission of rescue early in the morning, Tom?"

"The princess?"

"It seems imperative to check railroad and ship departures. I warn you this may be a fool's errand!"

I felt a familiar excitement; we were detectives again!

I was to meet him at eight o'clock at the Clay Street dock, where the Argentine freighter *Guillermo Fierro* was scheduled to depart.

CHAPTER 3

OPPORTUNITY, n. A favorable occasion for grasping a disappointment.
— *The Devil's Dictionary*

TUESDAY, JANUARY 13, 1891

In the morning, when I reached the Clay Street dock, Bierce was already pacing the paving stones, an elegant figure in a gray suit, polished boots, and a derby hat. He flung up an arm dramatically, finger pointing to the rust-streaked steamer farther along the dock. A blue and white flag drooped from a spar and thin smoke drifted from a single stack.

Stevedores bore burdens up a midship gangway, and a crane swung larger loads onto the upper deck, where an officer in a battered cap gesticulated and shouted.

Rimming the outer ends of the piers was a thicket of masts and spars. The place was rank with the stink of sewage.

"This steamer is departing for Buenos Aires with exquisite coincidentiality," Bierce told me. "We will inspect her for the victims of white slavers as soon as Sergeant Willsey arrives!"

Sensational stories of the white slavers appeared with regularity in the *Examiner*, less often in the less sensational San Francisco newspapers.

Bierce and I stamped along the oil-soaked planks to the

foot of the main gangway, where a whiff of fuel oil and grain dust mingled with that of sewage. Further along the dock two gulls fought over a length of red gut, wings flapping.

A heavy man with a sweep of black hair across his forehead beneath his mate's cap glared down at us.

Bierce called up to him. "I believe there are women aboard, sir!"

"No habla Inglés!"

A massive policeman approached us at a quickened gait, swinging his baton. Bierce beckoned to Sergeant Willsey and proceeded to mount the gangplank. The sergeant followed us up the splintery slanting boards. The mate stood at the head of the gangplank with a face as hostile as a Chinese devil.

He gave way as Bierce forged past him, heels cracking on the wooden deck, and disappeared into a passageway. Sergeant Willsey pointed his baton at the mate, and slapped it into the palm of his hand.

In the dark passageway Bierce pounded on the door of the passenger stateroom. It was thrown open on a lighted space in which a startled young woman stood facing us. She was red-haired, hair up, wearing spectacles, a white shirtwaist and a long, dark skirt. She was not Hawaiian.

Behind her was a pair of bunks. A cot covered by a gray blanket had been set up beneath a porthole.

Bierce skipped across the cabin to peer at the face of a figure who lay in the bottom bunk. I heard the small snort of a snore.

The Argentinian captain appeared beside us.

"We have been informed that these women are being kidnapped!" Bierce flung at him.

The captain rattled Spanish in reply, hands raised to shoulder height.

"I can assure you that we are not being kidnapped, sir!" the young woman said.

"Then why has this person been drugged?" Bierce said.

"She is Miss Simms," the young woman said. "She is the sister of Reverend Simms. She has only taken a seasickness potion, I assure you."

The captain racketed Spanish expostulation.

"Is these the white slave girls, Mr. Bierce?" Sergeant Willsey demanded.

"That is nonsense!" the young woman said. She indicated the woman in the bunk. "Miss Simms is prone to *mal de mer*, and has been given some powders so she will sleep through the passage of the Golden Gate, which is known to be very rough."

"And you are?" Bierce enquired.

"I am Miss Best. Miss Simms and I have been employed by the Reverend Simms to teach in the Claritas School in Buenos Aires."

"Hah!" Bierce said.

Sergeant Willsey said, "Don't you young ladies have enough sense not to go off to Buenos Aires with a stranger?"

"But he is not a—" Miss Best started; then she called out, *"Oh, Reverend Simms!"*

A tall man had come up behind the captain, clad in ministerial black, mustached face twisted with alarm. He was gone with a clatter of running steps down the passageway.

"Halt, Rube Slaney!" Sergeant Willsey shouted, and leaped out the door after him. I leaned out the door to see his coattail flying in pursuit of the Reverend Simms.

"You have been in grave danger, young lady," Bierce said.

Miss Best backed up to seat herself on the cot.

"You were to teach at this school of his?" Bierce enquired.

"I will teach English and Miss Simms is employed as head-mistress."

Bierce looked pleased with himself. He had not found his Hawaiian princess, but he had saved two young women from a fate worse than death. The other woman was now sitting up on her bunk, a pale chip of a face beneath a tangle of dark hair, hands in her hair as though holding her head on. Dark eyes peered from face to face.

"And who are you, madam?" Bierce asked.

Her eyes fixed on him, but she didn't respond. Sergeant Willsey returned, panting, with a shake of his head at Bierce.

"That is no reverend, ladies," Willsey announced. "That is Reuben Slaney. He is a malefactor. Captain Pusey has been on his track for three months now. You two won't be seeing any more of that bird, but *I* hope to."

"Miss Simms is the Reverend Simms's sister!" Miss Best protested.

"Bet she ain't," Willsey said.

The other shook her head silently. She was very pretty. Bierce assisted her out of the bunk, and to her feet.

"I am Mrs. Hansen," she said. She clung to his arm. "I don't understand—"

"We must leave this ship, madam," Bierce said, very courtly, and started her toward the door.

The ship's captain, now all bows and cooperation, led the two patrolmen who had arrived in a search of the freighter. Miss Best and Mrs. Hansen accompanied Bierce and me off the *Guillermo Fierro*, Miss Best with a small carpetbag of her belongings, her companion with a larger one. The bayside mi-asma soured my nostrils.

When Sergeant Willsey joined us he told the two young women he must take them off to Police Headquarters at Old City Hall to be questioned by Captain Pusey.

"We will miss our departure!" Miss Best complained.

I knew Bierce was disappointed that his hunch had not prevailed. His detection so far had not been of high quality. I thought I would not point out that a full-blood Hawaiian female could hardly be considered a white slave.

"I am certain that we will meet again, Mr. Bierce," the pretty woman, Mrs. Hansen, said, looking back at him over her shoulder as she moved off beside Sergeant Willsey, with a curious hitch to her step.

An intensity in her voice made me think that they would.

"I am glad to have this miscalculation behind me," Bierce said to me, as we watched them depart.

"I have promised Mr. Aaron Underwood that I will attempt to discover the why and whereabouts of the disappearance of the princess," he went on. "I hope you will assist me in this enterprise, Tom."

I said I would.

"Good! And I will offer us breakfast at the Palace Hotel," he said. We set off at a fast clip back along the docks.

"It is evident that Edward Berowne has brought your Miss Brown here to find a suitable young man among his socially prominent friends," Bierce said as we turned onto Market Street.

"That is correct."

His pale eyes met mine directly. "One perceives that you are in love with her."

"True," I said.

With Bierce the subject of relations between men and women was like a button pushed in some mechanical contraption, which elicited a pompous maxim. This time, however, the button remained blessedly unpushed, and I did not have to hear his prejudices against women and marriage.

"I feel a peculiar chill of awareness that the missing

princess will be a much larger endeavor than I at first considered," he said. "But no doubt it will not involve us in death
and destruction."

But it did.

———

In the Palace Hotel Grill, where Bierce was a fancier of the
chef's speciality of oysters and eggs, I ordered an omelette.

The usual sycophant appeared at our table in the sun-
bright room to beg Bierce for rules to be adhered to in order to
become a famous writer.

This was an intense, wide-eyed young man in a dark suit
with a big cravat, who stood at attention waiting for the delivery of the stone tablets.

Bierce rolled his eyes at me. I was afraid he would scarify
this interlocutor for his presumption, but he did not. He was a
scourge of hypocrites, but a friend to writers.

"These precepts," he said, holding up a finger. "Beware the
habitual case. The overuse of 'would' turns prose to wood. Beware the use of 'there': 'there is,' 'there are.' 'There' gives the
reader an announcement of the thing, not the thing itself. Beware the passive voice, which betrays masculine prose to ef-
feminacy. Beware the overuse of adverbs and adjectives.
Adverbs result in feeble verbs. More than one adjective will
castrate a noun." He leaned back and folded his arms on his
chest.

The young man thanked him excessively and took himself off.

———

Bierce sent off a message by a bellhop and presently a tall,
awkward-looking, frock-coated man in his early forties appeared at our table. This was Mr. Aaron Underwood, son of
the Hawaiian sugar magnate and director of his San Francisco operations. I was introduced as Bierce's associate. I felt a

twist of interest to meet a member of the family that had figured so largely in Haunani's young life.

I knew Bierce judged men by the quality of their hand-
shakes, and Underwood received a fair grade. He had a lined,
worried face with a scurf of chin whiskering, and a restless
eye. He ordered coffee with brandy.

Bierce had written of the sugar moguls in "Prattle": "The
whites of Hawaii, mostly American, are largely as selfish a set
of adventurers as ever sucked eggs and put the shells back into
the nest to be refilled."

Cigars were lit, except by me. I inhaled Bierce's and Underwood's expensive Cuban smoke.

"Why should the police not be called in?" Bierce enquired.
"Surely a Pinkerton operative, at least, would be more competent to conduct a search than Mr. Redmond and I."

"This is a very fragile business," Underwood said, frowning. "The king's high counsellor has been sent for. He has
been heading the Hawaiian delegation in Washington City.

"I can assure you of his majesty's gratitude," he added.
"The existence of the monarchy may hang in the balance."

Bierce must be flattered and intrigued: a missing princess, a
high counsellor, the king's gratitude. Although from the
newspaper accounts, it did not seem that his majesty had long
to live.

There was a digestive silence of cigar smoking and coffee
drinking. Then Underwood said, "I gather from your writing, Mr. Bierce, that you do not favor the Annexation of
Hawaii by the United States."

"That is correct," Bierce said.

"There are many obstacles to Annexation. The Chinese
problem, the racial problem in general, the noncontiguous
problem. The leprosy problem."

"Southern legislators," Bierce said.

"Color," I said.

Like his father, Underwood would be of New England missionary stock, the third generation. He raised his cup to his lips and nodded at Bierce over it, ignoring me.

"The government is, however, interested in certain naval leases," he said.

"Pearl Harbor, I believe," Bierce said.

"There is a contingency of the Pearl Harbor lease to the Reciprocity Treaty," Underwood said.

I knew that the Reciprocity Treaty had to do with tariffs on Hawaiian sugar, which was of importance to the planters of Hawaii.

Underwood had not met my eyes once.

"Liliuokalani objects to the Pearl Harbor lease," he said.

"Other candidates have been mentioned in newspaper accounts."

"There is the former queen, Emma, the wife of the last of the Kamehameha line. And Alexander Honomoku, the princess's fiancé, of whom we have spoken."

Underwood ignoring me must have to do with Haunani Brown. If my father knew of my interest in her, Underwood might know of her interest in me.

"King Kalakaua has made concessions to *haole* demands," he went on. "His sister would revoke those concessions. Queen Emma is even more intractable."

"So there is Alexander Honomoku," I said.

Underwood nodded again, but continued to address himself only to Bierce. "Alexander is moderate, flexible, and sensible, and not overwhelmed with Hawaiian pride. But in his anxiety over the disappearance of the princess Leileiha, he has become a different man. He considers her disappearance to be a judgment on his cooperative attitude. He is very changed. I thought it imperative to inform you of this change before you meet him."

"Does King Kalakaua know the princess has disappeared?"

Underwood shook his head. "He does not."

"You said you would find me a likeness," Bierce said to Underwood, who produced a photograph on stiff paper. Bierce examined it and passed it to me: a plain, dark-faced young woman in a tight-bodiced dress, hands clasped genteely before her. The princess Leileiha.

"I will keep this, if I may," Bierce said, and called for his check. Underwood and I rose with him.

We mounted to the sixth floor in the Palace Hotel's large groaning elevator, whose mirrored walls multiplied our images, with columns of Ambrose Bierces, squads of Aaron Underwoods, and crowds of Thomas Redmonds.

CHAPTER 4

WITCH, n. (1) An ugly and repulsive old woman, in a wicked league with the devil. (2) A beautiful and attractive young woman, in wickedness a league beyond the devil.

— *The Devil's Dictionary*

TUESDAY, JANUARY 13, 1891

In the antechamber outside the king's sickroom we met Alexander Honomoku, a stout young man in a cutaway, with Hawaiian jowls and a potato nose. His black hair was parted neatly. He looked tired and irritable.

We also shook hands with a uniformed Hawaiian man, Major Baker, who clicked his heels before returning to his newspaper spread out on a table.

I had a fancy of the Palace Hotel alive with the royal suspiration, the subtle inhalations and exhalations pervading the building, Market Street alongside it, all of San Francisco fanned by that dying breath.

The door of the sickroom was opened briefly and a female attendant, also Hawaiian, was momentarily visible within. A pale, frail, balding cleric in a dark suit appeared out of the interior darkness. Introduced to Bierce and me as Chaplain

Prout, he passed out of the anteroom after a perfunctory bow. There were sickroom smells, library hushes.

"Was that the nurse?" Bierce inquired, nodding toward the door of the bedchamber.

"Lydia Kukui," Major Baker said, looking up from his newspaper. "The handmaiden. Kalaua."

"There is a ritual massage," Underwood explained. "Has his majesty roused?"

"For a moment only," Honomoku said.

The handmaiden might perform the Hawaiian ritual massage, but the chaplain had surely been a Christian.

"Alexander, please tell Mr. Bierce and Mr. Redmond of the disappearance of Princess Leilei," Underwood said.

The young man glared down at his fists, which he held clenched together before him.

"Saturday I went out, only for a little while. When I returned she was gone." He had a slight British accent, like a catarrhal condition.

"Could she have been kidnapped, Alex?"

Honomoku gave his head the slightest of shakes. "She has taken some of her things."

"Had there been a quarrel between you?" Bierce enquired. Men mooning over lost women would strike him as somewhere between amusing and exasperating. Honomoku did seem haunted, with a mannerism of rolling white-rimmed eyes from one to the other of us.

"No quarrel," he said. "No argument ever."

"If we may be allowed to view the premises," Bierce said.

Honomoku received some communication from Underwood, and said, "Of course."

As we left the room he halted, his fists still balled before him, and said passionately, "It is a message to me! It is a message from my Islands. Others have been more loyal than I. She is trying to instruct me!"

"Ah, now, Alex—" Underwood started.

"No leases on Hawaiian lands! No foreign military! It is what she is telling me!"

"But those *are* arguments," Bierce said as we passed along a corridor.

"They were never articulated so, sir!"

Honomoku gave me a long glance, as though enlisting my sympathy. It was more than I had had from Aaron Underwood.

We halted before a door, where Honomoku produced a key. Inside, in a luxurious sitting-room January sunlight streamed through south-facing windows. The double bed stood in the center of the bedroom, light gleaming on the silk coverlet, cushions plump beneath it. Alexander Honomoku stood with his fists bulging his pockets, gazing on the bed with an expression of despair.

No personal effects of a princess were in evidence. I opened closet doors, which revealed only male suitings and boots.

Honomoku flapped a hand toward the vanity with its trio of mirrors. "Powder, perfume: the feminine things she has taken."

Underwood stood gazing out the window on New Montgomery Street, arms folded.

"She took all her clothing with her?" Bierce said.

"It has been removed."

"Why would that be?"

Honomoku licked his lips and said, "For safekeeping."

"Where has it been removed to?"

"The hotel has vaults for that purpose."

Underwood turned from the window, his eyes flicking past my face. I wondered what was his role among these Hawaiians.

A friend of the monarchy? An emissary of his father and the sugar power?

"No arguments," Bierce said to Honomoku.

"No, sir. She is the most amiable of persons."

"The reason you and the princess have not married is that you and she are related more closely than the clergy approves?"

"Relations among the high *alii* can be very complicated," Underwood said. His face had reddened.

"So this most amiable of persons perceived that her person was interfering with the ambitions of her fiancé?"

"That is a possibility which I mentioned to you," Underwood said.

Honomoku said, "We were to return to the Islands when the remains of David Kalakaua are returned. Admiral Green has offered the *Charleston*."

"Might it be that she does not wish to return to the Islands, and the disapproval of the clergy?"

"That is another possibility," Underwood said.

"Has she been long absent from the Islands?"

"Three years," Honomoku said. "In France, and in England this last year with me.

"I have loved her always," he went on. "From our childhood. We were as brother and sister. From the Alii School in Honolulu. On Maui, which was her home, in Baltimore where she attended the women's college there and where I joined her. In Europe after."

I reflected on Haunani Brown and Aaron Underwood knowing each other as "brother and sister."

"Tell me," Bierce said. "Are you in fact married? A secret ceremony, friends sworn to silence?"

"No! I promise you. It was not necessary, you see."

"You mean she did not require it?"

"She requires nothing of anyone, that darling!" Honomoku said in a breaking voice. "I will say this! I will give up whatever ambitions I have if she will only return to me!" He flung his arms out.

"You have responsibilities to others than yourself, Alexander," Underwood said severely. "You have responsibilities to Hawaii!"

Honomoku covered his face with his hands, shaking his black head.

Bierce meanwhile had been roaming the rooms. He seated himself in a chair before a folding desk and opened the lid. Inside were mahogany cubbyholes containing hotel stationery and envelopes, a squat bottle of ink and a blotter secured by Morocco leather corners. He detached the blotter, folded it four ways, and pocketed it. I was pleased to see him engaged in proper detective procedures.

"I will require a list of the princess's friends in San Francisco," he said. "Was there a servant?"

"Merely hotel staff."

"What do you think, Tom?"

I said it seemed strange to me that not a single item of the princess's effects remained in the room.

And there was the fact that Aaron Underwood had not met my eyes once.

———

It was cold and bright on Market Street when we left the Palace Hotel, with a steady breeze riffling along the thoroughfare, blowing papers down the sidewalk. Men hustled past with overcoat collars turned up, cheeks pink with cold. Women wore cloth coats or furs, and hats with windblown veils. A few beggars stood their ground, one with a barrel organ, another a fiddle, a match-seller on the corner. We passed a liquor-smelling bum tacking amid the foot traffic. The street was jammed with buggies, carriages, and horse-cars, in a concert of hoofs and the squeal of wheels on paving stones.

Opposite us California Street climbed Nob Hill to the mansions there, an ascending cablecar passing a descending one halfway up the slope.

———

In his office in the Examiner Building, Bierce found a magnifying glass in a desk drawer, with which he examined the blue blotter. I leaned over his shoulder. His desk skull regarded me with its empty eye sockets.

Among the loops and verticals of cursive script, I could make out "I am," further along "I will," part of a Hawaiian word, *pili*—.

Pilikia. Trouble.

He continued his examination, putting the glass away when his secretary, Fanny, came in to announce a Mrs. Pleasant.

Bierce and I promptly rose. Mammy Pleasant was a quadroon woman in a green cloak and poke bonnet who emanated an air of mystery and maybe menace, and who knew everyone's business in San Francisco. She did not look her age, which must have been seventy, although she did move slowly, with short steps, slightly hunched. She seated herself at Bierce's invitation and glanced hard-jawed from him to me. In her youth, I had heard, she had passed for white.

"How gracious of you to come, Mrs. Pleasant," Bierce said. "I'm sure you remember Mr. Redmond."

"How do you do, Mrs. Pleasant?"

Her ice tong jaw relented a bit, and she produced a nod. "I will come when sent for, Mr. Bierce." She had a hoarse, harsh

voice and a trick of hesitating before each word as though ex-
amining a coin's value before presenting it.

"I need your assistance, Mrs. Pleasant. A matter of delicacy
which requires a knowledge of the households of the City."

Mammy Pleasant was well known to have been employed
in many of the important residences in San Francisco, and to
have furnished colored servants to wealthy families. She could
be presumed to have connections on Nob Hill, South Park,
and the mansions of the peninsula. Mammy Pleasant was familiar with the corridors of power, and, it was rumored, with
the closets of the secrets as well.

"A young lady has disappeared," Bierce said.

"That Hawaii princess at the Palace Hotel," Mammy said,
with a curt wave of her hand.

"I wonder if you have any inkling of her whereabouts."

Mammy Pleasant was silent for an intense moment. Then
she said, "I have heard nothing."

"I wonder if you have a friend in service at the palace."

She rolled an eye at him. "I know of no *Kanaka* babies," she
said.

I understood this to be a joke. In addition to her fame as
San Francisco's voodoo queen, Mammy had been accused of
baby farming, disposing of unwanted ones and providing others as needed.

Bierce dutifully chuckled.

"The princess's young gent is concerned some harm has
come to her," she went on. "There's some new ones on hand
around the king's sickbed. A minister duck that combs his
hair straight across his bald head, for one. Mr. Underwood,
that his daddy holds the reins, do spend some time there, too."

"Concern for the king's illness, do you think?"

A flash of a smile split her face, which then turned sour
again like a murky pond recovered from a disturbance. "He

was the only one did anything about the princess gone. He went and got hold of *you*!"

"Mrs. Pleasant, you have mentioned *Kanaka* babies, I am certain in jest. But is it not true that you have claimed to have a *Kanaka* father?"

Her face in the poke bonnet thrust toward him. "That is so, Mr. Bierce, Mr. Louis Alexander Williams of Philadelphia."

"May I then count on your assistance in this Hawaiian matter?"

Drawing back, she recited slowly:

'Tis said they mean to take away
    The Negro's vote for he's unlettered.
'Tis true he sits in darkness day
    And night, as formerly, when fettered—

She stopped there, rose and swept her cloak around her, and was gone.

Bierce's face had reddened. "How disconcerting it is," he said. "When someone quotes your poetry to you."

"What was it?" I enquired.

"I'd written of the war veteran's view of the people of her race whom we freed from slavery. She is a powerful advocate for their progress, as you know."

I still didn't understand.

"She was saying that I may count on her," Bierce said. He leaned back in his chair with his arms folded.

"I was at Nashville in '64," he went on. "I saw the colored troops I had once declined to command sacrifice themselves in the frontal assault that turned the tide there.

"It was as fine an example of courage and discipline as I have ever seen," he said, who had fought at Shiloh and Chickamauga, and had been wounded at Kennesaw Mountain.

I had some sense by now of what had formed the bitter crux of his character, who in the war had killed and buried enemies who were as good and as bad as the men slaughtered on either side of him, and had come to an abiding hatred for the men and circumstances that made war, and for hypocrisy and cant in all their manifestations.

CHAPTER 5

POLICE, n. An armed force for protection and participation.
— The Devil's Dictionary

TUESDAY, JANUARY 13, 1891

Mammy Pleasant and the chief of detectives must have passed each other in the hallway.

In his brass-buttoned uniform and gold-braid forage cap, Captain Pusey stamped into Bierce's office, greeted Bierce, and nodded to me. He set his cap down beside the skull on the desk, and seated himself with a grunt.

Bierce had written in "Prattle" of Isaiah Pusey: "This hardy and impenitent malefactor, this money-changer in the temple of justice, this infinite rogue and unthinkable villain of whose service Satan is ashamed, and, blushing blackly, deepens the gloom of hell."

Captain Pusey had not, Bierce had remarked, chosen to take offense at this bolt of invective.

It was clear, however, that he was very pleased that Bierce had suffered a setback at the *Guillermo Fierro*.

"Well, Mr. Bierce," he said. "We did search that freighter top and bottom and didn't find a blame thing worth anybody's while, except Reuben Slaney that sped off like a jackrabbit."

"Did the women depart for the Argentine?"

"They did not, sir," Pusey said.

"Was there reason to detain them?"

"If duped by Rube Slaney was a crime, we'd have to incarcerate a pack of females. We'll catch up with that fraud of a clergyman, never fear, Mr. Bierce." Pusey smiled brilliantly.

It was his brag that he could recall any face if he had time to study the features. He kept an archive of photographs of criminals, city, national, and international. It was assumed that he also kept a blackmail archive. His corps of detectives was something of a scandal within a tolerably corrupt police department.

"The two women had been recruited to teach school in the Argentine," Bierce said. "It was a white slavery trick, surely."

"I just couldn't get much out of those two ladies, Mr. Bierce. I don't believe they will testify against that bird when we catch up with him. I will tell you there has been some fuss from the Argentine consul, however. Lit all over me! Ha-ha!"

Bierce looked austerely sour. "One of them had been drugged, Captain."

"Tell you who she is: she's a Mrs. Hansen. She's a spiritualist, a medium, like. Got a reputation in them circles. That is not your usual kind of young woman carried off by white slavers."

"And the other?"

"Miss Best," I put in.

"Schoolteacher not presently employed. Says she met Slaney at a church out on Washington Street. Mrs. Hansen's not much for information, either. Said she'd been drugged, but disremembers the circumstances."

Bierce grunted.

"Those ladies feel downright put out that you interfered

with their vacation in Buenos Aires." Pusey beamed at Bierce and me.

"It is often difficult for males to grasp the complications of female reasoning," Bierce said. I saw he was tired of the whole business and wanted to be rid of Pusey. He had been contacted by Aaron Underwood in the matter of the missing princess, and had thought to search the departing freighter, only to look a fool.

"Well, that is your business, ain't it, Mr. Bierce?"

"What is that, Captain?"

"Grasping complications. Now: I have a question for you. How was it that you and young Mr. Redmond here went down to that freighter this morning to rescue those ladies that don't understand yet they was rescued?"

"You must put it down to intuition, Captain."

Pusey chuckled. "That I don't," he said. "I surely don't put it down that way."

He took his leave.

———

I was in my office at the Chronicle Building not two hours later when a dirty-faced urchin from the Rincon Messenger Service, wearing an old federal forage cap, brought me an envelope. In it was a note to Bierce signed "Mrs. Mary Ellen Pleasant": "Miss Haunani Brown was seen two afternoons running at the notice-board at Woodward's Gardens. She did not find what she looked for there."

Bierce had added a note: "Tom, do you think this should be looked into? AGB."

He suspected, as I did, that Haunani knew the circumstances of the princess's disappearance, if not her whereabouts. Here was a challenge to my loyalties. I strolled down to the line of hacks in front of the Mint, still hesitating. After a while

I reassured myself that Bierce's and my efforts were in behalf of the missing princess and the Kingdom of Hawaii, and directed a hackie to Woodward's Gardens at Mission and Fifteenth.

In the street water sellers pushed their wheeled barrels, and Chinese vendors maneuvered along the sidewalks with fore and aft baskets of vegetables swinging from shoulder poles. A beer-wagon driver in a leather apron rolled a keg of beer through the swinging doors of a saloon, near a pushcart salesman hawking ducks that hung over his cart in racks. Street life South of Market was lively, and noisy.

————

The usual crowd milled around the entrance to the Gardens. On the wall above the entrance gates two great wooden bears held up the flagpoles with their slack flags. Inside, straight ahead was the museum, to the right a gigantic bust of George Washington on a high pedestal. Through curving lanes people ambled toward grand staircases, flowering terraces, a bear garden, deer park, conservatory, the lake. Farther along was the band platform flourishing streamers and banners, a roller-skating rink, the grand arena where the parades, the tribal dances, and the Roman chariot races were held. On the far side of the skating rink was the notice wall where notes were left for lost friends, missing husbands, mislaid family members.

Here I was to spy on my beloved, if she returned again today.

I found a slot on a balcony between a fat pot of artificial flowers and a low redwood box filled with genuine blooms, where, with my elbows propped on the railing, I could watch the notice board. I prepared myself for a long wait.

People came and went. A skinny young man in a derby hat explored a number of notes pinned to the board. A fat woman with a child by the hand turned away in disappointment.

Haunani appeared, the height of fashion in a broad-brimmed hat and a tightly fitted gray bodice with a voluminous skirt. Her gloved hand searched through the notices, paused uncertainly, searched again. She retreated from the board.

I was not her only observer.

He was watching her from behind an evergreen bush, poised in a position of tension, black-suited, a cloth cap cocked over his forehead so his face was invisible to me.

He made no move toward Haunani as she turned away from the board. With her long-legged stride, her many-gored skirt stretching and gathering with her movements, she passed around the far corner of the rink.

Only then did the other fellow appear out of his concealment. He had a distinctive walk, shoulders hunched forward so that his arms did not swing with his steps. He did not appear to be in any hurry to follow Haunani. I still could not see his face.

When I had hurried along the balcony and down the staircase both of them had disappeared.

I mingled with the people circulating before the entrance. A traffic of buggies, carriages, and drays passed in the street, some halting to debouch passengers, some passing swiftly. I moved from against the wall to the edge of the street for a better look at one of the departing hacks.

I was struck in the back so hard it knocked the wind out of me, and projected me stumbling into the street in a chorus of warning yells. I had a glimpse of a rearing brown horse, a frightened bearded face leaning over me, a whip raised as though to strike me. I managed to dodge to one side and was whacked by the side of a wheel so that I stumbled again with my knees giving way. I fell sprawling, catching my weight on my hands and drawing in my legs so I would not be run over.

I lay on my back on the planks of the boardwalk with half a dozen faces leaning over me.

"Are you injured, sir?" a man called out.

I struggled to sit up.

"Fellow rammed right into him!" another said. "God's blessing you wasn't run down, sir!"

"Who was it?" I said. "Who rammed into me?"

Someone held out an arm to help me to my feet. Another handed me my hat.

"Din't see who it was!"

My knees almost gave way again to think how close a call it had been. Those who had been attending me turned away when it was clear I was not hurt.

I wandered around the entrance for a time, not even knowing what I was looking for, before I departed from Woodward's Gardens.

I thought it about an 80 percent probability that someone had tried to kill me.

CHAPTER 6

TUESDAY, JANUARY 13, 1891

Edward Berowne was on hand late that afternoon when I
called on Haunani, who, he said, had just returned from a
visit to her dressmaker, and would produce herself momentarily.

He was very spruce in a silk smoking jacket, with his neatly
combed hair and his kindly tortoise face. He and I sat inside
with the gold and black Chinese screens on one side of the
room, and windows looking out on the bay and the Golden
Gate on the other. Before us was a brass-chased chest on
which a Chinese vase proffered pale blossoms of orchids.

Haunani had arrived in San Francisco just a month ago. I
asked about suitors.

"Gentlemen are b-b-beginning to congregate at the altar of
b-b-beauty," Berowne said.

Haunani swept into the room wearing a different suiting
than the one she had worn at Woodward's Gardens, this one

striped in tones of gray with a complicated fastening of the tight jacket. She seated herself beside me, with a pressure of her hip against mine.

Berowne remained in his chair, observing us with a bland smile. Subjects of conversation were limited by his presence, including that of the disappearance of the princess.

I told him and Haunani of meeting the king's entourage, including Alexander Honomoku and Aaron Underwood.

"You will be writing the king's obituary?" Berowne wanted to know.

I would probably be assigned a part of it. "There is a young woman in attendance on the king," I said to Haunani. "She was described as a handmaiden and a masseuse."

"She is called Kalaua," Haunani said. "David Kalakaua is very proud of the old ways. *Lomilomi* is the traditional massage," she added. "It is supposed to restore the life force."

Chang brought tea on a tray. Berowne poured and distributed cream and sugar.

"Alexander Honomoku sounded quite desperately in love with the princess," I said carefully.

"It has always been presumed they would marry," Haunani said.

"Young p-p-people are very concerned with love," Berowne said. "When you are older and wiser it is less imp-pportant than other considerations."

"Yes, money and social position, Uncle," Haunani said, laughing.

He laughed indulgently with her. "How I loved the Islands as I knew them so long ago!" he went on. "Ancient times! A simpler, sunnier, happy-memoried—no doubt falsely so—Hawaii!"

"These are more troubled times, Uncle," Haunani said,

and she said to me, "Mauna Loa has been in eruption for months. It is frightening! Villages are burned, there have been deaths. Pele is angry. Is she angry at David Kalakaua?"

Pele was the volcano goddess. It was best not to get on her bad side, I knew. Haunani took Pele as seriously as she did her Christian religion.

"If Pele is angry it may be that an *alii* must be sacrificed. The *kahunas* would say so."

"My dear, surely you do not b-b-believe that tiresome ab-b-borigine b-b-business about Hawaiian magicians," Berowne said gently.

"Yes, I believe!" she said, with her chin raised. "And you had better, Uncle. For *your* brother—*my* father—died of the *kahunas*."

"My dear! Your father died of cancer!"

Berowne's cheerful features had turned grim. I had a sense that he was suddenly angry. He sprang into action in a flurry of collecting his overcoat, hat and a packet of manuscript, and departed for an appointment downtown.

As soon as the door closed behind him, Haunani flung her arms around me and kissed me.

"My dear Tom Redmond!" she said, kicking off her slippers. Lounging back on the settee, she propped her pretty bare feet with their pale soles up on the corner of the Chinese chest, her arms hugged around herself.

I returned to the subject of Aaron Underwood. "He wouldn't look me in the eye," I said.

She made an interested sound.

"You lived with the Underwoods in Honolulu."

"In Uncle Silas's mansion there. Like a hotel. Uncle Silas was a good friend to my Papa, good to *haoles* in trouble. He'd say *haoles* had to stick together."

"Was Aaron part of that?"

"He's older. He was away at school most of the time."

"Now he's in charge of his father's sugar refinery over here?"

"He lives here, but he comes to Honolulu twice a year, sometimes with his wife and Walter."

"Walter?"

"Sweet, unfortunate boy, son of Aaron and Gwendolyn."

"Is there a Mrs. Silas Underwood?"

"Auntie Edith died last year. *Ma-ke*. Gwendolyn is sick, too." She glanced casually away and said, "Aaron Underwood wants me to marry him when Gwendolyn *ma-ke*."

I felt suddenly shaky. I said, "It occurred to me to wonder if you might have come to San Francisco on account of Aaron Underwood."

"To get away from Underwoods!" Haunani said.

"He's too old!" I protested.

"Twenty-one years older than I am! No thank you," she said, shaking her head. "Too much Uncle Silas. His father runs him! No."

"He's a rich man."

She continued to shake her head, but after a moment she continued: "Fine Christian gentleman. No *panipani*, no hanky-panky, nothing such. Honorable! Good! Religious, too! But he is not his own man."

"I see why he would be unfriendly, if he knows of us. I wonder just how unfriendly. Would he wish me harm?"

She looked puzzled. She studied her feet braced against the chest, toes flexing. "There is somebody else in the City who might wish you harm, if he knew of us."

"Who?"

"Charley Perry."

It was another name on the list of Princess Leileiha's friends in San Francisco.

"Who's Charley Perry?"

"He's *hapahaole* like me. He loves all the *wahines*, the most *alii wahines* the most. Charley went to France, to military school there. He married a French lady, very French *alii*, very ambitious like Charley."

"His wife is in France?"

"She is here in San Francisco. Very tiny lady." She grinned at me.

"Every *wahine* Charley Perry ever had he thinks still belong him," she went on. "I was twelve. Isn't it terrible?"

"A virgin," I said, before I could stop myself.

Haunani just grinned, but stiffly, and shook her head.

"Do you belong to him?"

"I belong *me*," Haunani said. "Don't you forget that, either, Tom Redmond."

I found it difficult to confess that I had spied upon her, but I confessed it.

"You damn *haole*!" she said through her teeth. "You *meddler*!" She jammed her folded arms over her bosom.

I tried to excuse myself.

"You do that again and I will never see you again!"

"But you know why she has disappeared."

"She has disappeared for a good reason!"

"It seems that finding her is important to the future of Hawaii."

She made a face.

I said, "Does the fact that there was no note for you mean that she is in danger?"

"It means she did not write a note for me."

"But you are the one she communicates with?"

"None of your business."

"But you do know where she is."

"Leave her alone! Leave *me* alone!"

"There was someone else watching you," I said.

Her hard face collapsed into anxiety.

"I couldn't see his features. He had a queer way of walking. Like a second baseman going after a grounder." I rose to illustrate.

She shook her head. She was clearly frightened.

I told her what had happened to me.

"Serve you right!" she said tight-lipped. "So that's why you wanted to know who would wish you harm."

"Why would they have put the princess's clothing into storage so soon?" I asked.

"So no *kahuna* could use them to make trouble for her."

"Is there a *kahuna* in San Francisco?"

She shrugged, her face stiff and expressionless.

I got up to go. She patted my arm to show we were still friends.

———

"Miss Brown has forbidden me to spy on her," I told Bierce, sitting by his window watching the traffic in the street below in the fading daylight. Some of the carriages had their lamps burning. At the intersection a helmeted policeman wheeled and semaphored his arms.

"No doubt you are inclined to observe that prohibition."

"I am," I said, and told him of the other observer. "Probably he was the one who knocked me into the street."

"If you were watching Miss Brown in the hopes of discovering the whereabouts of the princess, maybe the other was doing the same," Bierce said.

"Miss Brown believes in Hawaiian witchcraft," I said. "Her uncle chided her about it. *Kahunas*. It is the only subject that I have seen frighten her. More than the Calvinist claptrap about the elect and the reprobate.

"She thinks she is not among the elect because of the color of her skin," I added.

Bierce shuffled some papers, and said, "I hope this investigation will not involve the peculiar Calvinist views of the lapsarian event."

CHAPTER 7

MORAL, adj. Conforming to a local and mutable standard of right. Having the quality of general expediency.

                — *The Devil's Dictionary*

WEDNESDAY, JANUARY 14, 1891

The next morning Bierce and I called on the chaplain in the king's suite at the Palace Hotel.

We sat with Jonathan Prout in a small room off the ante-room where the major perused his newspaper. Prout slumped in his chair, painfully thin in his black suit with a high collar and muted cravat. Colorless hair was combed sideways across a skull delineated through transparent flesh, and black eyes that flared like candles. He had a mannerism of speaking in profile rather than head-on, as though deflecting a noisome breath.

Bierce regarded him with interest.

"So, Reverend Prout," he said. "You are here to lend theo-logical support?"

Prout's bloodless lips turned down like a carp's mouth. I didn't think he would be much help with anyone's immortal soul.

"The king is a communicant of the Anglican church," he said. "I am here at the command of his sister."

"You and King Kalakaua are not well-acquainted, then?"

"We all in Honolulu know one another. It is a small place. Very quiet. It is not like this great rushing metropolis."

Bierce asked if he had any ideas about the disappearance of the princess.

"I have."

"Will you share your opinion, sir? I have been charged with solving this mystery."

"There is a strong line of incest running in the *alii*," Prout said. "It has to do with bloodlines, but also with lust and propinquity. They have no sense of what is proper, not to speak of what is iniquitous. Alexander and Leileiha are actually stepbrother and sister. They are also cousins by blood. In any other nation their depravity would be threatened with prison terms. In present-day Hawaii it is a wonder that it is actually a detriment to the career of that young man."

"So she has disappeared so as not to be a detriment to his career?"

"I believe that to be the case."

"How would one search for her?"

"I would not bother."

"You do not approve of the princess Leileiha."

"She is a godless, frivolous young person."

"Her sacrifice does not sound like that of a frivolous young person."

"You asked my opinion," Prout said, glaring.

"And I am very grateful for it," Bierce said. "So, am I to understand that the clergy would interfere in the matter of a marriage between these two young people?"

"*I* would interfere," Prout said, with a jut of his jaw.

"I understand, then, that members of the royal family belong to different Protestant denominations."

Prout nodded curtly. "But their old religion is never

forgotten," he said. "The king has promulgated an article in the constitution calling for the study of the ancient sciences. The *Hale Naua*! These are prejudices so savage, pagan, and ungodly that it is impossible to believe that a monarch of a modern state could even consider them. He has even suffered a sorcerer to practice his healing arts upon him. Here! In this City!"

It was the answer to the question I had put to Haunani. "A *kahuna*," I said.

Prout frowned at me with a jerk of his head that turned aside again like a screen door on a spring.

"I prefer the term 'sorcerer'," he said. "Sorcerers have their terrors. A sorcerer may get hold of a hair cutting, a clipped fingernail, or a discarded bit of clothing."

I met Bierce's eye.

"There are good sorcerers as well as evil ones?" Bierce enquired.

"There are native healers as well as sorcerers who can deliver curses. If David insists on the old healing arts he cannot separate the healings from the maledictions. They have their healing herbs and their poisonous ones." He wiped his hands together as though brushing Hawaiian evils from them.

"What do *kahunas* do?" I asked.

"They design spells and administer potions. It is a ridiculous, dangerous, and obscene proceeding.

"The presence of Satan is everywhere visible in the Islands," he went on. "The volcano is in eruption, there are earthquakes and floods. There is a plague—unaccountable illnesses." His skeletal hands flipped at his own breast. "Someone must take upon himself these sins and torments. Will it be the king, in some satanical mimicry of our Lord's passion?"

"Your religion has not won its battle for Hawaiian hearts?" Bierce said.

"We are in the midst of that battle," Prout said. It seemed he brightened. "But there are not so many natives anymore. It is as though their sorcerers have cursed their own race."

"The stillbirths," I proffered, who knew something of stillbirths.

Prout swung one of his skeletal hands toward the doorway to the king's sickroom. "The Hawaiians die, they become a minority. The Islands become *haole* and Chinese. The race is doomed."

"You do not approve of the race," Bierce said.

"I do not!" Prout said. "They are improvident, lazy, lustful, superstitious—it has been our sacred duty to try to change them."

"I understand the *alii* can trace their genealogies back to their own Adam and Eve," I said.

"Eight hundred twenty-five generations, in David's case," Prout sneered. "I believe the present is some twenty-five thousand years from the *kumulipo*, the beginning. Of course if one finds his ancestry not sufficiently impressive he can hire a genealogist to improve upon it."

"Not unlike some of our own countrymen," Bierce said.

"What can you say of a race that honors its genealogists more than its ministers of the church?" Prout said. He smoothed a hand over the horizontal hairs on his head. His eyes were deeply pouched, his face lined with a yellowish fatigue. "As to the missing young woman, my advice is to let her be.

"Now, if you will pardon me, gentlemen . . ."

He pulled himself to his feet with an effort and started away from us, round-shouldered and slow-moving in his black suiting, placing his feet carefully, steadying a hand on the table as he passed it, jerking irritably at the door before it opened for him, and was gone except for the shuffling sound of his feet.

In the silence of his departure I listened for the kingly suspiration from behind the closed door opposite us.

Bierce said to me in a lowered voice, "Fear of sorcerers, then, is the reason for the disposal of the princess's clothing."

"So Haunani told me."

"It appears," he said, "that Hawaii is afflicted with Christianity of a particularly malignant type."

———

When we returned to the anteroom, in conversation with Alexander Honomoku was an impressive gentleman of erect carriage, a tall, thin, aged, dark-faced Hawaiian who had proud cheekbones above sunken cheeks, deep-cut creases at the corners of his lips and dark eyes that flickered from Bierce's face to mine. His features were so noble that it seemed the king himself must have risen from his deathbed, although I knew that the Merrie Monarch was a stout fellow. Major Baker stood at attention before his chair.

With Honomoku and the other was Kalaua, the handmaiden, in a shapeless gray garment, looking up into the old gentleman's face as though to gain some strength or wisdom from him.

Kalaua slipped back into the sickroom as Honomoku introduced Bierce and me to the distinguished newcomer, who was Judge Akua of the Hawaiian *Aupuni*, the royal counsellor, arrived this morning from Washington City.

"David is resting easily," the old man said in a voice like sounding brass.

Honomoku announced that the famous journalist Mr. Bierce had agreed to investigate the disappearance of the princess Leileiha.

"I have come on that same urgency," Judge Akua said.

"And this is his associate, Mr. Redmond."

The counsellor's dark eyes took me in with a registering

glance. Hands were not shaken. I was interested that Honomoku seemed diminished by this aged Hawaiian.

"May I ask the meaning of *Aupuni*?" Bierce said.

The counsellor spoke carefully: "The *Aupuni* are those who do not wish their islands to become an almshouse of cheated and degenerate natives, like those of the mainland. We are a political party seeking to hold out against the domination of whites."

Honomoku stuck his jaw out, nodding.

"You have written in criticism of the sugar and commercial interests that seek to enslave us, Mr. Bierce," Akua said.

"That is correct," Bierce said.

"It is, of course, a matter of where the Hawaiian salvation lies," Honomoku said, as though he was expected to say something. The company of this proud old man seemed to have reduced him to a schoolboy.

"Salvation is a word our religious teachers have used to ensure our obedience to their ways," Akua said.

"So has it been used to secure the general obedience," Bierce said.

Akua said, "One may believe in the Lord God while recognizing that his ministers are mortal men even as you and I."

"The churchman's ticket entitles him to a reserved seat in the dress circle of heaven," Bierce said. "Commanding a good view of the pit." It was a tidbit I remembered reading in "Prattle." I knew that Bierce carefully honed these items in writing, and he delivered this now in a solemn voice. Akua smiled his appreciation.

Honomoku cleared his throat and said, "The *Aupuni* disapproves of the constitution as it limits the powers of the king."

"The Bayonet Constitution was imposed unconstitutionally," Akua explained. "It disempowered the king, who now reigns rather than rules; it imposed a property requirement for the suffrage, which disempowers the natives. It has many advantages for *haoles*, none for Hawaiians."

Bierce asked if he thought the princess had disappeared for political reasons.

Akua looked thoughtful. "Perhaps," he said. "She is greatly opposed to a sale of lands on the Island of Maui."

"To whom?" Bierce said quickly.

"It is one of the associate companies of Silas Underwood," Akua said.

With that the royal counsellor excused himself, bowed and passed on out of the room in his dignity.

"That is an impressive personage," Bierce said.

"He is a paragon of a man," Honomoku said.

The major had slumped into his chair again.

"But bitter against the *haole*," Honomoku went on, after a moment, as though it had come to him that he should not seem so subservient to the royal counsellor.

"His life has had its tragedy," he added.

"And what is that?" Bierce enquired.

"His son was drowned. *Haoles* were guilty. It is a legend that has been embroidered upon like a Massachusetts sampler. Always the *haoles* are shown as villains, the Hawaiians as victims. It has become a banner waved by such men as Charles Perry, who wish to inflame relations between the races of the islands. The arrogant *haoles*, the naive Hawaiians."

I glanced sideways at Bierce, who had straightened to stand tall with his hands stretched at his sides. Two years ago his sixteen-year-old son, Day, in a quarrel over a girl, had shot his best friend and then himself.

Bierce's enemy Fred Pixley had taken the occasion to kick Bierce when he was down, in the *Argonaut*: "May not the death of the younger Bierce teach the older man, his father, how sinister have been the bitter, heartless and unprovoked assaults which he has spent his life cultivating that he might more cruelly wound his fellow men?"

I had a sense of Bierce relaxing the taut cord of his emotion inch by inch, until he said in a perfectly normal voice, "The old gentleman has a regal bearing."

"Judge Akua is descended from the last kings of Maui before the island was conquered by King Kamehameha," Alexander Honomoku said.

"And is the counsellor considered a possibility to succeed as king?"

"It is well known that he is not interested," Honomoku said.

"How old was the young man who was killed?" Bierce wanted to know.

"Oh, I think nineteen, twenty," Honomoku said. "It was many years ago!"

CHAPTER 8

DIVINATION, n. The art of nosing out the occult. Divination is of as many kinds as there are fruit-bearing varieties of the flowering dunce and the early fool.

— *The Devil's Dictionary*

WEDNESDAY, JANUARY 14, 1891

I supposed Bierce wanted to attend a suffragette meeting in order to savage the presumptions and pretensions of "them loud," as he called feminists in "Prattle." I was invited to accompany him.

"By female suffrage is meant the right of a woman to vote as some man tells her to," he had written. And, "The woman most eager to jump out of her petticoat to assert her rights is first to jump back into it when threatened with a switching for misusing them."

Of the women posted on the announcement, the first lecturer, Rose Blessing Hansen, billed as a "medium and trance speaker," was the drugged, dark-haired young woman from the *Guillermo Fierro*, who had prophesied that she and Bierce would meet again.

Although I knew of the genre of female lecturers called "trance speakers" I had never heard one in action.

I was uncomfortable seated in the audience at the Hopkins Hall, where there was a handful of men and at least two hundred women, in a reek of mingled perfume and perspiration. There were women with complicated hats in magnificent dresses, and women in plain bonnets and plain dress, young women and old, cutting glances at Bierce and me from beneath hats and bonnets, a few with smiles but most without. They seated themselves in a hushed cyclone rustle of fabrics and muted conversation.

A jockey-sized gent in a dress suit introduced Mrs. Hansen with a peculiar offhandedness, as though all in the audience shared some secret together. Bierce sat beside me with the corners of his mouth slashed down in disapproval or concentration beneath his fair mustache.

Mrs. Hansen was seated in a straight chair farther back on the stage, with her head tipped back so that her face was turned up to the design of the gold ornamentations on the ceiling.

When summoned, she tripped forward in a halting gait that made her appear half asleep. She was dressed in a collection of variously colored scarves that floated about her as she moved, from which thin bare arms protruded, and her small face beneath a cloud of upswept dark hair.

She tipped her head back again as she began to speak, in a low, mild, carrying voice. With her pale throat, her raised chin, her inclined face resembled that of a pretty frog.

She spoke of the religion in which she had been raised: "And I said to my minister, 'Why has God made the singing birds so happy and I must be miserable?' And I said to him, 'Why must a little child with a living soul live with this terrible fear, like a phantom sweeping between me and the beautiful earth that God has made for his creatures?' And I said to him, 'Why must this terrible fear of the hereafter steal into my dreams each night with its ugly grimaces, and casting its black pall between me and the beautiful sunlight?' "

Her minister had not had acceptable answers to these queries. Bierce poked my ribs with his elbow and nodded judiciously when I glanced at him. I could hardly believe his response to this peculiar female.

Later, still apparently in the somnolent state, Mrs. Hansen said, "Why must wives be brutalized by their husbands' passions? Threatened with death from physical drain by pregnancy after unwanted pregnancy? Why is the husband empowered to enforce his legal rights upon her body? Why do the priest and minister, the law and the marriage institution, support him? I have cried to heaven, 'Nothing short of giving a woman the right to the control of her own person, nothing short of her freedom to take on the material relation, or not, will remedy this evil'!"

This ending of her peroration resulted in a great stirring, then applause, and, after an interval, as though each must wait to see how the others had responded, cheers and "Hear! Hear!"s. Upon which pretty little Mrs. Hansen wandered back across the stage with her scarves drifting and settling in some kind of breeze she kept about her. I was impressed again by her sidling gait, as though she were indeed entranced, or inebriated. She disappeared to applause, in which Bierce and I participated.

Bierce did not feel constrained to listen to any more of the suffragist ladies, and we passed out of our row and aisle, and into the empty lobby.

Market Street was a blaze of light. It seemed that each month there was more illumination, shimmering pools of it splashed along the great thoroughfare from the high light standards. Because there was more light, the buildings that lined the street seemed to have retreated into shadows, like

•

grand ladies sweeping their cloaks about them when they came under the observation of commoners in a public place.

"What did you think of our little person, Tom?" Bierce inquired.

I didn't know whether I was supposed to be ironic or frank, so I said, "Remarkable!"

"I have done some investigation," Bierce said, when we had settled at a walnut table in the nearest saloon. "Mrs. Hansen is a well-known medium. She is a divorced woman. There was a scandal involving her and her assistant who was thought to be her lover. This was in New York State."

"She looks very young for so much experience."

"She may not be as young as she looks."

Our drinks were brought, his whiskey, my lager.

"There was some manipulation of a manifestation of spirits," he went on. "She and her collaborator were publicly exposed by one of those cranks whose pleasure it is to expose frauds. Her spotted reputation was the reason for that curious introduction."

"Is there any explanation for her presence aboard the Argentine freighter?"

"I have not spoken to the lady. Pusey got nothing out of her, or so he said.

"I intend to make her acquaintance," he went on. "One recognizes that Spiritualism is a profession in which clever ladies may make their mark. Some of these women are convinced that they have actually made contact with the spirit world. Although always there is fraud; contrived spirit-rappings, the noisy toes of the Fox sisters, the charlatan sisters Victoria Woodhull and Tennessee Claflin, who so charmed Commodore Vanderbilt.

"The trance speakers are usually very young women who, because of some contact with a near-hovering and personal spirit, can discourse with wisdom on a variety of subjects: astronomy, astrology, history, ecomomics. Their range is quite astonishing."

"Mrs. Hansen is billed as one of them."

"Many of these women become mediums," he said, nodding. "Their spirits are contacted for personal messages, and certainly for personal gain. As what I perceive to have been the case with Mrs. Hansen, corrupt and profiteering men take over the show, so to speak. Manifestations become a requisite of the séance. And so are hatched the exposers of fraud, such as Harry Houdini. Sometimes there is enormous baggage to these events, with mediums confined in sacks in their cabinets, the sack nailed to the floor. Still, manifestations have been managed.

"I have this information from my friend Mrs. Chandler, who is a believer. She points out that many of these women—because they are self-confident and good speakers, and some of considerable intelligence, have been recruited to the suffragist cause. Also, of course, to the temperance movement, its close ally.

"Which is why women's suffrage is continually opposed by the power of the liquor interests," he added, and paused to sip his whiskey.

"As I say, I will pursue Mrs. Hansen's acquaintance in order to observe some exhibition of her powers," Bierce said. "I would like to test her with our fugitive princess."

THURSDAY, JANUARY 15, 1891

The next to last of the names on the list of the princess Leileiha's acquaintances in San Francisco was a college friend, whom I discovered had moved back to Baltimore with her family after Christmas. It was a frigid day and I strode along California Street with my fists doubled up in my overcoat pockets, returning to the *Chronicle* after this fruitless investigation.

Halted at an intersection was a fine carriage with a matched team of grays and, up on the seat, a husky, dark-complected driver in a magenta uniform. I had a glimpse of a female brown face glancing back at me out of the rear window.

When the traffic policeman signalled the carriage on I flagged a hack and we joined a line behind an express wagon and a hansom, swinging right on Market Street west toward Van Ness Avenue under low clouds.

The Hawaiian face in the window had been too young to be that of the missing princess. It might, however, be the handmaiden Kalaua. There seemed a possibility that Kalaua, like Haunani, could lead to the princess.

In Hayes Valley the carriage swung into an alley where I hopped off, gave the hackie four bits and trotted after the carriage on foot. It had halted, the grays pitching their heads beside a hitching post. The occupant or occupants had disappeared.

The carriage was drawn up in a cobbled courtyard behind a brick building. A window was open and a curtain flicked in the wind like a signal. I ducked down cellar steps. After some hesitation I tried the door there. It gave way under the weight of my shoulder, scraping open onto darkness. Inside, I followed a passageway blind, sliding a hand along a brick wall.

When I came into another room I halted to focus my senses. The place had a presence to it, as though a soundless crowd surrounded me.

"Hello?" I whispered.

A rectangle of light lines indicated a window with a drawn blind, with an array of objects adjacent to it. I moved carefully to raise the blind, and gray light bathed the room.

Against the wall was a kind of altar, waist-high, covered

with a stiff cloth of brown and white figures. On the cloth were several objects. A feather casque in the shape of a Trojan helmet was formed of tightly shingled yellow feathers. Next to it was a patch of newsprint held down by a round, smooth fist-sized black stone, and, lastly, a figurine of gleaming dark wood about three feet high.

The figurine's oversized face was so ugly, I stepped back from it. The blind eyes were almonds of some gleaming white material, the mouth warped into a figure eight, depicting ferocity or anguish.

My breath came hard as I stared at the carved figure.

It was too dim in the room to read, so I took the newsprint from beneath the stone and stuffed it into my coat pocket for examination later.

On the far wall another of the stiff brown and white cloths was fastened with tacks. In this the brown spots were discernible as human forms in a variety of postures and gestures, frozen in immobility as though trapped trying to escape from the stiff matrix that held them. An open door led into another room, where the light from the window stretched out before me.

A Hawaiian man sat on a cot across the room, staring at me. He had a kind of halo of white hair, a high-cheekbone visage, and eyes that showed quarter moons of white beneath the pupils, a phosphorescent white like the blind eyes of the idol, a white that was both alive and totally still, and captured the light and my own eyes powerfully. The man on the cot did not move.

I backed quickly out of his field of vision, as though I had entered a water-closet in use, and I escaped from that airless, evil place. I had encountered a *kahuna*, and he had frightened me so that I had to consciously stop myself from breaking into a trot, with any attempt to track the handmaiden Kalaua forgotten.

It came to me that this was the man who had spied on Haunani at Woodward's Gardens, and who had tried to kill me.

I was a block away before I discovered that I had carried away in my overcoat pocket the black stone as well as the torn-out square of newsprint.

It was a news item: "The Reverend Jonathan Prout arrived from Honolulu yesterday to add his prayers as Royal Chaplain to those of King Kalakaua's entourage at the Palace Hotel—"

CHAPTER 9

DISABUSE, v.t. To present your neighbor with another and better error than the one which he has deemed it advantageous to embrace.
— *The Devil's Dictionary*

THURSDAY, JANUARY 15, 1891

My adventures in Hayes Valley sounded especially bizarre in the circus hubbub of the *Examiner* offices. Messengers trotted along the hall past Bierce's door, reporters called to each other in their cubicles, and a brief shouting match resounded farther along the floor.

Bierce had had a message from Captain Pusey that Reuben Slaney had been captured and was locked up in the city jail.

I had hardly had time to wonder why that matter concerned us when Judge Akua was announced. The dignified old Hawaiian appeared in the doorway, his white head inclined under the transom.

Bierce and I were on our feet. This time hands were shaken. Akua did not look well, with a grayness beneath his eroded cheeks. Bierce ushered him to a chair.

"Mr. Bierce," Akua said, in his voice that seemed to rise from some lower part of his body. "I have come with a new aspect of the matter in the disappearance of Princess Leileiha. There is another possibility."

"What is that, Judge Akua?"

"Silas Underwood is trying to acquire land on Maui. Princess Leilei has inherited a huge tract there. She has rebuffed his interests, even though David Kalakaua has sought to assist him."

"But Underwood is not here in San Francisco, surely?"

"An agent acts for him."

"His son?"

"Not his son," Akua said. He held his palms to the sides of his head as though smitten with a headache.

"Are you ill, Judge Akua?" Bierce asked.

"I am very distressed, Mr. Bierce," Akua said. "I have just come from a conversation with Jonathan Prout. I wonder if you are aware that he collapsed yesterday, and was taken to a hospital? I am in the position of Hamlet hearing from the ghost upon the ramparts that there is something rotten in Denmark. There is something rotten on the Island of Maui, which is my home, and there is something rotten in the City of San Francisco as well.

"Jonathan is very ill," he went on. "He is afraid that he is dying."

"Tom and I had a conference with him yesterday," Bierce said. "He does not seem to have much sympathy for the problems of Hawaii."

"I have known him for a great many years," Judge Akua said, shaking his head. "As a young man he had a congregation on Maui, where he was a friend of my son. At that time he was a serious and dedicated young minister. Later on, in Honolulu, he became something else. He has not been a well man for years."

He said with a sigh, "No, he is not a friend of Hawaii. Lili-uokalani must have sent him to her brother's bedside on the theory that ill-tasting medicine is bound to be effective."

"Because he is afraid he is dying he related something to you that has made you feel like Hamlet on the ramparts?"

"Yes, Mr. Bierce, but it is not a matter which I am free to describe to you."

The judge did look deeply ill, as though his conversation with the chaplain had been even more indigestible than ours had been.

"Powerful interests are provoked by the succession," he said. "You may know that the Akua name is of some royal significance."

"Are you concerned about political involvement?"

"My conversation with the chaplain has caused me to be concerned about everything in my life."

"*For* your life, do you mean, sir?"

"Even that," Akua said grimly.

"Then here is a coincidence," I said. "At Woodward's Gardens yesterday someone tried to shove me under the wheels of a carriage."

Akua's dark eyes with their yellowish whites fixed on me. "What is Woodward's Gardens, Mr. Redmond?"

"It is a place of public entertainment. I had gone there on a tip that Miss Haunani Brown might be meeting the princess there. Another man was watching Miss Brown also."

I had not meant to tell the judge all that.

He gazed at me steadily. "And did you see your assailant, Mr. Redmond?"

"I did not."

His eyes flickered away as down the hall there was a burst of reportorial bellowing and laughter.

"Haunani Brown, whom I had not seen since she was a

child, has become a lovely young woman," he said. "Should she be warned? Although I would think this surveillance would have to do with Princess Leilei."

"She has been warned," I said.

"Judge Akua, are you residing at the Palace Hotel with the rest of the royal entourage?" Bierce asked.

Judge Akua shook his head, sinking down in his chair so that he looked not quite so long and angular. "It would be well if the king's entourage did not accumulate expenses that already overburden the monarchy. I am comfortable at a very pleasant rooming house on California Street."

"Chaplain Prout told us he thought the king was being attended by a sorcerer," Bierce said.

Akua closed his eyes for a moment. "When I said Silas Underwood had an agent here, that is whom I meant. The man is named Kanekoa."

"Would such a sorcerer have to do with a society known as the *Hale Naua*?"

"Yes, he might."

"And is the *Hale Naua* allied with the *Aupuni*?"

"In certain ways, yes."

"Is the creed of the *Aupuni* 'Hawaii for the Hawaiians'?" I asked.

The dark eyes fixed on me again. "It is the creed of the several parties that seek to stop the whites from devouring our islands, Mr. Redmond. But 'Hawaii for the Hawaiians' is the actual slogan of the Reform Party. It may be that you will meet Charles Perry, who is presently in San Francisco. He is one of the leaders of the Reform Party, and commander of the Diamond Head Rifles, a patriotic group of young Hawaiian men."

Who thought Haunani Brown still belonged to him, and whose name was the last on the list of Princess Leileiha's friends.

"We would be grateful if you would tell us something of these parties," Bierce said.

Judge Akua said, "There are a number of nativist parties that support the monarchy and detest the Bayonet Constitution. They are fragmented, however, while the Annexationists are single-minded. Of the organizations we have mentioned, the *Aupuni* is the most moderate. The Reform Party is erratic and perhaps prone to violence. Charles Perry's adherents sometimes appear in red shirts in the Garibaldian manner.

"Both the *Aupuni* and the Reform Party call for the revocation of the 1877 constitution, and universal suffrage, with no economic or property requirement. The king would rule rather than reign. The Reform Party, however, threatens armed rebellion if its demands are not met.

"The *Hale Naua* is a not-very-secret secret society of powerful *alii* who are powerful because David Kalakaua has pledged allegiance to their cause. The *Hale Naua* seeks the return of a Hawaii David never knew, but which I knew as a boy. It is not a Hawaii one should wish back. The priests would regain their *kapu* power, the *alii* would be elevated to the ascendancy, the commoners reduced to powerless and fearful peasants. Such changes could not occur without an armed insurrection by much more competent foreigners, a war that natives could not win."

"Does the *Aupuni* support Liliuokalani to replace her brother?" Bierce asked.

"We believe that to be the proper constitutional course. The Reform Party supports Queen Emma, who was the wife of the last of the Kamehameha line, and rather reactionary. The *Hale Naua* also supports her."

"And where is Alexander Honomoku's support?"

"Mostly moderates and Americans."

"Aaron Underwood told us that he believes that anyone but Alexander Honomoku will result in the armed insurrection you spoke of."

"That is his assessment, not mine."

"The Annexationists are the white merchants?"

Judge Akua nodded.

"And what of the United States government?"

"The envoy in Honolulu is improperly and noisily pro-annexation. Have you met the U.S. commissioner, Mr. Regan?"

We had not.

"I believe it is important for us to discover what you have come to see is rotten in the City of San Francisco," Bierce said.

"It is not a political matter, Mr. Bierce. I am sorry I mentioned it. It has come to occupy my mind so that I can hardly see around it."

"So the princess may have taken herself off in order to avoid Silas Underwood's agent?" Bierce said.

Akua blew out his breath again. "Silas has been very loyal to David Kalakaua. To the monarchy. He loves Hawaii, but his embrace is rather like that of a bear. Kanekoa may well have been brought to the mainland on one of Silas's freighters. Silas has always had an unhealthy association with the old *kahunas*. Perhaps they have served him well."

"Is the princess in a position to thwart his ambitions in a land dispute on Maui?"

"She has certainly interfered. That is a part of my uneasiness about Leilei."

"Is Silas Underwood a member of the *Hale Naua*?"

Akua shook his head. "Distinguished *Hawaiian* genealogies are required."

"He would be a powerful enemy."

"Yes."

Bierce said to me, "Tom, tell Judge Akua of your adventure in Hayes Valley insofar as it might concern the illness of the chaplain."

The counsellor gazed at me as I told the story of the face that might have been Kalaua's glimpsed in the carriage window, the evil shrine, the cross-legged fellow, and the newspaper clipping of Prout's arrival in San Francisco.

"A volcanic rock?" Judge Akua said in a sharp tone. "Pele was invoked."

I did not mention that I had kept the stone.

"Could it possibly be," Bierce said, leaning back, "that the illness of Chaplain Prout can be attributed to this stone and this clipping, *in San Francisco*?"

The counsellor was silent. I could see the rise and fall of his shirt over his chest.

Bierce said, "And in his illness he communicated to you some poison out of the past?"

Judge Akua passed a hand over his forehead. His voice shook:

"Jonathan has just told me of evils and connections I had not known."

"I understand your son died tragically," Bierce said. "You have my great sympathy."

The counsellor licked his gray lips. "It was at a time when I was serving as minister in London. There was a surfing accident. It was thought that the Brown brothers could have saved him. That they failed to do so was taken as evidence of racial contempt or enmity. William Brown already had a reputation for arrogance. It was the kind of event, however, that is subject to endless reinterpretation."

The Brown brothers would be Haunani's father and Edward Berowne.

"The great virtue of Christianity is the doctrine of forgiveness," Judge Akua said, and struggled out of his chair and to his feet. He seemed to rise in sections, as though connecting tissues had loosened in his great age, in his anxieties. He rose to his full height, and Bierce and I rose with him.

"Tell me, Judge Akua, are you related to the Princess Leilei?" Bierce asked.

"No, I am not related to *her*, Mr. Bierce." He stood before us, inches taller than Bierce, lean and frail, with those strong bony lines and reefs in his gray face.

I thought to ask what he meant, but my nerve failed me.

"I did not mean to infect you with my own cancerous thoughts," he said. "I really came to speak of Leilei." And he dipped his head to me.

"You understand that I can be of no assistance without information," Bierce said.

"I understand that," Judge Akua said, and, moving slowly, departed.

CHAPTER 10

THURSDAY, JANUARY 15, 1891

I spent some hours in the Mechanics' Library looking into Hawaiian history for a piece on the Islands to accompany the news story on King Kalakaua's demise, which day by day appeared more imminent. Back in my office I typed a rough draft:

"The first incursion of whites was in 1779 when Captain Cook discovered the archipelago. He was murdered by natives shortly thereafter. King Kamehameha conquered the islands of Hawaii, Maui, and Oahu in 1796, with the help of European arms and advisors. Liholiho, the son of Hawaii's conqueror king, succeeded him as Kamehameha II.

"Hawaii's religion was a fabric of taboos. *Kapus* pervaded all of life; religion, politics, heritage, genealogy, food, war, play. The penalty for disobeying *kapus* was death. It was a fearful religion for a sunny population. The nobles, with the authority of the gods, were superior in every way to the commoners, and, with the priests, held power of life and death over them.

"Kaahumanu was Kamehameha's favorite wife. When the great king died she persuaded Liholiho to eat with the women at a feast, thus breaking one of the strongest *kapus*, which prohibited men and women from eating together. It was a decisive moment. The new king had broken a *kapu*, and the gods had not punished him. The *kapu* system was mortally wounded, just in time for the arrival of the New England missionaries, with a new set of taboos.

"The missionaries did not like what they found in the Islands. One of them wrote: 'The appearance of destitution, degradation and barbarism, among the chattering, and almost naked savages, whose heads and feet, and much of their sunburnt swarthy skins, were bare, was appalling. Some of our number, with gushing tears, turned away from the spectacle. Others, with firmer nerve, continued their gaze, but were ready to exclaim, "Can these be human beings? Can we throw ourselves upon these rude shores, and take up our abode, for life, among such a people, for the purpose of training them for heaven?"'

"Mark Twain visited Hawaii in the sixties, and said of the missionaries that they were 'pious; hard-working; hard-praying; self-sacrificing; hospitable; devoted to the well-being of the people and the interests of Protestantism; bigoted; puritanical; slow; ignorant of human nature and the natural ways of men.'

"As the whaling industry declined, sugarcane became the economic savior of the Islands. The Hawaiians would not work the necessary long hours for low pay, and there were not enough of them anyway, so the planters brought in coolie labor. The Chinese were accompanied by leprosy, which swept through the Hawaiians as syphilis, smallpox, and measles had before it. In combatting the disease, the kingdom has dumped its victims, of high as well as low estate, on a barren mountain-walled lazaretto of a peninsula on the island of Molokai.

"The Hawaiian race has begun to die out, from disease, liquor, early death, a lowered birthrate, stillbirths.

"There are still strong feelings for the ancient Hawaii. Some of the old *kapus* live on underground, *kahunas* practice their black as well as their healing arts, with a resurgence of their power whenever Mauna Loa erupts and earthquakes shake the islands, which they do at frequent intervals, and are doing at this moment.

"Hawaii's present problems have to do with Reciprocity and the Pearl Harbor lease, and a large personal debt owed by the king to a powerful sugar planter descendant of the missionaries, Silas Underwood. Reciprocity would give Hawaiian planters an advantage on import duties, and its success in the U.S. Senate is dependent upon the Pearl Harbor lease. Pearl Harbor is one of the greatest natural harbors in the Pacific, and recent U.S. administrations have been interested in expansion to the Pacific Ocean. The merchant forces in Hawaii are intent upon Reciprocity, and many ultimately on Annexation, but the native parties resist ceding or even leasing Hawaiian lands to a foreign power."

———

"My great-grandmother may have been the princess Nahienaena," Haunani said, leaning back against my pillows. "Do you know who she was?"

We had been talking of what I had learned of Hawaiian history. Hearing her speak of old Hawaii was like listening to fairy tales related by someone who believed in them unquestioningly.

"She was the sacred daughter of Kamehameha."

I asked what "sacred" meant.

"The one to whom the *mana* passes. She was the only

daughter of Kamehameha by his sacred wife. He had many other wives, but their children had no *mana*. In those days if someone stepped on Nahienaena's shadow he must die. As she grew out of her younger clothes they had to be destroyed, because they contained her *mana*."

"That makes the missionaries sound sensible," I said, and wished I hadn't spoken so lightly. This was a solemn matter. Her blue eyes had a bright glare to them.

I could see the stretch of her nostrils, hear the whisper of her breath. I understood that when she said they were trying to make her crazy, this mood was what she meant.

"She loved her brother," she continued after a time. "Often in the old days brothers married their sisters. Nahienaena and her brother would have married if it had not been for the missionaries. Later she had a *haole* consort. His name was Abraham Robbins. He was a ship's captain from Massachusetts. He could be my great-grandfather."

"I see," I said, with pity for her.

"I can chant the names of my ancestors back to the beginning," Haunani said.

"So your grandmother may have been *hapahaole* also," I said.

She was silent for a time before she said, reluctantly "Yes." She sighed, and smiled, and seemed to come back from somewhere, and said, "I would be very proud if my ancestor were Nahienaena, and also Abraham Robbins. I went to call on Andrew Akua yesterday. I told him that. He said that is all nonsense. I am a Maui girl. Nahienaena lived on the Big Island." She laughed at herself.

"I asked him about my mother," she went on. "My mother is a great mystery. Surely she was Hawaiian, but no one seems to know of her, or they won't tell me— All my life—" She stopped and drew a deep breath.

"He said I remind him of his son," she said. She laughed. "He said, 'I guess there was a blue-eyed *haole* in the woodpile!' I love that grand old gentleman! He is descended from the kings of Maui."

Akua had said his name had royal significance.

Haunani was shocked that I knew so little about the Redmond family. I had never had any contact with my grandparents and only knew that Redmonds came from county Clare, where I supposed they had resided since some Irish *Kumulipo*, or Adam. There was certainly no royal or noble significance.

"He came to call on Bierce earlier this afternoon," I said. "He said there is a *kahuna* who treats the king, the *kahuna* is Silas Underwood's agent, and the princess may have disappeared because she and Silas Underwood have a contention over some land on Maui."

Haunani stared at me as though she had not taken in what I had said. I could see the rise and fall of her bosom.

"It seems that Princess Leileiha has interfered with Silas Underwood purchasing land on Maui."

"Leilei has land on Maui," she said nodding. And she added, "Uncle Silas gets what he wants. David Kalakaua will see to that."

"Who is dying."

"Yes."

"And Chaplain Prout is dangerously ill in the hospital."

Haunani laid her hands to her cheeks. She whispered words in Hawaiian. I told her what Judge Akua had told Bierce and me about Prout.

"That pig!" she spat out.

She was silent for a time. Then in a slow, storytelling voice she said, "When I was eleven we moved to Honolulu. My father was very ill. There was a minister who was his friend who came to Honolulu also. Who betrayed his faith."

"What do you mean?"

"He made *panipani* with a virgin child. *Puupaa*. And blamed her that she had enticed him. He hated the half of her that was Hawaiian. He said there was a curse on Hawaiians. He said they would never be elect because they were brown. They would have eternal death instead of eternal life because God did not love them." Her voice began to shake. When I tried to hold her she jerked away. "He hated Hawaiians because he'd made *panipani* with a twelve-year-old *hapahaole* girl!"

"That damned religion!" I panted.

"You are a nice Roman Catholic man," Haunani said more calmly. "That is a religion for sissies!" I saw the gleam of tears on her cheeks.

When I embraced her warm, brown, abundant flesh, she did not respond. The piano's notes tinkled through the wall. Signora Sotopietro began to sing, softly, sweetly; long, sinuous melodies through the thin wall that were not ones I had heard before.

"So if I am damned I will make *panipani* with whom I please!" Haunani said.

"You are not damned!"

"I don't even know who I *am*!"

"That is infernal nonsense!"

"Not nonsense," she said, weeping. "Someday soon, Tom, there will be no more Hawaiians."

"What was his name?" I demanded. She did not answer, but I knew who he was. He was ill in St. Francis Hospital.

Last year with some fanfare, the Texas legislature had raised the age of female consent from seven to ten years of age.

Haunani, who in her full female finery was as beautiful and tall as a sailing ship, had been seduced and reviled as a twelve-year-old. Mrs. Hansen had complained of the "material relation" that forced women to make marriages for sustenance rather than love. Former slaves could vote, but not women. Men treated worse than slaves the gender they pretended to love and admire.

Signora Sotopietro's aria sweetly soared.

———

Later I escorted Haunani to Raffaello's for dinner, where I ordered a Chateaubriand for the two of us, four inches thick and six inches across, with a quarter-inch of black crust and the meat inside as red as the blood of patriots. I was in a state of rage and tension and love so fierce that I could hardly think to order. But good food had its effect, on me and on Haunani.

The waiter brought Roquefort cheese, and I showed her how to blend in the paprika, butter, and Worcestershire sauce, and a clove of garlic. Raffaello himself appeared, his hairy arms wrapped in his white apron, to beam down on us.

Because he approved of Haunani's appetite, he said, "Ah, *signora*, regard what I will bring you now!"

And he produced his renowned banana fritters, light as lamplight, heaped with whipped cream seasoned with cloves, and black coffee with it.

Haunani made a humming sound in her pleasure, and clasped my hand under the table, and with a different kind of tears in her eyes, said, "You are so good to me, Tom Redmond. Why aren't you the rich gentleman who will marry me and give me his name and make me happy forever?"

When I apologized, pretending it to be a joke, she clutched my hand so hard I could feel the bones grate.

I was not rich enough even to bring her to this kind of dinner very often.

FRIDAY, JANUARY 16, 1891

In the morning I encountered Signora Sotopietro on the stairs, clinging to the rail and making her slow downward progress. Her cheeks were sucked in with the effort.

"What was that beautiful song you sang last night, Signora Sotopietro?" I asked. "It was very lovely."

She managed a hulking curtsey, her face alight with pleasure. "Thank you, young sir. It was 'Casta Diva' from Vincenzo Bellini's opera *Norma*, which I have sung so many times in the great opera houses of this country and Europe."

"I hope you will sing it many times more, Signora Sotopietro," I said.

———

On Montgomery Street it was a sparkling morning with the shadows of the buildings splashed across the paving stones, where the street cleaners wielded brooms and shovels, which squealed on the stones along with the grating of iron-rimmed wheels. It was not a morning when *kahunas* seemed dangerous.

Bierce was already at his desk. He looked pleased. The Reverend Slaney had escaped.

"Captain Pusey is fit to be tied! The jailer was called away by a message that his wife was taken ill. A handsome young woman in a cloak with a hood appeared and brought the warder a bottle of champagne from an admirer. He thought the admirer was the young lady. The champagne had been treated with a chemical compound that rendered the warder helpless. Keys were taken, the Reverend Slaney's cell unlocked. He and two other felons escaped. They donned and took away with them three overcoats that were hanging in the anteroom there. One of these was Captain Pusey's. I find that gratifying, Tom," he said.

"I wonder if the woman was Miss Best, or Mrs. Hansen."

"The warder was not, in fact, able to make much of a description, except that the woman was young and comely."

He laughed and said, "It sounds like the kind of trick Mammy Pleasant used to contrive."

———

In the *Chronicle* files of four years ago I found the article on Mammy Pleasant that I remembered. There was a cut of her grim face framed in a bonnet like a bucket, with the headline:

ANGEL OR VOODOO QUEEN?

Mary Ellen Pleasant is the daughter of a slave who had been the Voodoo Queen of Santo Domingo, and a free man named Williams described by Mammy as a Kanaka. Although she was born into slavery on a plantation near Augusta, Georgia, she was considered too pretty a girl for fieldwork and was sold to a wealthy Missourian, who treated her as a member of the family. She spent much of her youth in New Orleans where she was tutored by the New Orleans Voodoo Queen Marie Laveau, and also learned the fancy cooking which was to prove important to her future career in San Francisco. She married an abolitionist named Smith, who left her a fortune when he died. She used her inheritance to assist the Underground Railroad. In danger of prosecution for her activities, she took ship to San Francisco. News of her expertise as a cook preceded her, and she was beseiged by would-be employers. She cooked for a number of bachelor clubs and private families, including the former governor and U.S. Senator Milton Latham. She made good use of her position with powerful San Francisco families, listening to conversations of both scandals and financial dealings, which were to serve her well in her pyramiding fortunes.

She invested in three laundries, and also in houses of assignation. She became the leader of San Francisco Negroes, who were indebted to her because she found them positions with her influential white friends, and feared her as a Voodoo practitioner.

Although California's state constitution outlawed slavery, Negroes were not allowed to testify in court, attend public schools or ride on public transportation.

Mammy Pleasant regularly tested these laws, and was arrested several times on the street railway system but never jailed.

With some $30,000 of her own money and funds she had collected from the San Francisco Negro community, Mrs. Pleasant returned to the East to give financial support to John Brown in his plan to raid the arsenal at Harpers Ferry, and to buy land in Canada to house the slaves he planned to free in his slave insurrection.

John Brown was captured and hanged, and Mammy Pleasant returned to San Francisco, where she became known as the western terminus of the Underground Railroad, and the high priestess of the Voodoo serpent god Jango.

CHAPTER 11

ALONE, adj. In bad company.
                    — *The Devil's Dictionary*

FRIDAY, JANUARY 16, 1891

That Friday Edward Berowne was honoring himself with a celebration at his house.

The Poet of Telegraph Hill had been offered a position as the editor of the *Atlantic* in Boston at a salary of ten thousand dollars a year, an unheard-of sum. In the effort to keep him in the City the publisher of the *California Monthly* had pulled strings for his appointment to the faculty of the University of California, across the bay in Berkeley, and he was selected as the Poet Laureate of California, with laudatory items in the City newspapers. His poetry was praised, and his *California Monthly* stories of Hawaiian lads surfing in the old days given more attention than seemed to me warranted.

His change of name from the plain Brown to the ornate Berowne was treated indulgently, as a kind of San Francisco quirk.

I received an engraved invitation to the celebratory party, with a handwritten note that I was to come early. I was the first guest on hand, and I realized that Berowne wanted to have a talk.

Seated on the porch with the famous poet I watched a cluster of fishing boats with their hennaed lateen sails heading past Alcatraz. Berowne's amiable face was friendly but severe. I knew what was coming.

"Haunani will be attending Senator Hearst's b-b-ball with young Richard Goforth," he said. "Richard's father is one of San Francisco's most highly regarded lawyers, Thomas."

My father passed out boodle in the state legislature.

"Well, that's fine," I said.

I did not approve of the defensive note in my voice.

"He is very well connected," Berowne said.

"And *I'm* here for a lecture on not being well-connected?"

Bierce referred to well-connected people as "instant aristocrats."

"Thomas, you know I am fond of you, but may I ask what are your resources?"

"Let's see," I said. "I own three suits, four hats, and three pair of shoes. And a typewriter. I have a very fine badger hair-shaving brush, a gift from my father; a valise, six cravats, maybe seven presentable shirts—"

Berowne chuckled. "You have enumerated your wardrobe for me, Tom. I can't b-b-begin to enumerate Haunani's."

I felt myself sinking into my chair. I couldn't afford to support Haunani's appetite, much less her wardrobe.

"It is true her father, my b-b-brother, was not a rich man," he continued. "Nor am I, heaven knows. But the dear girl was b-b-brought up in p-p-prodigal circumstances by Silas Underwood. She is his ward. Silas Underwood is the most p-p-powerful man in Hawaii, and ranks very high among the world's financial aristocracy."

I knew all this.

"I am aware that she is attached to you, Thomas," Berowne said.

"And I am to say, yes, and I am very attached to her also, to which you will respond that if I am truly fond of her I will get out of the way so that she can marry someone of serious social and financial connections."

Berowne cleared his throat. A glint of anger appeared in his eye, and faded.

"I do not consider myself to be in her way," I said. "I am pleased she will be attending Senator Hearst's ball with the well-connected young Richard Goforth. I am someone with whom she amuses herself while awaiting the proper social young gentleman of whom her uncle will approve."

"Thomas, I am afraid 'amuses' may be a more elastic term than San Francisco society would approve of."

No answer to that.

"In Hawaii a young lady, especially an *alii*, has considerably more leeway than on the Mainland," Berowne said. "Haunani is used to having her way. She is very headstrong, as I am sure you know. She is not sufficiently aware of the degree of criticism that may be incurred, and of the p-p-penalties thereof."

When I thought of afternoons and evenings alone with Haunani in my rooms, they seemed so precious, so improbable, and so fragile, I could only conceive of my life without them as lonely nights weeping for my dead wife while Signora Sotopietro sang "Caro Nome" next door.

Haunani had told me that her dear uncle did not care how she comported herself, but I had known this was coming.

"A young woman of high rank in Hawaii has a great deal of autonomy," Berowne went on in his friendly voice. "Chiefesses were able to order their lives as they saw fit. I am trying to make Haunani understand that there are many more strictures in San Francisco."

I slipped a finger inside my collar to loosen it.

"I know in time you will come to understand," Berowne said, "that in San Francisco it is not what you know, but who you know. I am not a rich man, but I am able to move in the highest circles in this b-b-blessed City b-b-because I have made friends with well-connected people, I have entertained my dinner p-p-partners, I have kissed the b-b-eringed hands of ugly old women, I have laughed at jokes that have caused my gorge to rise. It is a kind of initiation one must go through. One must cultivate, before one comes to be cultivated. Some, of course, like our friend A.G. B-b-bierce, will not p-p-perform this function. And does not need to b-b-because he is naturally endowed and esteemed. B-b-but lesser geniuses must cultivate."

My gorge had already risen.

"What do you want me to say?" I said after a deep breath.

"I want you to say you will do what you know must b-b-be done."

"I will think about it," I said.

———

Presently literary San Francisco began to gather. Haunani was resplendent in gleaming white, a fitted and ruffled Mother Hubbard that enhanced her exotic appearance. With her pale brown hair swept up at the back of her head, she was taller than anyone but Joaquin Miller, the Poet of the Sierras.

The endowed and esteemed Bierce was on hand, along with a passel of female poets and a number of literary gents.

Bierce was accompanied by his new friend Rose Blessing Hansen. She wore a black gown which showed off her white arms, and her pretty face beneath a mannish soft hat with the brim turned down over her forehead.

Aaron Underwood stood alone by the window, a tall sandy-graying Puritan with cheeks wrinkled in lines of worry that made him look more compassionate than he probably was. His eyes always returned to Haunani.

I watched him watching her. She had been brought up since her eleventh year in a household in which he had also lived as a young man. While she had engaged in *panipani* with Jonathan Prout, with Charles Perry, and what other *alii* had caught her fancy, he longed to marry her when she became an adult and his sickly wife was finally out of the way.

Because his intentions were honorable he seemed more threatening than the men who had actually possessed her body.

Chang passed glasses of Sonoma Valley wine, and a couple of young male poets with Oscar Wilde bow ties helped with crackers and cheese. There were toasts to Berowne, who beamed and chirped in a frock coat and striped trousers.

Calls for a speech resounded.

Berowne stood, holding his glass, pink cheeks flushed and smiling. "It is lovely to b-b-be celebrated!" he said.

Applause. Aaron Underwood glanced at Berowne only briefly, before he resumed his gaze at Haunani, who stood near me. Aware of Underwood's jealousy, I could laugh at the ache of my own economic resentment.

"What I appreciate is consideration!" Berowne continued. "A volume of my p-p-poems will b-b-be p-p-published by the Harrison P-p-press next month. And I have b-b-been laboring over my autob-b-biography." With a dramatic gesture he laid his finger to his lip. "B-b-but that is only to b-b-be p-p-published p-p-posthumously!"

"By a Californian or a Bostonian?" someone called out.

"Oh, I would so like it to b-b-be b-b-both!"

"Can't be both, Edward!"

"Which is it to be? Please tell us!"

"It is so nice to know that California loves its Telegraph Hill P-P-Poet!" Berowne said. He had a way of swaying on his feet, his big belly swathed in a striped vest with a gold watch chain across it, like some large, tame tabby.

"We love you, Eddie!" a group of the lady poets called out together.

Aaron Underwood had seated himself so that I could no longer see him past the crowd around Berowne. Bierce and Mrs. Hansen stood side by side, her arm looped through his. They looked comfortable with each other.

Out the window Alcatraz gleamed in the late sun. A rusty freighter with a rack of bare spars slipped past its barren flank.

Entering at a jaunty stride was a slim young fellow in fine broadcloth and a blue cravat, with a hairline mustache and a high-nostril look of contempt for lesser beings. With him was a tiny delicate-featured lady with dark reddish hair and flashing eyes.

Charles Perry and his French wife.

I watched this handsome young man steer his wife through the guests to Berowne, whom he saluted with a flourished hand and a bow. Berowne kissed the hand of the tiny woman.

Perry saluted Haunani also. I saw her hand raised to her cheek, the tilt of her head. Then the flash of her blue eyes met mine, and she grinned in mockery.

Perry had managed to focus attention on himself and away from our host. Bierce and Mrs. Hansen had retreated to stand at the window, he in his sartorial and tonsorial ease, Mrs. Hansen's pale face raised to his attentions. Mrs. Perry had taken a post beside Berowne.

She clapped enthusiastically when someone called, "Speech, Charley!"

Perry struck a pose.

"Our king is dying!" he proclaimed. "Who will succeed David Kalakaua? Will it be his sister, and his likeness in every way? Will it be Alexander Honomoku, the favorite of the merchant interests, who would cede Hawaiian lands to the United States? Or will it be the good Queen Emma, widow of the last of the grand Kamehameha line, who will bring Hawaii back to integrity and glory?"

He spoke in a mock-heroic tone, with broad gestures. Laughter spilled out all around at his sideshow.

I thought the admiration with which Perry's little lady regarded her husband's posturing was forced.

"Oh, King David!" he continued. "Do not leave your loyal subjects in this horrid suspense. If you do not speak Lili-uokalani ascends to the throne of Kamehameha. Name Queen Emma, David Kalakaua! Down with the Annexationist traitors! Down with the Chinese! Hawaii for the Hawaiians! Pearl Harbor for the Hawaiians!

"How much does David Kalakaua owe Silas Underwood now?" he said, swinging suddenly toward Aaron Underwood.

All eyes turned to Underwood, who did not speak, his mouth compressed into that lipless missionary line my father had described.

Perry waited. After a moment he said, "Still adding, eh, *Miliona?*"

Another round of laughter.

"*Maikai!*" Perry cried out, and pushed his way over to Haunani, picked her up and swung her around. I had a glimpse of the pink of her face. She was inches taller than he was.

"*Waiho!*" she whispered.

Promptly he put her down.

He sang a song whose verses ended with the word *auwe*,

which Haunani said when she had hurt herself or was sad about something. The rest of the verse was in words I did not understand, but seemed to be a parody. I glanced around to see who understood the words: Haunani, Underwood, maybe Berowne, who looked embarrassed.

Chang appeared with champagne. Perry in his golden good looks and the surety of them stood laughing into Berowne's face. His little wife pulled at his arm. Haunani made her way over to join me, still pink-cheeked.

"You see?" she whispered.

Perry performed another of his arrogant crowd-cuttings to join Haunani, standing beside her possessively.

She made introductions. My hand was given a brief shake. Of this pair of *hapahaoles*, Haunani was one notch closer to the haole side, Perry's skin a shade darker than hers. His brown eyes were completely cold where her blue eyes were warm. He looked straight into my face.

"So this is your *haole* friend, Nani." Even the nickname had a possessive note to it.

"I hope he will be yours also, Charley."

I doubted that.

"You are a journalist, Mr. Redmond?"

I admitted it.

"I am afraid we have not much respect for journalists in the Islands."

Bierce would have had a killing response, even though he himself had no respect for his profession. "I am sure the lack of respect is well deserved," I said, and felt the pressure of Haunani's hand on my arm.

"Nor in France, where I have spent some years of my life," Perry said, eyes boring at me.

"They are highly regarded in Greenland, I believe," I said. "In the mountains there."

"I must doubt that," Perry said. The pressure on my arm increased.

"And have you resided in Greenland also, Mr. Perry?"

An expression of fury passed over his face like a rain cloud quickly gone. He said to Haunani, "And what have you done with Leilei, Nani?"

"I have done nothing with her, Charley."

"Surely you know where she has gone. Alexander is devastated."

"I don't know where she is, Charley," she said. Her hand fell away from my arm. I thought she didn't like to lie.

"Am I to suspect that she has left for the mountains of Greenland, where the journalists are respected?" Perry said, and turned away. His wife had called to him, in her small, imperious voice, and he went to her.

Haunani and I faced each other. "Thank you," she whispered.

"The commander of the Diamond Head Rifles," I said, nodding toward Perry and his wife. Champagne was being passed again.

"He is certain of his importance if the king selects Queen Emma as his successor," Haunani said. "He sees himself as counsellor. More than that! Maybe Queen Emma will select *him* as her successor. A *hapahaole*! He can make himself so darling to older ladies. Young ladies, also. But he can be a nasty fellow, Tom. You have seen this just now."

"Thank you for the grip on my arm that reminded me that I am not a nasty fellow also."

She laughed in my face. "Tell me: Who is the pretty little person with your Mr. Bierce?"

"She is a medium, Mrs. Hansen."

"I must go to speak with Cousin Aaron, if you will excuse me." She left me on her own expedition through the crowd around her real uncle, to her so-called cousin, who wished to be more than that.

I went to join Bierce and Mrs. Hansen. She smiled at me with a tilt of her head. Her wide-apart eyes and narrow chin gave the effect not so much of beauty as of otherworldliness, as though she had taken on the appearance of the denizens of the spirit world with whom she kept contact.

Bierce was posturing in that way he had that meant he was pleased with himself, his companion and his prospects.

"I wonder if it is significant that the royal counsellor has not appeared at this affair," he said. "I assume he was invited."

"Alexander Honomoku is not here, either."

Mrs. Hansen smiled up at her escort. "Am I not to be included in this conversation, Mr. Bierce?"

"I would like to see you included in almost everything, my dear Mrs. Hansen," Bierce said, with ironical courtliness.

He addressed himself to me. "Mrs. Hansen has volunteered the assistance of her spirit guide to help us discover the whereabouts of the princess Leileiha. Is it possible for you to attend a séance with us this very evening, Tom? After this event?"

I said I would certainly attend.

CHAPTER 12

SPOOKER, n. A writer whose imagination concerns itself with supernatural phenomena, especially the doings of spooks.
— *The Devil's Dictionary*

FRIDAY, JANUARY 16, 1891

Mrs. Hansen occupied rooms on Clay Street with a bay window view of the lights of Chinatown. Bierce helped her off with her coat and brought her a libation of some kind, maybe whiskey, which, seated, she imbibed with her neck stretched up so that she gave the impression of a birdling ministered to.

She spluttered, coughed and laughed, passing a small hand over her forehead. I had an impression of Bierce as one of the "corrupting and cynical men" he had lectured me on, who manipulated the female mediums to their own profit.

The sitting room was sparsely furnished, with a rag rug on a pine floor, a sofa somewhat the worse for wear, straight chairs and a cheap carved sideboard. A big armoire stood in the corner, doors open. Beyond it a curtain of strung eucalyptus acorns rippled in some unfelt draft.

Bierce saw to moving a tiny table inside the armoire, with a straight chair beside it, and set a lantern on it, which he lighted. Meanwhile, Mrs. Hansen brought a small cut-glass bowl of milk as for a pet and placed it on the table.

She wandered between the sitting room and the hall bedroom, seeming to float in her filmy garments in which, against the light, a full though small figure was outlined. Her white throat and bare arms had an almost phosphorescent quality in the splashes of shadow and light from the electric bulb on its twisted cord. She moved at a curiously ritualistic pace, with her twisting half-limp.

After circling like a dog preparing to bed down, she seated herself inside the armoire at the little table, and, motionless, head bowed, looked as though she were napping there. She seemed in a trance, as she had at the suffrage meeting.

When she made a signal with her hand Bierce moved to extinguish the central light. Now she was in semidarkness, framed in a more concentrated dark within the armoire, with the slashes of illumination from the lantern making bright planes and heavy shadows of her face. Hairs prickled on the backs of my legs as I watched from my end of the sofa. Bierce, who had been moving restlessly, at last seated himself also.

It seemed a quarter of an hour must have passed. My hairs prickled again when I heard the triple tinkle of a tiny bell she must have secreted on her person.

After another wait I heard a faint whispering. It came more loudly. *"Miles?"* she whispered, an intensity in the pale planes of her face within the closeted dark.

"Miles? *Miles?*"

The triple bell tinkled again.

This was effectively theatrical.

Another voice, when it came, was a whisper also, but a powerful one that sounded as though it reverberated within an empty skull. *"ROSIE!"*

I was certain that Mrs. Hansen's lips had not moved with that responding whisper. Bierce's hand tapped my knee.

Mrs. Hansen's whispering seemed to be relating to her attendant spirit what Bierce must have told her of the disappearance of Princess Leileiha. This took some time, and was barely audible. It was followed by another interminable silence while within the cubicle Mrs. Hansen's head sagged over the little table so her face was concealed in shadow.

When it came again the huge whisper was electrifying: *"NOTHING IS KNOWN!"*

Silence again. The sensation that the spirit had absented himself again was very strong. Then he was back: *"NOTH-ING IS KNOWN!"*

"I know the spirits know nothing, Miles, for no one has passed to the other side." Mrs. Hansen sounded like a schoolteacher rebuking a careless scholar. "It is your assistance I am requesting."

"NOTHING IS KNOWN!"

"Miles, I want you to *think*. What could have happened to the princess?"

"Pa!" a new voice said, a young man's voice. I could feel Bierce galvanized beside me. *"Pa!"*

"Here," Bierce said.

"I am over here, Pa!"

"I know that, Day."

"Pa, they don't give a fellow a second chance!"

Bierce cleared his throat and said, "I'm afraid they don't."

"She wasn't much good, Pa. But I thought I loved her, and then she run off with Neil Hubbs, and I couldn't stand it! I was such a dang fool. I have made you and Ma ashamed of me, Pa!"

"I'm proud of you, son," Bierce said in a deep voice.

I almost jumped out of my suit at the clanging of a bell that was not within the room. It was the firehouse over beyond California Street. As the bell ceased its noise there was a clamor of voices; the fire must be nearby. Bierce had risen.

In the armoire I could dimly see that Mrs. Hansen had her hands to her cheeks. Bierce hurried to bend over her so that I could no longer see her face. "Turn up the light!" he called to me.

I did so, and the room sprang to brightness. Out the window I saw that the fire was blocks away. Orange illumination rose like dawn over a rooftop higher up the hill. The firehouse bell was clanging again. Ten years ago I had been a fireman with an engine company, and I would still hasten to the scene of a fire if one was nearby. The old impulse tugged at me, and I wanted to leave this uncomfortable place.

The session with Mrs. Hansen and her spirit guide was surely over.

Bierce half helped, half carried her past me and into the bedroom. I could hear her sobs. I saw with a shock that the bowl of milk was half-empty.

Finally Bierce came out of the bedroom, pulling the door closed behind him.

"That's the end of that for tonight," he said. "If anything interferes it seems to rend her nerves."

His eyes looked like burnt holes in his face. In a lowered voice he said, "It is all trickery, Tom."

I didn't know what to say about Day Bierce's voice, trickery or not.

I said I would be going.

"I will have to stay to see that she does not comfort herself with an excess of laudanum," Bierce said.

———

The fire, in a tall shingle rooming house up California Street, was out by now, the firemen standing around the pumper in their black helmets in a circle of light under a street standard. There was still that burnt-toast stench of the aftermath of a blaze. The chief had taken off his white helmet and parked it on the fender of the pumper, the canvas hoses had been recoiled. The crew was drinking coffee spiked with Chilean rum that one of the neighbors had supplied. I chatted with them about the fire. The chief was Jimmy Gallagher, whom I had known long ago, a fat fellow with a meaty Irish face and a balding head gleaming in the lights. What hairs were left to him were swirled into a pixie coil from the band of his helmet.

"Well, hello Tommy!" he called to me. "Come to look us over?"

The fire hadn't caused much damage but they had discovered a dead man in the room where the fire had started. "Murthered!" Jimmy said.

"Dark-skin fellow," another said. "Not a blackie, though. "High tone from the look of him. Somebody'd whacked him right in the middle of the forehead and laid him out on the bed."

"Wasn't robbers," a pale-faced young fellow said. "There was a poke bag of greenbacks there that Ernie set a watch on till the coppers came."

"Don't want any bad name for corpse-robbing for number seven," Jimmy said.

"Hawaiian fellow," another fireman said. "There was Hawaiian goods there, a feather thing and some photographs of places with palm trees and ocean to them."

"What did he look like?" I asked.

"Tall, skinny as a whip, all cheekbones and sunk-in cheeks. Head busted in."

"Can I take a look inside?" I said to the chief, and he waved a hand in permission.

Judge Akua's room was a mess of knocked-about furniture

and charred walls, mainly the window wall. The bed had not been burned. The little fireplace caught my eye, where a packet of papers had been burned on the grate. When I fingered through it the paper crumbled to ash in my hand except for a pasteboard card that seemed to be a menu, with a peculiar crest. It was charred along one edge. I tucked it into my pocket and looked around for the murder weapon. I couldn't seem to focus on anything, thinking of the royal counsellor. I had started to open a curved-top trunk when one of the firemen came in, carrying an axe with a red-painted head, and it seemed best to get out of his way.

——

I rode the cable car down California Street, and hailed a hack to take me to the morgue. Judge Akua was a long, skinny corpse, gray flesh with paler skin on his palms and the bottoms of his feet. His forehead was caved in, gray lips gaping open. The blood had been washed away. Death had cancelled his regal aspect, his royal significance, and the secret that had horrified him.

He had been murdered in his room in his boardinghouse, which had then caught fire. It was the kind of murder that was common in San Francisco, a traveler assaulted in his room, a fire set to conceal the crime, and the murderer never identified or apprehended.

But this had not been a crime of robbery.

I felt a weight of depression. That old Hawaiian gentleman had impressed me, and Haunani had loved him.

It seemed to me that Bierce and I should have known and acted to prevent this murder.

SATURDAY, JANUARY 17, 1891

Bierce and I were discussing the death of Judge Akua when a Mr. Regan arrived in Bierce's office. It was precisely ten o'clock on Saturday, the sixth day of Bierce's investigation into the disappearance of the princess Leileiha.

Regan was a short, stout gent smelling of rose water as though he was right out of the barber's chair, with a round face gleaming with tonsorial attention, and his pink scalp showing through thinning hair. He introduced himself as a U.S. commissioner for Hawaiian affairs, shook hands with Bierce and me, and plumped himself down in the chair by Bierce's desk, examined the skull and, squinting down his nose, addressed himself to Bierce: "Are you aware of the fact that Judge Akua, King Kalakaua's counsellor, was murdered last night?"

"I am aware of that tragic event," Bierce said.

"Judge Akua was not viewed as a friend of this country."

"Is that so?" Bierce said, finger to his chin.

"In my position," Regan said, "I must be aware of U.S. policy, but also of what U.S. policy is to *become*. The present and the future, you see."

This was a personage with a high opinion of himself.

"There is this administration, in other words," Regan went on. "And there is the administration that will follow it."

"Am I to understand that there has been a change of policy?" Bierce said.

"Manifest Destiny," Regan said. He had sharp little eyes, which he switched from Bierce's face to mine.

"Fateful words," I said.

"Manifest Destiny has completed itself to the edge of the continent. But what of the islands of the Pacific? Will the next administration wish to extend the scope of our destiny? Pearl Harbor is one of the great natural harbors in the Pacific."

"That is well known."

"In the present, we want that harbor. In the future, if Manifest Destiny is to be extended, we must *have* that harbor. King

Kalakaua has *reluctantly* supported a lease in exchange for reciprocity and low tariffs on sugar. Alexander Honomoku will also support such a solution."

"But the counsellor would have been against it."

"Judge Akua had thrown his considerable weight against it."

"You are building a case against this country as the perpetrator of this foul business, Mr. Regan."

Smiling with a show of teeth, Regan said, "One can regret the tragedy while praising its salutary effect on the American interest."

Bierce said that if he thought that by grinding up Alexander Honomoku and casting the residue upon Judge Akua's bier that fine old gentleman could be restored to life, he would set out immediately for the Palace Hotel with a meat grinder.

"Ha-ha," Regan said. "U.S. policy is just a bit more complicated than that, Mr. Bierce! On the surface of it, it might seem that this country should support the Honomoku claim to the crown. Princess Liliuokalani has announced her opposition to the leasing or ceding of Hawaiian lands. Queen Emma is even more strongly opposed.

"And what will be the result of such opposition? No reciprocity. Ruin of the sugar planters and commercial interests, which are American in the majority."

Regan clapped his hands together and spread them wide.

"Rebellion! Establishment of a republic! Pearl Harbor ceded, not leased!"

He laughed at his cleverness.

Bierce said, "The difficulties of Annexation have been described to me as the Chinese problem, the noncontiguous problem, the leprosy problem, and the Southern senators problem."

"Circumstances alter cases, Mr. Bierce," Regan said.

"And in the altered case is Annexation now the policy of this country, which has pretended to be a friend to the Kingdom of Hawaii?"

Regan shrugged elaborately.

"And the United States supports Emma as queen?"

"Precisely."

"And not Liliuokalani?" I said.

Regan shrugged. "Emma would be most easily overthrown. You are in a position to be helpful to your country, sir!" he said to Bierce.

"In what way, Mr. Regan?"

"As I have said, Mr. Bierce, cases have been altered. It is now to our benefit that the princess *not* be located. We prefer that Alexander Honomoku remain a force that need *not* be reckoned with. I call upon your patriotism, sir."

"Samuel Johnson contends that patriotism is the last refuge of scoundrels," Bierce said. "I believe it to be the first. U.S. policy as you state it is to stir up a rebellion in Hawaii for the purpose of promoting Annexation. I decline to be a party to perfidy, Mr. Regan. Good day, sir!"

When Regan had taken himself off Bierce said to me, "Diplomacy is the patriotic art of lying for one's country."

I said, "I would hate to do any favors for that bamboozler."

"I wonder if we were bamboozled," Bierce said.

———

Charring flaked off the edge of the card I had recovered from Judge Akua's fireplace as I handed it to him. He perused it carefully.

It seemed to me to be of interest because it was among papers the murderer might have burned, and because of the crest, which consisted of numbers and letters woven together, PO–8 and EC–4, beneath a curve that might be a hill, bearing an upright with upslanted arms like the same-length hands of a clock pointing to 10:10, or 1:50.

Above this crest, handwritten, was the word "Jongleurs."

I reminded Bierce that Lillie Coit, in her association with San Francisco firefighters, had been honorarily inducted into Knickerbocker #5, and thereafter her signature was always followed by a "5."

EC–4 could be Engine Company #4 of the Fire Department.

"Ah!" he said.

"What about the clock hands?" I said. "Time of day?"

Bierce assumed a baffled expression. "Jongleurs were medieval musicians."

The menu was dated August 4, 1885. It was ordinary enough:

"Baked veal, potatoes, salsify, cabbage salad, sweet pickles, minute pudding, cakes, mince pie, Sally Lunn, coffee, tea."

"Pastry," Bierce said, brushing crumbs of char from his desk. He dropped the menu card into his desk drawer with an eyebrow hooked up interrogatively.

I nodded permission.

"I had no idea that old gentleman was in danger," Bierce said unhappily. "Who could have done this?"

"A burglar?"

He shook his head grimly.

CHAPTER 13

SORCERY, n. The ancient prototype and forerunner of political influence.
— *The Devil's Dictionary*

SATURDAY, JANUARY 17, 1891

En route to the Palace Hotel I asked Bierce what he knew of Mrs. Hansen's spirit guide, Miles.

The corners of his mouth tucked in in reluctant amusement. "Rose lived in England, in Surrey, as a child, and a gentle old man there came to play with the children in the house where she was. She loved him. According to her his spirit sought her out. He's been with her ever since she first became a medium. I said to you that it is all trickery. For instance, if you had noticed you would have seen that the milk in the little bowl was half gone, as though Miles had imbibed it. She has a little sponge, which she empties into a little metal box she keeps about her."

"But are we to think that Miles really speaks?"

"He speaks through her. I believe she actually thinks he is speaking."

"Her lips did not move."

"She is very clever. She has convinced herself."

"And you had told her of Day's tragedy?"

"Yes, I had," Bierce said, in a tone that meant we would hear no more of *that*.

———

Unless I misunderstood him, Major Baker of the king's retinue explained that "Kalaua" was a title in the king's service, for handmaiden. Bierce and I sat with the major at the table in the anteroom outside the king's bedroom where that vast suspiration still continued, degrees weaker.

The king's attendants already knew of the royal counsellor's murder, and that the chaplain lay in a coma at St. Francis Hospital. It did not seem that we would learn from Prout the information out of the past that had afflicted Judge Akua.

Summoned, Lydia Kukui sat straight-backed opposite me, big-eyed, brown hands folded primly before her. Major Baker, short and erect, with a puffy clean-shaven face, clearly considered himself translator and guardian. The girl's eyes were white-rimmed. She was not pretty, her features too large, but she looked young and healthy, and frightened.

"Who would kill Judge Akua?" Bierce asked her.

"I don't know!"

"You knew him well?"

"Everyone knew Andrew Akua!"

I recalled the sense of intimacy in her stance beside the counsellor when we had first seen him.

"Are you from Maui also?"

"Hilo," she whispered.

"Kalaua is from Hilo on the Big Island," Major Baker put in.

"When did you last see the counsellor?"

"Yesterday!"

"Where?"

"Here!"

"And you, sir?" Bierce said to the major.

"Here. Yesterday."

"He was very upset yesterday? Why was that?"

The major and Miss Kukui looked at each other. The major frowned. "He did not seem upset."

"He went to see the chaplain, who told him something that upset him. What would that have been?"

"No idea," the major said, and folded his arms.

"Miss Kukui?"

"Kalaua!" she whispered. She chattered at the major in Hawaiian.

"Kalaua says Mr. Prout was like that," the major said. "Always, when you talked to Mr. Prout, you felt less good about everything than before you talked to him."

"Judge Akua said whatever it was was not political," I said.

"He suggested that Princess Leileiha may have disappeared because of the *kahuna*," Bierce said. "And that the *kahuna* was sent by Silas Underwood."

The silence had dimension and weight. Lydia Kukui examined her fingernails.

"What is the *kahuna*'s name?"

"Lapidus Kanekoa," the major said.

"Is he here now?"

The major and Kalaua gazed at each other again.

"Mr. Kanekoa has not been here for some days."

"How many days?" Bierce said, addressing Kalaua.

She rolled her eyes at Major Baker, and whispered in Hawaiian.

"Kalaua must return to the bedside," Major Baker said.

Bierce sighed and watched her go, a big hurrying girl trying to get out of our sight. Before she disappeared into the king's bedroom, he said, "One last question, Kalaua."

She swung back toward us.

"How is Mr. Kanekoa treating the king?"

She looked as though she would faint, clinging to the doorknob. Then she drew herself up and spouted Hawaiian to Major Baker, who cleared his throat.

"Kalaua is forbidden to discuss his majesty's treatment," Major Baker said, and Kalaua disappeared inside the sick-room.

Major Baker refused to answer Bierce's question on the same grounds.

When we left the palace, I said to Bierce, "Did you notice that Kalaua kept her fingers crossed all the time we were talking to her?"

Bierce blew out his breath in a whistle.

"Maybe crossed fingers means something in Hawaiian. A charm against the evil eye or some such. Against a *kahuna*."

"They are very frightened, both of them," Bierce said.

———

By a visit to the Spring Valley Water Company, I ascertained that the house in Hayes Valley belonged to Mr. Aaron Underwood, although his residence was around the corner on Van Ness Avenue.

Bierce did not need persuasion to accompany me to the house to which I had followed Kalaua, and where I had encountered the *kahuna*. This time we mounted brick steps to the front door, and I rang the bell.

A skinny, gray-haired woman in a maid's uniform opened the door. Slick as a Bible salesman, Bierce slipped past her, and, as she turned to confront him, I stepped inside also.

In a sunny parlor a kind of human spider reclined, arms in motion rising and falling, flexing and straightening. The movements increased in velocity as the being became aware of Bierce and me at the opposite end of the room. In the center of these moving arms was a human face, a boy's face, tousled black hair, mouth open.

"Madam, I am Ambrose Bierce and this is my colleague, Mr. Redmond. We are investigating activities known to have taken place in the cellar below this room."

"He's gone," the woman said. "Cleared out."

The boy was trying to speak, the lips mouthing a word I couldn't make out: "Hel— Hel— Hel—"

"Hello," Bierce said, who had understood.

"Hel— Hel— Hel—"

"Hello," I said. We both moved away from the door, toward him.

The room was furnished with a piano in one corner, a lamp with a purple velvet shade, a settee, a little closed-up desk, an oriental carpet on the floor. The afflicted young man reclined in a black iron adjustable arrangement padded with beige pillows. A brindle cat was seated, licking herself, on the piano bench.

"Who was he, madam? There have been complaints—"

"He was a Hawaiian gentlemen acquaintance of Mr. Underwood's. Mr. Underwood is always hospitable to visitors from Hawaii."

"Hel—lo!" the boy got out. I went over to stand on the fringe of the flexing and rippling arms. A hand flapped at me. I understood I was to shake it. The boy was grinning ingratiatingly with a great show of teeth, gums and tongue.

"Wal— Wal— Wal—"

The woman said, "Walter," and I said, "Hello, Walter. I'm Tom Redmond." I shook his hand some more while he grinned up at me like a puppy.

"And you are?" Bierce said.

She was Mrs. Mulberry.

Walter was engaged in an inarticulate statement accompanied by weaving hands and the loopy smile. I could not get the gist of it.

"Walter did not like Mr. Kanekoa," Mrs. Mulberry said. "He frightened Walter. I think Mr. Silas Underwood had sent him here because he is a doctor in Hawaiian medicines. It was hoped that he might help King Kalakaua, and Walter."

"Tom— Tom— Tom—"

"Yes, Walter?"

"*Bad*—" He was nodding excessively, jerkily. "*Kah— Kah— Kah—*"

"*Kahuna?*"

"Walter is Mr. Aaron Underwood's son?" Bierce said. I glanced at him in surprise, for it had not occurred to me that this was the youngest Underwood, whom Haunani had mentioned.

"Mr. and Mrs. Underwood's son," Mrs. Mulberry corrected me.

"*Kah— huna!*" Walter got out.

"What did Kanekoa do for you, Walter?" I asked.

The treatment had had to do with feathers. Walter made motions of brushing at his cheeks and chin. He seemed a bright, interested, and eager person; and lonely.

"It was not successful," Mrs. Mulberry said. "Of course the finest proper doctors in San Francisco have been unsuccessful, also."

A shadow of irritation passed over Walter's features. His hand flapped toward Mrs. Mulberry as though to silence her.

The cat jumped down from the stool and trotted across the room, vertical tail with a crook in the end. She disappeared out a far door.

"Hawaii people think every affliction is the result of a

curse," Mrs. Mulberry went on, in a sour voice. "Imagine Mr. Silas Underwood sending that medicine man from the Islands to wave his feathers over poor Walter's head!"

"Dough— Dough— Dough—" Walter started.

There was a silence.

"Don't talk!" Walter said.

"Well!" Mrs. Mulberry said.

"We are investigating the disappearance of the Hawaiian princess Leileiha," Bierce said.

Mrs. Mulberry only looked puzzled, shaking her head. Walter said, "Ask— Ask— Ask—"

There was a scraping, a thumping of footsteps and through the far door came Aaron Underwood himself, carrying his plug hat. He halted, staring at Bierce and me, then he strode toward us, calling out in a loud voice, "What is this, Mrs. Mulberry?

"Ask how—" Walter said. "How—"

"Bierce!" Underwood said, halting again. He gave me a glance like a thunderhead.

Walter's hand pawed at my arm. "Ask how— how—Haunani!"

"Allow me to explain," Bierce said. He managed to give the effect of lounging at his ease, where he stood with Mrs. Mulberry. "Mr. Redmond followed a carriage here the other day in which he had seen a woman he thought might be Princess Leileiha. In the cellar he discovered disturbing evidence of malevolent Hawaiian rites. He brought me with him today to investigate further."

"He's gone," Underwood said. He crossed to Walter, laying hands on him in a curiously ceremonial way. He swung around to face Bierce.

Bierce said gently, "I must follow any suspicious activities among your countrymen in my effort to find the lost person."

"That would have been Lydia Kukui," Underwood said. "She was being taken for a ride in the park. Lydia seldom gets out of the sickroom and I have asked Amos to take her for an outing when it is convenient. Mrs. Mulberry, will you serve us tea in the parlor?"

Mrs. Mulberry led us into another room.

Behind us Walter was silent but not motionless in his patent wrought-iron chair.

The parlor was fitted out with red plush overstuffed furniture, and a gold-framed painting of brown deer drinking at a brown pond. The cat, recumbent on the settee, regarded us disapprovingly.

"Are you aware of the murder of Judge Akua?" Bierce asked when we had seated ourselves.

The news had to be explained. Underwood looked unmanned. "Who can have done this thing?" he whispered. "My father's life has also been threatened, in Honolulu," he added.

His father runs him, Haunani had said.

"By whom, sir?" Bierce asked.

"Annexationists. The message was, 'Gold and silver cannot stop lead.' "

"Your father is sometimes spoken of as the uncrowned king of Hawaii."

"That is a canard, Mr. Bierce. My father has never wavered in his support of King Kalakaua."

"The monarchy owes him great deal of money," Bierce said.

"In the neighborhood of a million dollars."

I whistled.

Bierce said, "The monarchy has been spendthrift, as, I believe, is customary with monarchies. Mr. Underwood, was the *kahuna* in the cellar sent here by your father?"

Underwood raised his chin, his lips clamped closed. He

seemed to have kept his physique in youthful condition, for there was no fat on him. I was having difficulty maintaining my dislike.

He said, "If Kanekoa was sent by my father it was at David Kalakaua's request. David is convinced of the efficacy of priestly healing. He feels it should become a part of recognized medicine in Hawaii."

"Priestly healing has two faces," Bierce said. "There is also the opposite of healing."

Underwood nodded reluctantly.

"In his previous visit to this house Tom discovered a newspaper piece announcing the arrival of the Reverend Prout in San Francisco, displayed with a lava rock placed on top of the newspaper clipping."

"Mr. Prout has long been a sick man," Underwood protested.

"I understand that *kahunas* are more pervasive in a time of volcanic action in the Islands," Bierce said. "And perhaps in times of political upheaval as well as geological. I wonder if these Hawaiian convulsions have to do with the disappearance of Princess Leileiha, and now the death of Judge Akua."

Underwood looked flustered. "I cannot believe these matters are connected."

"Where is Kanekoa now?"

"I don't know where he has gone, gentlemen. He is not a personal friend, and hardly an acquaintance. I suggest that you inquire of him among the king's aides."

I said, "Does Miss Haunani Brown come here often, Mr. Underwood?"

His big fair-haired hands clasped before him, he said, still without looking at me directly, "Miss Brown is the best medicine that is available to my son." He nodded toward the other room.

He seemed so anxious to be rid of us that Bierce rose and said, "I think we will take our leave now, Mr. Underwood. Thank you for the refreshment."

Outside he said to me, "I cannot think of any reason why Aaron Underwood would have urged me to search for the princess if he were concealing her in one of his various establishments."

———

On the newsstands the headline on the afternoon *Examiner* was, "**KING COUNSELLOR MURDERED.**"

CHAPTER 14

SATURDAY, JANUARY 17, 1891

Late that day I joined Bierce for the Saturday evening saloon round. Before we could set out from his office, however, a heavy tread sounded in the corridor, and the chief of detectives appeared.

Captain Pusey placed his cap on Bierce's desk beside the skull, and displayed his fine teeth in his irritating got-the-goods-on-you, better-come-across grin.

"Now, Mr. Bierce . . . this young lady missing at the Palace Hotel . . ."

Bierce sighed.

"There is juju business I don't know whether to pay attention to or not. I have been told a high-rank person has to die to make the volcanoes settle down out in the Islands."

"The king is dying."

"A princess is also a high-rank person."

"As was Judge Akua, the counsellor."

"How about that young Honolulu lady you are known to be acquainted with, Mr. Redmond? Is she high rank?"

In my estimation. I nodded.

There was no point disliking the chief of detectives for a heavy-handed persistence, which, in fact, sometimes must pay off.

Pusey scrubbed his fingers through his beard. He bent forward to thrust his face closer to Bierce's. "Mr. Bierce, what is your involvement in this matter?"

"Mr. Aaron Underwood asked me to assist him in discovering the whereabouts of the missing princess."

"And what are Mr. Underwood's considerations, if you please?"

"He and his father are closely involved in the affairs of the kingdom."

"Somebody that is closely involved in the affairs of the kingdom went and brained that judge over on California Street, and set fire to the place. And maybe has disposed of this princess person, too." Pusey leaned back with a sigh. "Fellow that coshed the judge wanted us to think robbery, but it has been a long time since I thought the way a perpetrator wanted me to think."

"And who is the perpetrator?"

Pusey jerked a thumb at the ceiling, as though calling upon the Almighty.

"Victim resided in Mrs. Gale's rooming house," he said. "Mrs. G. didn't see anybody, but whoever it was knew where the victim's room was and went there and brained the good judge. There's a nob end on the poker that most likely did the job. Turned his pockets inside out, but missed a stash of money. Burnt some papers in the grate, set fire to the curtains and skedaddled.

"That is a *bad* business, setting a fire in this tinderbox city," he said, shaking his head.

Bierce propped his fingertips together. "There would be a bowl on a hall table in a rooming house where calling cards are placed. Was there such a receptacle at Mrs. Gale's?"

Pusey brought a folded piece of paper from an inner pocket, unfolded it and presented it to him.

When the paper was passed to me, it proved to be a typewritten list of maybe twenty names. Some had a business listing after them. One name caught my eye: Charles Perry, Reform Party of Hawaii.

Pusey watched my face as I studied the list. He knew as well as I did who Charles Perry was, whose name had now appeared on two lists. Pusey repocketed the paper.

He said, "I will ask you to sort out for me that bunch of Hay-wy-yans that is in and in-and-out at the Palace, waiting on the king dying. If you would, Mr. Bierce."

Bierce said, "Mr. Charles Perry is Hawaiian, as I am sure you know. His card pronounces his political allegiance."

"There is a minister fellow in the hospital, I understand."

"Jonathan Prout," Bierce said. "There is Major Baker, the military aide; and Aaron Underwood, the son of the sugar magnate Silas Underwood."

Pusey brought out a little notebook, wet the tip of his pencil with his tongue, and wrote.

Bierce continued. "The masseuse Lydia Kukui, called Kalaua, and Alexander Honomoku, whom some hope the king will appoint his heir. There *was* Princess Leileiha, Honomoku's intended, and there *was* Judge Akua, the royal counsellor. There are doctors with whom I am not acquainted, and a Hawaiian practitioner named Kanekoa, also unknown to me."

Pusey wrote.

"I understand the judge and young Mister Perry had political differences," he said. "The judge was a conservative kind of fellow, Perry is all fire and go-it. One old and in charge, the other young and wants to be in charge." He gazed at Bierce with an eyebrow hooked up.

Bierce nodded, as though impressed by Pusey's analysis. "No doubt you will be pursuing that line of enquiry," he said. "And now, Chief, may I inquire as to the search for the escaped Reverend Slaney?"

Pusey scowled ferociously. "That devil!" he growled.

"Have you made any determination as to the identity of the young woman who assisted in his escape?"

"We have not!"

When Pusey had departed Bierce produced from his desk drawer the charred card from Judge Akua's grate with its mysterious letters and numbers: PO–8 and EC–4 under clock arms indicating 10:10, and the handwritten "Jongleurs." I pointed out that there was of course an Engine Company #4, and said I'd look into that. PO–8 was pure mystery.

"Might the raised arms indicate a theological aspect?" Bierce said. "The Sermon on the Mount? A preaching? A blessing?"

He sighed and said, "Jongleurs! I remind myself that Judge Akua's murder is Captain Pusey's business, not mine. Princess Leileiha is my concern. And your Miss Brown knows her whereabouts."

I did not dispute him.

"Mammy Pleasant's observers have seen her in a hired buggy, alone, in a certain part of town."

I did not inquire where. "Underwood wants Miss Brown to marry him when his consumptive wife dies."

"He is a very wealthy man. Isn't that what young women are in the marriage market to attract?"

"There are complications that have to do with his father," I said. "The father controls the son to a degree of which she disapproves."

Bierce drew his gold watch from his vest pocket and consulted it.

"Come, it is past five o'clock, time to tread the Cocktail Route."

———

The Route led along Market to Montgomery with frequent stops for drinks and lavish saloon buffets. Someone had counted twenty-one possible stops between Geary and Montgomery. Bierce and I began the celebration of the end of the working week at Hacquette's before we even turned onto Market Street. We would end up either at the Bank Exchange in the Montgomery Block, or the Palace on Market. Bierce was usually accompanied on the Cocktail Route by his *Examiner* cronies Arthur McEwen and Petey Bigelow, but this time I was the one to try to keep up with him.

On a saloon counter there would be a huge rosy ham holding the place of honor, close by a yellow cliff of cheese; surrounding these, platters of salamis, sausages, sardines, smoked salmon, olives, and pickles. Working away at the food and drink were crowds of men in suits and cutaways, in a din of conversation.

Bierce explained satire to a fat gent with a noble mustache: "Satire is directed at a specific individual, not an abstraction. It is punishment, you understand, for civic and personal unworth."

And he added, "Despite my continuing efforts there is still manifested a deplorable propensity for felonious behavior among the civil servants of the city."

Mustache didn't know whether to look concerned, insulted or amused.

"No doubt it is congenital," Bierce added, and turned to address another importunate who had been tugging at his coat sleeve.

We moved on along Market Street, in the January early dark. At Crowell's Saloon Bierce was happily hailed by a new pack of cronies. This time he was asked about writing.

He illustrated with a thumb up and thumb down. "Specific" (up); "Abstract" (down); "Particular" (up); "General" (down); "Individual" (up); "Type" (down); "Peculiar" (up); "Generic" (down); "Precise" (up); "Ambiguous" (down); "Detailed" (up); "Summarized" (down); "Definite" (up); "Indefinite" (down); "Distinct" (up); "Indistinct" (down).

When he began repeating himself, he halted with one eye closed and the other fixed on his interlocutor.

"Prose expression lives on the specific and dies in the general, you see, sir," he said.

We passed on. About seven o'clock I told him I intended to go home now and he gazed at me with one eye closed and the other half open, and nodded. I snatched my hat from its hook and carried it outside to put it on. It slipped down over my eyes. I thought I had picked up the wrong hat until I realized that someone had ripped out the sweat band.

I tried to assure myself that it was only a malicious joke.

CHAPTER 15

GENEALOGY, n. An account of one's descent from an ancestor who didn't particularly care to trace his own.

— *The Devil's Dictionary*

SATURDAY, JANUARY 17, 1891

When I came home to Sacramento Street Haunani was seated on the steps, a shawl wrapped around her shoulders, rising as I came up to her. I couldn't see her face in the darkness, beneath a cartwheel hat.

As Berowne would have pointed out, a proper San Francisco young lady would not be found sitting on the steps of an apartment house waiting for a male friend to return.

In my room, with the lights turned up, I saw that her face was swollen with grief. She plumped down on the sofa, removed her hat and shook her hair free. She plucked a handkerchief from her sleeve and scrubbed her cheeks. I tossed my own ruined hat onto the bureau and sat beside her.

"They've killed him!" she said.

"Judge Akua?"

"He was going to tell me about my mother! He had sent me a note to meet him today, at the Palace. I know he was going to tell me something!"

She leaned heavily against me. She smelled of flowers. "When my mother died, my father burned everything of hers, clothing, photographs, letters, all her *things*. I was not a year old, so I have no ... recollection. I have nothing! My father wouldn't speak of her. Her name was Alma Puunene, but there is ... no record of her anywhere! When we moved to Honolulu no one knew of her. At the school they made fun of me! And Andrew Akua *knew*. He was going to tell me, and they killed him!"

"Who killed him?" I said.

"I don't know!" She buried her face in her handkerchief again.

I put my arms around her but she shrugged me off. Her teared blue eyes gazed into mine. "It's as though I am being punished, Tom! It is so important in Hawaii, your ancestors. It is what you are! It's as though they won't let me be the person I truly am! Why would my father be that way? As though I was responsible—as though my mother had died giving birth to me! But she didn't! You know, when I had no mother—I made one up! I pretended that she was a chiefess, a princess out of a storybook. I made a fool of myself—pretending!—that I was descended from Nahienaena. And I learned the dances and the *inoa*—the name chant—I made up Nahienaena because I had to have someone! Andrew Akua told me that was foolish!"

I kissed her tears.

"This terrible *thing*!" She made herself small in my arms, shivering. She thrust her wet face into my throat. "Tom, they're trying to make me *pupule*!"

"I won't let you be crazy," I said.

"You don't know what it's like—not to know who you are! If you are Hawaiian, even *hapahaole*, that is the strongest thing—knowing exactly who you are all the way back. And I'll never know now! Oh, that poor, dear man!

"There is no sad beautiful song tonight!" she wailed.

"Signora Sotopietro is visiting her son in Stockton."

We made love, which pleased her as some kind of contest which she always won, and presently she was purring.

I told her that I had met Walter Underwood.

She lay silently for a time, her head on my arm. "He is the sweetest boy in the world," she said. "His mother is ashamed of him. He has to stay in a separate house from her. She can't stand to see him. Like a big spider, she says. Cousin Aaron does everything he is supposed to do, but it is just *duty*. Uncle Silas is terrible! He acts as though Walter is Cousin Aaron's fault!"

"It seems strange that Aaron Underwood would engage Bierce to search for Princess Leileiha, who has hidden herself because his father has sent the *kahuna* here."

There was a moment of intense silence.

"That is not true," Haunani said.

"Why has she disappeared, then?"

"I told you to leave her alone!"

"Has it to do with the succession?"

"I can't tell you."

"But you know where she is?"

"I don't know where she is at this moment!" She pulled away from me, stretching, pointing one breast with its dark nipple. Her skin fit her so beautifully.

"She is safe," she said. "Why is it so important to you?"

I said it was important to Aaron Underwood and Alexander Honomoku, and maybe to Hawaii.

"Oh, Hawaii!" she said contemptuously.

She lay back with her eyes closed. I watched the depressions of her eyelids brighten with tears.

"He was a man people loved," she said. "The Akuas had been kings of Maui! He told me I was foolish to pretend I was the great-granddaughter of Nahienaena.

"I can dance the ancestors of Nahienaena, who is not my ancestor," she whispered. "I can chant the names, the names, the names."

———

We went to the seafood restaurant in the California Street Market for crab legs meuniere and a bottle of Chablis, and then I took her home in a hack. In her uncle's house were Berowne and Alexander Honomoku, who kissed Haunani's hand, and shook mine firmly. I sensed a meeting to which I was extraneous, but Haunani urged me to stay.

"David was conscious this morning," Honomoku said. "He called for me!"

Berowne made ushering motions to chairs. Haunani and I seated ourselves on the settee. I couldn't make out the expression on her face as she watched Honomoku—respect but mockery of the respect?

I wondered if they were all conspiring in hiding the princess. At least, Haunani was.

"He did not give Alexander his b-b-blessing," Berowne said to her.

Honomoku's pouter-pigeon stance was one of great gravity. "We spoke of the succession, however. He asked me my views. He was almost his old self!"

King Calico, the irreverent pun on King Kalakaua.

"I said that Leilei's disappearance had changed my notions. That darling person was trying to tell me I had been wrong. And I have listened!"

So Berowne had been informed of the disappearance.

"What have you and Mr. Bierce discovered?" Honomoku asked me.

"We believe that she is not in danger," I said.

Haunani wouldn't meet my eyes. "Does David know that Andrew Akua is dead?" she said in a low voice.

There was a silence. "He does not know, Nani," Honomoku said.

"I told David I had come to agree with the spirit of the Reform Party," he continued. "I have renewed my friendship with Charley Perry. Charley and I will move forward together, whatever David's decision as to the succession!"

Haunani said, "I would be surprised if Charley moved forward with anyone but his own self."

Honomoku's brown countenance creased into a frown. "I will not hear the old canards against Charley, Nani. I believe it is what Leilei wishes of me!"

"Does Amb-b-brose have any idea why she has taken herself off?" Berowne asked me.

"There are several possibilities," I said.

"It is to make me come to my senses, Edward!" Honomoku said. He seemed a good deal more forceful than the man I had first met.

"I am a Hawaiian man!" he continued. "I am *alii* of the most noble genealogy. But I must prove myself to Hawaiians, not to *haoles*!"

His face showed a flush.

"Leilei has made a patriot of you, Alex," Haunani said.

"And what did David Kalakaua say?" Berowne asked.

"He approved of my decision! He gripped my hand. He said he, too, had been too much influenced by haoles."

"B-b-by which he means Silas."

"He knows he has compromised too often with the mercantile and sugar haoles. He hopes his successor will not be so influenced by them."

"B-b-but he did not say that you were to b-b-be that successor."

"He did not say that." Honomoku strode two steps

forward, and back, and struck an orator's stance. "We agreed that there should be no sacrifice of Hawaiian soil!"

That would refer to Pearl Harbor.

"You should have told him that Andrew Akua is dead," Haunani said.

"David does not like righteous men," Honomoku said somberly. "David does not like people criticizing his ways. Certainly he has faults, but he is the monarch of the Hawaiian people!"

It was interesting that the king had not liked Judge Akua, who was considered a hindrance to U.S. policy. And who had also interfered with Silas Underwood's land acquisitions.

"Andrew Akua spoke to me of the death of his son," Haunani said. "That old tragedy."

"More than a tragedy!" Alexander Honomoku said.

"Of course you know I was p-p-present," Berowne said grimly.

Haunani gazed at him with her lips pressed tightly together.

"It was a surfing accident," Berowne said, who wrote sunny little pastiches of Hawaiian boys. "There is a surfing ground near Hana, the *Nalu Kuono*, where the waves can come up very large. Suddenly huge. I had never seen anything like them that day. The seventh wave came up to obscure the heavens. Daniel Akua and I were swept into the rocks. My b-b-brother William chose to save my life rather than Daniel's. It has not b-b-been forgotten or forgiven."

He stopped to clear his throat.

"Never forgotten," Honomoku said pompously. I thought he had remembered that he now had to reconsider his attitudes on everything. He seemed to me quite changed.

"So I was saved b-b-but Daniel Akua was drowned,"

Berowne said. "We had been friends, the four of us. It was a tragic day."

Judge Akua had spoken of the Christian doctrine of forgiveness.

Beside me Haunani was sitting so still it was as though she were holding her breath.

"It was William's instinct to save his b-b-brother," Berowne went on in a muffled voice. "I can understand that, certainly. I am here b-b-because of that decision!"

"And your brother had a *kahuna*'s curse on him?" I said.

Berowne's face paled in stripes. "He died of cancer! There are those who consider it the work of a *kahuna*. I b-b-believe that to be nonsense!"

I could hear the sibilance of Haunani's breath.

Honomoku said to me, "The death of Daniel Akua was taken as evidence that the *haoles* consider their lives to be of more value than the lives of Hawaiian people."

"The instinct of a b-b-brother to save his b-b-brother," Berowne said obstinately.

"The *Nalu Kuono*," Haunani said in a calm voice. "Big Surf Point." She had spoken to me of the surfing tragedy as though it was a Hawaiian legend.

"Charley Perry makes much of the *Nalu Kuono*," Berowne said. "It is the Reform P-p-party's design to find differences between the races to exploit."

"We will reexamine the *Nalu Kuono*!" Honomoku said.

I inquired who would want the counsellor dead.

"I understood he was murdered by a burglar!" Berowne said. His thinning white hair was mussed, and Haunani rose to smooth it for him.

He smiled his fond smile. "Thank you, my dear!"

"I believe with Charley that if the *haoles* continue to press us we will have to resort to arms," Honomoku said sullenly.

"Leilei would not approve of that!" Haunani said.

Honomoku jerked his chin up arrogantly. "Leilei has never had to confront unprincipled men! She believes the best of everyone."

It was Bierce's theory that the way to gather information in conversation was to get the conversants angry at each other. Here there was disagreement at least, but conversation lagged.

"Why is a *kahuna* in the City?" I asked.

Haunani looked sick, Berowne steadied himself with a hand on a chair back. No one spoke.

"Kanekoa," I said. "The king is interested in ancient Hawaiian healing."

"Hale Naua," Honomoku said, nodding.

"Believes in it?" I said.

"David thinks he should believe in his Hawaiian heritage. In Hawaiian medicines."

"Can a *kahuna* cure Bright's disease? Can a *kahuna* kill Jonathan Prout?"

"If they b-b-believe, you see," Berowne said. "It is not so different from the Christian religion, Thomas."

"Is Kanekoa here for good or ill?" I asked.

"Good!" Honomoku said.

Gazing into my eyes, Haunani shook her head. Her tongue flicked out to moisten her upper lip. She returned to seat herself beside me.

I said, "Why would he have a newspaper clipping of Prout's arrival at the king's bedside placed with a volcanic rock on top of it?"

"Tom," Haunani said, gripping her arms to her bosom. "How did you—encounter this person?"

"I followed Aaron Underwood's carriage because I'd seen a Hawaiian woman's face in the window. Kanekoa was in the basement of a house that belongs to Underwood. Objects were laid out on a kind of altar. I think the stone on the newspiece might be a curse."

There was a heavy silence.

"Could Kanekoa have had to do with Judge Akua's death?"

Berowne rubbed his hands over his pale face.

"What I'm trying to get at . . . " I said. "Kanekoa may be here to try to treat the king. But is he here for something else also? The murder of Judge Akua? Some endangerment of Princess Leileiha? Something I don't know about?"

The three of them stared at me. I could almost hear the revolving of Hawaiian mental gears. But Haunani knew why the princess had disappeared, and considered her "safe."

There was no more discussion of *kahunas*. There were no answers, only, I supposed, resentment at a pushy *haole*. When I departed Haunani walked with me onto the veranda in the chill January dark. A necklace of tiny lights ranged along the Marin side of the bay.

"Tom," she whispered, holding my hand in her two hands, eyes fixed on mine. "You no mess wid dis *kahuna*, you hear me?" she whispered in pidgin. *"You no mess wid him!"*

CHAPTER 16

> *Work not on Sabbath days at all,*
> *But go to see the teams play ball.*
> — *The Devil's Dictionary*

SUNDAY, JANUARY 18, 1891

On Sundays, off-season, I would get together on the ball field in the park on Market Street with Frank Grew, a police sergeant, and Parris Hoffman, an editor at the *Chronicle*, to peg a baseball around. We would rig up different combinations, but often Frank would pitch to me and I fire a cut off out to Parris at second base. It was a throw I had practiced until sometimes in a game I had to slow it a hair so as not to halt the base runner halfway along. I had a good arm.

People would stop by to watch, especially half-grown boys. There were other games going on further along in the park, mostly kids, with a lot of yelling and pleasant times had.

When we took a breather we sat on a slat bench to chat things over.

"How are your investigations of Hawaiian royalty proceeding, Tom?" Parris asked. He would be rewriting the historical piece I was working up for the death of Kalakaua. He inclined his thin, mustached face at me past Frank, who leaned back with his arms extended along the back of the bench.

"Mysterious doings," I said. "Royal prerogatives, dynastic considerations. Handmaidens and royal counsellors."

"Murder," Frank said. "Get a turbine turning up the revolutions, lots of stuff around starts moving and shaking the same."

"Revolutions?" Parris said.

"If the king chooses the wrong heir. He hasn't made a sign of a choice yet."

"In a coma, I hear."

"In and out," I said.

"Did you know the judge who was murdered, Tom?" Parris asked.

"As fine and honorable an old gent as you'd ever meet."

"Rough strife," Frank said.

"The U.S. is involved. Pearl Harbor leases and the Reciprocity Treaty. There's an eye on Annexation, too."

"What's Bierce say?" Parris inquired.

"He's got a rant going. A republic founded by religious bigots and slave drivers is now turning into an empire. Variations on that theme."

They both laughed.

I squinted at the traffic on Market Street, bicyclists, hacks, fancy carriages, a halted horsecar with pedestrians lined up to board it. A buggy was drawn up at the curb fifty feet away from us, canopy up, bay horse with his head down.

I asked Frank if Captain Pusey had anything on the murder of Judge Akua.

"I don't think there's much. It'd just lay out as a burglar caught in the act except for the doings upstairs in the Palace Hotel." Frank paused before he said, "There's that princess missing."

"Is Captain Pusey looking for her?" I said.

He shrugged.

"A princess?" Parris said. "Is she a part of your researches, Tom? There's always interest in princesses. Willie Hearst would do handsprings for a princess. Princesses do make gee-whiz front pages."

"She ought to be easy to find," I said. "She's a big Hawaiian woman."

"I understand you've been seen in some fancy gastronomy establishments with such," Parris said gravely. "It wouldn't be this princess, would it?"

"A different Hawaiian lady." I stopped myself from saying "half Hawaiian."

When we got our gloves back on we spread out into double-play formation and began to fling the ball at one another. The buggy with the bay horse was still at the curb. The occupant was invisible under the hood.

We made a date for next week and said our good-byes. I collected my cap from the bench. My course took me toward the buggy. As I donned my cap I thought of my missing sweatband, and just then a headache like an iron ring clenched around my skull. I halted, gasping. The pain slowly receded as the horse and buggy turned out from the curb and started on along Market Street.

You no mess wid him!

———

I was still nursing a tender head and a case of nerves when I sat over coffee with the Sunday *Examiner.* An item in "Prattle" caught my eye in a paragraph devoted to one of Bierce's favorite targets, San Francisco's preachers:

"It is the steadfast position of our ministry that the most neglected part of church work is that of educating people to give money to the church. It is considered that the proper way is 'to begin with the children and train them in the duty of giving.'

Wherefore I mean to search my pockets for the churchly hands, and, finding them, shake them warmly in token of approval. The people must be educated to give money—there can be no doubt of that; and we must catch them young. On minor points I venture to differ with the holy men. For example, I am persuaded that the money should be given, not to the church boards but to writers for newspapers. If one will kindly set up a givery I will open a receivery close by.

"The most successful receivery of the era has in fact been set up by the Reverend Simms, alias Reuben Slaney, for whose maintenance God fashioned gullible ladies. Slaney is now vigorously being sought as the finest example of his craft by San Francisco's finest under the direction of Captain Isaiah Pusey."

Slaney did not seem to me to be worth Bierce's sarcasm, unless this was some kind of gibe at Mrs. Hansen.

MONDAY, JANUARY 19, 1891

When I raised the question over lagers in Dinkins's saloon the next day, Bierce punished me for my impertinence with one of his lectures on men and women:

"It is nature's imperative," he said, "to continue the species by the tried and true method of the female attracting the male by whatever means comes to hand. One of these of course is the distribution of a layer of fat beneath the female skin into concavities and convexities that blur the male's sanity with visions of abiding pleasures. Another is the anticipation of grounding those high-flying and tantalizing creatures by the effective process of making them pregnant."

I was aware that my own sanity had been blurred by Haunani Brown's concavities and convexities, and the pleasures were not mere visions.

"But it must always be remembered," he went on, "that the man's role is polygamous, to spread his seed as widely as possible. While it is the female role to demand monogamy in order to provide nest and care for her offspring according to the imperatives of nature. Since that is not to the benefit of the male, she must beguile him by her several arts."

I inquired about Mrs. Hansen.

"Perhaps you would join us for dinner tonight?" he said.

I said I would be glad to, and mentioned that I had seen her photograph on a poster in a drugstore amidst a cluster of hard-jaw, them-loud females: "The Past History, Present Condition and Future Prospects of the Women's Movement."

"Yes, there is a grand meeting. She will be speaking." And he squinted at me to ask about Miss Haunani Brown.

"She insists that the princess is safe. She will only say that there is a good reason for her disappearance."

Bierce sighed. I was to take it that he would not have been content with such a response.

I told him of my experience in the park on Market Street. "Someone stopped to watch me playing ball with some friends at the ball grounds this morning," I went on. "Tell me: How could a Hawaiian medicine man give me a headache at fifty feet away?"

Bierce looked thoughtful. "Impossible," he said.

I laid a hand on top of my head.

"A coincidence."

"I don't have headaches. Was this headache a threat?"

Bierce clucked uneasily.

"Something has made Chaplain Prout dangerously ill."

He sipped his beer, eyeing me over the rim of the glass. "Mammy Pleasant should be consulted in Voodoo matters," he said.

———

Mammy was often to be seen on Market or Montgomery streets hurrying in her cloak and black straw hat and carrying her baby-sized basket. I spent an hour walking the sidewalks before I spotted her on Mason Street, and invited her to take a cup of tea with me in a teashop there. She came along with a show of reluctance, as though I had broken into a string of important errands.

We seated ourselves in the steamy atmosphere. A pot of Darjeeling and cups and saucers were placed before us. I tried to fix an amiable expression on my face. Mammy Pleasant did not make a similar effort, her face hard as an ax blade watching me.

"Mrs. Pleasant," I said. "It was interesting to me that when the princess Leileiha had only been missing three days, her wardrobe had already been placed in storage in the Palace Hotel vaults."

She granted me a nod.

"So it was felt necessary to protect her clothing from someone who might wish her ill."

Another nod, a slight relaxing of her expression.

"Night before last I hung my hat on a hatrack at a saloon on Market Street. When it came time to put it on again, I found the sweatband had been ripped out. I have a sense that that has to do with the same sort of thing as the princess's wardrobe being stored away."

"That is correct, Mr. Redmond." She lifted her teacup with a long-fingered dark hand and held it level with her chin. A haze of steam from the cup masked her eyes.

I told her what had happened at the ballpark yesterday. "The sensation was like an iron band compressing my head," I said.

"Your hatband," she said.

I didn't say that this had already occurred to me. "This man is a Hawaiian *kahuna*. What can be done, Mrs. Pleasant?"

"What does he want?"

"It may have to do with the missing princess, who will inherit land on the island of Maui that Silas Underwood covets. He may be working for Uncle Sugar. No doubt he knows that Mr. Bierce and I are looking for the princess. But then why wouldn't he go after Bierce?"

"He has your hatband."

"There is also the fact that I am writing about Hawaii and the king for the *Chronicle* obituary."

She nodded.

"Or it may have to do with my friendship with Miss Brown."

She nodded more vigorously.

I asked again what could be done.

"You must get back your hatband."

I didn't know how to go about that.

"You will see him again. He will be stronger now that you know to fear him. I could defend you if I were present."

I didn't know how to go about that, either.

"You would do that for me?" I said.

"I would," she said, and now seemed more at ease in my presence as she sipped her tea.

————

At eight o'clock I met Bierce and his Mrs. Hansen at a French restaurant on Montgomery Street, where the headwaiter fawned over the famous journalist. Champagne was poured.

Mrs. Hansen wore her usual peculiar raiment, variously colored layers of fabric that concealed her attractive figure and made her resemble an autumnal tree. She fingered a bright-stoned necklace on her smooth neck, and bracelets rattled on her arms.

I asked if she had been able to persuade Bierce to the feminist cause.

"He is very stubborn," she said, smiling at me with the

gleaming pearls of her teeth. Her fingernails gleamed on her champagne glass.

"I have explained to her that the world is damnably feminized as it is," Bierce said. "The masculine tone is missing in this generation, the male virtues of daring and enduring and facing the challenges of reality quite vanished. We live in an hysterical, chattering, falsely delicate world of feminized sensibilities."

Mrs. Hansen said gently, "The male virtues he refers to have kept the female ones imprisoned since the beginning of history."

"Imprisoned by the male homage to beauty," Bierce said, and Mrs. Hansen laughed delightedly.

I did not understand his interest in her. Was it simply to garner ammunition for an attack of invective on the feminist movement, which he detested? Did he intend to exploit her, as he had complained that the female mediums had been exploited by commercial males, in fact with a commercial motive himself since such attacks were his stock in trade?

"Am I overly suspicious to weigh these garlands of flattery Ambrose proffers me?" Mrs. Hansen asked me.

"No," I said, and she laughed again. She was very charming, in fact quite disarming. But I was not certain that Bierce was disarmed.

I raised my glass. "To the beautiful Mrs. Hansen and the cause she espouses!"

"Thank you, Mr. Redmond! How very nice!"

"He is very nice because he is in love," Bierce said.

Mrs. Hansen's face brightened. "What a lucky young lady!"

"My prospects with her are exceedingly remote."

"Can it be the ample young lady who is the niece of Mr. Berowne? What amazing eyes she has!"

"Yes."

"Tom's wife died about a year ago," Bierce said.

Mrs. Hansen's face was suffused with a sympathy so genuine that tears like claws scratched at my eyes. "I'm so sorry!" she said. "Have you had communication with her?"

For a moment I didn't understand what she meant. "I'm Roman Catholic," I said.

It was her turn to look puzzled. "Communication can be a great assuager of grief, Tom."

I thought of the communication with Day Bierce; that was clever trickery, Bierce had said.

"I do not urge you, you understand," Mrs. Hansen said. "But I have seen it many times."

"Thank you," I said. "I have come to terms with it."

Bierce urged Mrs. Hansen to tell us something of her life, for my benefit surely.

Her English parents had been abolitionists, she said, sipping her champagne with birdlike cocks of her head. They were active in Pennsylvania in the Underground Railroad, and supporters of John Brown. Her father spent a term in prison for his activities. She was brought up by her mother, an outspoken woman who gave lectures, and she began to lecture also at a very early age. Her mother had become a Spiritualist, as had many women from the abolitionist movement.

"Young women were able to engage themselves in professional activities in the Spiritualist movement," she said in her clear, unchallenging voice. "I found contact with a friendly spirit, who advised me."

"Trance speakers were required to be well educated," Bierce said.

"There were only so many subjects on which one was called upon to inform the public," Mrs. Hansen said. "The abolitionist movement, the women's movement, Spiritualism, astronomy—the stars! I can discourse most effectively on the Wars of the Roses, the history of Britain, Mary Queen of Scots. On Mary Magdalene! On great women through history. On a dozen subjects. I am afraid Ambrose will say I am a very flimsy expert, dependent upon style rather than content."

"Not at all," Bierce said fatuously, and added, "It was an economic necessity for Spiritualists to become mediums."

I saw from Mrs. Hansen's mobile, beautiful-frog face that this was not a subject she wished to pursue. She stroked her chalk-stick arms nervously.

"And mediums were required to produce materializations," Bierce said.

"Many of us have become active in the suffragist movement," Mrs. Hansen said. She smiled up at the waiter as our dinners were brought to the table. I thought she was relieved by the interruption.

She had ordered a plate of spinach with garlic and olive oil, upon which Bierce and I looked with disapproval while Bierce consumed his sweetbreads and I my cutlet.

I pointed out that although Mrs. Hansen's spirit had produced no information about Princess Leileiha's whereabouts, now there was a murdered man.

"There is obstruction," Mrs. Hansen said.

"Interference," Bierce said.

"From other spirits?"

"It is from this side of the divide," Mrs. Hansen said. "It is very strong."

When she had excused herself to "restore her face powder," Bierce said, "She is a divorced woman. Her husband beat her. She claims he lamed her. You have noticed her peculiarities of locomotion?"

"What about her presence aboard that freighter?"

"She will not speak of it. She claims not to know what

happened after tea was served her in a tearoom on Stockton Street."

"With Slaney?"

"A man she is not certain she can identify. She met him at a church function." And he said, "Which I am inclined to doubt. She is not much for church functions.

"I wonder if the obstruction is your *kahuna*," he added.

"That gives me a chill," I said.

Now Mrs. Hansen was coming toward us between the tables where others were engaged in Gallic gustation. Her "locomotion" was half a limp, half a kind of twisting stiffness of her body.

"It is a defect of the spine," Bierce whispered. "It has affected her life, her way of speaking, her reception by large audiences, her way of thinking, I believe. Yet I find it very charming."

We rose to receive her back at the table.

Her smile for us was a little tipsy. I recalled Bierce saying that he was called upon to protect her from an excess of laudanum.

When we had parted I dropped in at Carlson's Saloon for a whiskey to dispel the chill of thinking of Kanekoa standing guardian at the gate to the astral plane.

CHAPTER 17

FUNERAL, n. A pageant whereby we attest our respect for the dead by enriching the undertaker, and strengthen our grief by an expenditure that deepens our grief and doubles our tears.

— *The Devil's Dictionary*

TUESDAY, JANUARY 20, 1891

In the rain the black blossoms of the umbrellas sheltered the funeral-clad figures in procession following Judge Akua's shiny mahogany coffin up the hillside of the Laurel Hill Cemetery. I joined the tail of the procession, rubbers sloshing through the damp grass. Ahead of me were Hawaiians bulky in black, some I recognized and some I did not. Major Baker in a bedraggled uniform, and Haunani, on Berowne's arm, were among them.

I wondered if a murderer was also there.

Dark faces, half concealed by the petals of the umbrellas, glanced back at me on the slow ascent. We arranged ourselves around the coffin that was braced on planks above the grave. The minister's head was covered by a rubber bonnet, his face pale among the darker ones. At his right hand was Aaron Underwood. With Aaron was tall Lydia Kukui, Kalaua, her eyes flashing at me out of her brown, broad face. She concealed herself behind Aaron.

Haunani gazed down at her hands in black gloves clasped before her. Berowne, holding a prayer book, mouthed words accompanying the minister's prayer, a low mumble unrecognizable to a Roman Catholic. Also holding a prayer book was Charley Perry, standing with his tiny French wife who was properly in black but with a drift of red scarf showing on one shoulder beneath her coat. I looked for Kanekoa but did not see anyone who could be the *kahuna*. Nor Princess Leileiha. I gazed from face to face looking for guilt.

When the coffin had been let down into the grave, the minister led the way back toward the street. Sloshing through the soaked grass again I trailed fifty feet behind Haunani, whose black bonnet sailed among the men's plug hats. Perry appeared beside me, his wet cheeks, black mustache and neat little cleft chin turned up to me under the brim of his topper.

"So, Mr. Redmond," he said, "what brings a journalist to this sad affair?"

"Journalists attend funerals," I said. "The deaths of famous men."

"You consider Andrew Akua a famous man?"

"He was one I respected."

"We are in agreement, Mr. Redmond." I did not like to think of big Haunani Brown engaged in *panipani* with this arrogant little fellow.

"Andrew Akua had not sold himself to sugar," he added solemnly.

"As everybody else in Hawaii has?"

"I have not, Mr. Journalist!" he said through his teeth. His wife followed ten feet behind us, arms wrapped around herself, looking miserable.

"Would the fact that he would not sell himself for sugar have anything to do with his demise?"

"That is the kind of question one might expect from a journalist," Perry said, trudging along beside me. From time to time he mopped his dripping face with the end of his scarf.

"And what answer might a journalist expect from a man who has also not sold out to sugar?"

"Hawaiian answers lie in the past, Journalist," he said, with a laugh that had no amusement to it. We trooped on down the hill away from Judge Andrew Akua's grave in silence.

"I am also looking for a *kahuna*," I said.

His wet face jerked up toward me.

"A *kahuna* who treated the king," I said.

"The king has his *lapa-au*."

"That's the good kind of *kahuna*, to cure him? But is he also a sorcerer?"

"*Ana-ana,*" Perry said. "There are many kinds of *kahunas*, Journalist. Some bad, some good, some who examine the heavens for portents."

"*Ana-ana* ones can cause headaches?"

He produced the humorless laugh again. "Yes, *ana-ana* ones cause headache," he said.

"Can they kill chaplains?"

"If that chaplain is already ill, perhaps yes."

"Would he kill the king's counsellor?"

His eyes widened. "I would not think so, Mr. Journalist."

"Why would Silas Underwood send an *ana-ana kahuna* to San Francisco?"

"For David Kalakaua's comfort," Perry said. "'Because he's *lapa-au* also." He laughed.

"If Judge Akua wouldn't sell out to sugar and was murdered, what about you?"

He didn't reply.

"What about Princess Leileiha?" I asked. "I thought she might be here."

"Oh, Leilei," he said, as though she was of no importance. "Run off with some *haole*, probably. She is a woman, Journalist."

He halted so that I was forced to move on ahead of him. I looked back to see his wife take his arm. He stared ahead at me with a doleful face, pacing slowly so the distance between us increased.

———

In the carriage returning to the City with Haunani and Berowne, I inhaled Haunani's scent of flowers and damp wool. Berowne held her hand.

"Andrew Akua would have told me about my mother, wouldn't he, Uncle?"

"I don't know, my dear. Is that what he said?"

"Why don't *you* tell me? Why *won't* you?"

"It was what William wished, my dear," Berowne said. "It is very complicated." He kept patting her brown hand. "It was to do with old family attitudes ab-b-bout color that your father was never ab-b-ble to relinquish."

"Then my father was ashamed of me?"

"He loved you very much."

"Do you hear this, Tom?" Haunani said, her eyes flashing blue at me. "Do you see how they try to make me *pupule*? I will never know my true mother!"

Berowne said uncomfortably, "She was very . . . handsome."

"But brown."

"Yes, she was b-b-brown."

"But was she *Mrs.* Brown?" Haunani said, handkerchief clutched in her hand. "What I suspect is true, is it not, Uncle?"

Berowne did not answer, sunk down in his seat beside

Haunani. I watched his face. I understood what Haunani was getting at, but I had no idea what illegitimacy might mean to a Hawaiian, to whom genealogies were all-important. Nor could I understand why Haunani would pursue this subject in my presence. From the first it had been as though I meant something to her that I did not fully comprehend. More than a provider of expensive dinners.

"So they were young people on Maui and they made *pani-pani* even though my father was a Southerner and thought my mother was just another kind of darkie. . . . And she had his *keike* who was me, and then she died."

"You were hardly six months of age," Berowne said.

"So I can only know what my father chose to tell me—what *you* choose to tell me!"

"You must trust me, my dear," Berowne said, with a worried look at me, who was a party to this conversation.

It was an inappropriate time to bring up the subject of the princess Leileiha.

———

Later that day I called on Bierce in his office to tell him that I had had no luck with Engine Company #4. When the chief discovered that EC–4 had to do with a murder investigation, he became protective and suspicious. As he pointed out, EC–4 might have a lot of meanings other than that of a fire department company.

Bierce sat at his desk with his fingers knitted together and his legs crossed, frowning down his nose at me. The big eye-holes of the chalky skull at his elbow regarded me similarly.

He asked about the funeral, but not as though he was much interested. He had brought from his drawer a sheaf of papers.

"Wet," I said.

"There is a lesson I have learned in a life of dedicated cynicism," Bierce said. "There are many motives for some of the major matters of life, for murder, for disappearance, for malfeasance and corruption and offenses against heaven and earth. And the chiefest of these is greed. So in these Polynesian calamities we should look for the procession of greenbacks that leads somewhere."

It seemed I was in for a lecture. For my part I thought that the answers lay, as Charley Perry had said, in the past.

I saw that the papers Bierce held contained figures. "I have had Fanny doing researches for me," he said.

"Uncle Sugar is the principal creditor of the Kingdom of Hawaii." He leafed through the papers with a manicured forefinger.

"He is owed some $920,000, including 6 percent bonds of $500,000, and the rest on open account at 9 percent. At present the government is negotiating a loan for $2,000,000, Silas Underwood is willing to take it on—another $1,080,000, that is. For this he would receive a 5 percent commission, plus 2 percent discounting. He would clear close to $90,000, not including the interest he is to receive. Not bad!

"However, the king has been anxious to get out of his clutches. He has had an agent negotiate a loan in London, for two million—to pay off Uncle Sugar. In this situation, 6 percent bonds are exchanged for 6 percent bonds, with, however, the same 5 percent commission and 2 percent discounting. In other words it will cost the kingdom $50,000 to begin with to get rid of Uncle Sugar. Plus, however, some $75,000 to the agent negotiating the loan. And more plusses.

"These are some powerful motivations, Tom!"

"Motivations for what?" I enquired.

"For the disappearance of a princess, the murder of a royal counsellor, and other matters with which we are not yet acquainted.

"It is estimated that the London loan will cost about

$169,000 not including interest," Bierce went on. "That is a lot of money to get rid of Uncle Sugar. Nor is that capitalist pleased at the evidence of ingratitude. Moreover, although the United States government disapproves of the Underwood grip on the kingdom's economy, his loan is unsecured, while the London loan would be secured by the 'consolidated revenues' of the kingdom. Thus, in case of default, England could come to control Hawaii as she controls Egypt—which would not be acceptable to the American government.

"Our government desires leases on Pearl Harbor. We would be even more pleased if Pearl Harbor were ceded to us—our own grasp on the sovereignty and independence of the kingdom, which is not pleasing to Hawaiian nationalists, as you are well aware. The Reciprocity Treaty, which is so favorable to the bank balances of the sugar planters, is dependent upon the Pearl Harbor lease.

"The fly in the ointment is the McKinley Tariff, which removes duty on *all* sugar imported, and gives domestic growers a bounty of two cents per pound—thus nullifying the blessings of reciprocity.

"Fanny has discovered that under the McKinley Tariff the price of sugar has been reduced from about a hundred to $60 a ton. This has been a blow to sugar profits. Many plantations are losing money. Smaller ones, facing bankruptcy, may be gobbled up by larger fish. Does this temporary situation benefit the largest fish of all, Uncle Sugar?"

He put down Fanny Porter's figures and frowned at me. His blue eyes gleamed under his shaggy eyebrows.

"My understanding is that there are these complaints against the king, these royal malfeasances." He extended his fingers, point by point. "Appropriations are made without reference to tax receipts. Members of the legislature favorable to the regime are rewarded in many ways. The royal franking privilege is regularly abused, particularly in regard to the imports of liquor—which liquor is much used to influence elections. Lands are sold illegally, without public auction. A vast section on Maui, as we know, may be sold to Silas Underwood, who wishes to purchase still more. Licenses to sell opium have been illegally and scandalously put up for bid.

"Apparently exemptions of lepers, condemned to Molokai, are *not* sold, as has been rumored; that is quite inviolate.

"I have been reading the prose writings of Edward Fairchild Berowne," Bierce went on. "Some of these have appeared in the *California Monthly*, others elsewhere. There is a thin little collection entitled *Island Idylls*."

"His reputation as an editor is worth ten thousand a year to the *Atlantic*," I said.

"His prose idylls are informative. My friend Clarence King—who has also contributed to the *California Monthly*—is beguiled by what he calls 'the old gold girls.' Women of color, that is. He would be beguiled by your Hawaiian young lady, for instance. Half-breeds, Polynesians, Mexicans, mulattos. It seems that Berowne was beguiled by old gold boys."

I stared at him silently.

"He does not celebrate the customary beautiful brown maidens with their firm breasts and generosities with their persons, but the strong-backed handsome young men driving their canoes through the crashing surf. One of these welcomes Berowne to his compound and calls him his brother."

I also was familiar with *Island Idylls*, and we exchanged stories from that thin little book. I recalled a tale about a Hawaiian lad who had befriended the white-skinned *malahini*, Edward, on the island of Maui. The high-spirited native, Joe Kane, was Edward's special friend, who whistled to him in church until Edward came outside, where Joe borrowed money from him to buy fine clothes to impress a dark young beauty. Later Edward encountered him again in the leper colony on the island of Molokai, where Edward had gone to meet the famous Father Damien. His friend Joe was suffering from the disease, crippled, his features horribly deformed, but still full of cheerfulness and charm, a charm that the author had managed to render to the reader despite a decorative and sentimental style that set my teeth on edge.

"His is an example of the poisonous style of a poet writing prose," Bierce said.

————

Haunani had spent the day buggy-riding with her promising new friend Richard Goforth. Because of the expectation of a proposal of marriage, there was to be no more *panipani* until the issue was settled.

She lingered, so that I saw there was some possibility of changing her mind. Instead there were kisses and tears in a queer mood that did not, however, appear to be one of renunciation. I thought she was preoccupied with her parentage and the death of the counsellor.

I took her home to Telegraph Hill with our hands clasped tightly together, and came back to my empty rooms.

Signora Sotopietro had returned from her visit to Stockton, and through the wall came the opening notes of the piano, then her voice, "Caro Nome." The song ceased in a bout of coughing followed by a frightening silence.

The piano tinkled a few notes as though to reassure me, before it was still. My tears were no longer so imperative because of my concerns with Haunani, but in time they faithfully produced themselves.

CHAPTER 18

KING'S EVIL, n. A malady that was formerly cured by the touch of the sovereign, but has now to be treated by the physicians.
— *The Devil's Dictionary*

WEDNESDAY, JANUARY 21, 1891

"I have spent nine days in this futile effort to discover the whereabouts of Princess Leileiha," Bierce reminded me and himself, tipping his hat over his eye against the afternoon sun, where we sat in our hack rattling out Market Street.

"The murder of Judge Akua is the province of Captain Pusey," he went on. "Malevolent island *kahunas* and beautiful part-Hawaiian ladies are your to-do."

We were heading west in thinning traffic. Bierce had sent me a message by the Rincon Messenger Service that it was important that I accompany him. He wore a grim expression.

"So you have located her," I said.

"Mammy Pleasant has informed me where she has been seen, and I now understand the cause of her departure. It is not cheerful news, Tom.

"She is not 'safe' at all," he added, and said no more. He looked very troubled.

It was a brilliant blue day with the sun like an omniscient

eye gazing down on us. We turned finally into 21st Street, rows of small wooden houses with steep roofs, front stoops and laundry on angles of clotheslines in a shrugging dance in a little wind. Bierce halted the driver before a two-story structure set back fifty feet from the street. Sunlight flashed off windows.

"What is this?" I asked.

"It is the San Francisco Smallpox Hospital."

We clambered out. The driver was instructed to wait. We mounted brick steps to a broad veranda where there was a row of fat bundles of laundry. These proved to be patients wrapped in white blankets reclining in steamer chairs. They watched our approach, one of them a Chinese man with a face blasted with smallpox. Others were white men, a few women, maybe ten in all. Bierce made a saluting gesture with his hat, and I followed suit.

Inside a heavy door I was half-blind in sudden darkness and a stench of carbolic. A plump nurse in a white cap and striped blouse sat at a desk.

"Dr. Sanford?" Bierce said.

We were shown down the hall and into an anteroom, where the nurse knocked on an inner door and called out, "A Mr. Bierce to see you, Doctor!"

Dr. Sanford sat at a desk with his fingers steepled together. He had a weary face framed by muttonchop whiskers.

"Please sit down, gentlemen," he said in a thin voice. "And tell me what I can do for you. I have exactly ten minutes to spare."

A fat gold watch was placed faceup on the green blotter on his desk.

"We are looking for the princess Leileiha."

Sanford only frowned.

"She is a Hawaiian young lady."

"Matters concerning our patients are private, gentlemen. May I ask what are your credentials to be making these enquiries?"

"We are journalists," Bierce said. He sat at his ease, legs crossed, his hat on his lap. He had assumed his expression of a kind of fair-haired Satan, brows knit, lips twisted into an unreassuring smile. "I am employed by the *Examiner*, Mr. Redmond by the *Chronicle*."

Sanford rearranged the watch on the blotter.

"I am aware that there are patients in the hospital suffering from disfiguring diseases other than smallpox," Bierce said.

"Yes, we have syphilitics and lepers here, also."

And so I understood.

Bierce gave me a prideful glance. "In Hawaii a sufferer of leprosy would be exiled to the Island of Molokai in primitive conditions. Here she is free to come and go within some regulations. Is this not true?"

"There is no rigorous enforcement," Sanford said.

"Tell me, is there any effective treatment for the disease?"

"It will run its course," Sanford said.

"It is invariably totally disfiguring, and fatal."

Sanford steepled his hands again.

I was appalled to think of Princess Leileiha a doomed victim of that biblical curse. I connected her looks with Haunani's large beauty, who complained that "they" were driving her insane. The fate of Leileiha must be one of the factors.

"Will you tell me where I can find this unfortunate lady?" Bierce said, leaning forward.

"No, sir," Dr. Sanford said.

"Will not?"

"Cannot."

"Do you mean that you are prevented from revealing this information by some regulation—"

"By the fact that I do not know where this person is presently to be found."

"But she comes here for treatment?"

Dr. Sanford rearranged his watch again.

Bierce thanked him and rose. "We will meet again, Dr. Sanford," he said.

"I will not be available should you return," Dr. Sanford said, rising.

We passed down the dark corridor, and outside under the concentrated gaze of the patients on the veranda, and mounted into our buggy.

"What a horror," I said, as the hack swung away from the curb with a grating of wheels on paving stones. "How did you come to it?"

"Mrs. Hansen's married name reminded me of the fact that leprosy is known as Hansen's disease. There have been cases of leprosy in Chinatown. I enquired where local sufferers were incarcerated."

"At the Smallpox Hospital."

"There was one other matter that prompted my mind," Bierce said. "There has been an effort to forget my son's death, but the matter came up recently—as you will recall. The name of the young lady in the quarrel was Effie Atkins. At the station where the trains bearing the coffins of the two young men went their separate ways, she is reported to have said: 'One goes this way and one goes that way, and I am left here like I have the smallpox.' That was what settled it," he said.

"What will you do now?" I asked.

"I wash my hands of the matter," he said.

———

In Edward Berowne's house on Telegraph Hill, Haunani was ensconced on the settee with her bare feet displayed against the edge of the Chinese teatable. They were curiously wedge-shaped, toes with shiny nails, tan on their tops, pale bottoms. She was proud of her small feet.

I had never seen my wife's feet bare. I had only seen my wife bare by accident. Always she had managed to cover herself. Haunani was proud of her flesh as she was proud of her feet. I had been embarrassed by her free display of her nudity, but was no longer.

When I sat next to her and pressed my lips to the side of her neck, she clapped her hand there. "Tom," she said.

"Here."

"I must be a lady now."

"Why?" I said, with a sinking in my chest.

"A proper gentleman has been found for me. He is a widower like you, he is tall like you. He is taller than me! He owns lumber mills! He has lumber mills in Mendocino County." She waved her hand to the north. I saw that her cheeks were flushed. The sinking sensation continued.

I didn't ask what had become of Richard Goforth.

"His name is Albert Grady," Haunani said. "Isn't that a nice name?"

"Is Albert Grady appropriate?"

"Yes!" She clutched my arm and leaned her weight against it. "Tom, if he is the right gentleman all the *pilikia* will be *pau*!"

"Will it?" I said.

"Oh, yes. Yes! Yes! Yes!"

My anger was dissolved by the gleam of damp in her blue eyes.

"I want you to say that this is very good news, Tom!"

"This is very good news, Haunani!"

"He has a deep voice." She pointed to her waist: "From down here somewhere. It makes me shiver." She clutched my arm again.

"Is your uncle pleased?"

"He is pleased!"

I wanted to get out of here and go to a saloon for a glass of whiskey to consider my griefs, but there was the matter of Princess Leileiha.

"Haunani, Bierce has found where Princess Leileiha has been, but is no longer."

She was silent for a long time, contemplating her toes. "At the hospital."

"Yes."

"So he knows."

"He knows."

"If she goes back, you see—"

"There is no other course, in Hawaii?"

"There is only Kalaupapa."

"How does she know she has it?"

"Anybody in Hawaii knows what to look for. There are signs, on your body, on your face. Terrible signs. Not terrible at first. That dear honest good Leilei does not deserve the *mai pa-ke*!"

"But wouldn't Honomoku have noticed?"

"Not if she didn't wish him to."

"So she will stay here when he and the others return with the king's remains?"

"There is no Molokai here. There is nice Dr. Sanford. It is more complicated than you can know," she continued. "Alexander loves her very much. She is afraid, if she goes to Molokai, he will come with her *kokua*—to care for her while she dies. So that is the end of him. But she does not know whether he is too good for such an ending. If he becomes king he would be less king than David Kalakaua. He would be a good king for the *haoles*. But she is not the kind who will harangue him over this. She will run away so that he will think and think again how Hawaiian he is. He must be more for Hawaii than he is. That is her way. So there are the two matters; that, and the *mai pa-ke*. So you see why I did not wish your Mr. Bierce to find her."

"She seems a considerable person," I said.

"She is a considerable person who will not live to be an old person. I do not wish Mr. Bierce to send her to Kalaupapa, Tom."

"He won't," I said.

She said, "I do not like people who hold a club over other people."

"He told me he had washed his hands of it," I said.

She shook her head without speaking.

"Listen to me," I said. "There is the princess, there is the king dying, there is Judge Akua murdered, there is a *kahuna* who gave me a headache and may have tried to kill me. What does Silas Underwood have to do with all this? Isn't he in Hawaii?"

Her lips tightened. Her cheeks were still flushed from speaking of Albert Grady. Always there seemed to be an inner light in her that suffused the flesh of her face. She had removed her feet from their prop on the table edge.

"Uncle Silas thinks Hawaii is his business," she said, tight-lipped.

"Everything in Hawaii his business?"

"Everything in Hawaii, and everyone, *Kanaka* or *haole*."

"Judge Akua?

"Certainly."

"Including *you*?"

"Including me."

"He thinks you should belong to his son?"

"Belong *him*," Haunani said in pidgin, tight-lipped. "Every ting belong *him*!"

———

On my way home, trying to digest what Haunani had told me before she had fled to her room in tears, the afternoon *Examiner* was on the racks. "Hawaii Murder Arrest" was the headline.

Charles Perry had been taken into custody for the murder of the royal counsellor.

———

As I walked along Post Street there was a rattle of heels on the sidewalk behind me and a voice called, "Mr. Redmon'!" It was the wife of the incarcerated Charley Perry, trotting to catch up with me, wearing her black dress from the funeral, with the slash of red scarf across her bosom. She clutched my arm with her black gloved hands, and thrust her pale face up at me.

"Please, I must speak with you!"

In a tearoom two storefronts up the street she seated herself uncomfortably close to me with her heavy scent of musk. Her hands worked at each other removing her gloves. Her tinny, imperious voice was heavily inflected.

"They have taken my Charley to prison!"

I said I'd seen the evening paper.

"Why, please?"

"They think he has knowledge of the murder of Judge Akua."

"But he knows nothing!"

A pot of tea was brought. Steam rose in our faces. Hers was pink and lined with emotion.

"Mr. Redmon', what must I do? I have no one to turn to!"

I said I would give her the name of a lawyer who would get her husband out of jail instanter, and wrote down Bosworth

Curtis's name on a slip of paper. I explained how to reach the address. Bos Curtis would enjoy a pretty Frenchwoman begging his assistance.

She tucked the slip of paper into her bodice, poured tea, sipped it and seemed instantly relaxed.

"You are very kind, Mister."

"It is thought that your husband and Judge Akua were enemies," I said.

"Ah, no!" she said. "Both loyal to the king, but in different manners!"

"I'm sure lawyer Curtis will clear up that misunderstanding," I said. I had to resist the impulse to shrink away from her skinny, tension-filled physical pressure and her powerful scent.

"Poor Charley," she said, gazing down into her teacup.

"Why do you say 'poor Charley'?"

"He will be disappointed, is it not so?"

"The king will not select Queen Emma as his successor?"

She shook her head vigorously in her black crinkly bonnet. "The king is very sick. I believe it is too late."

She did not seem to be in much of a hurry to engage Bosworth Curtis to free her husband from jail.

"So, Mr. Redmon', you are love with the big dark-skin girl!"

I mashed a smile onto my lips. I sensed more of a personal interest than was warranted.

"She is a very fine young woman," I said.

"Ah!" she said, with a knowing smile.

"She has come to San Francisco to find a proper husband. I am not that person."

"It will be difficult, will it not, that she is a bastard?"

Nothing to say to that.

"Charley says it was difficult for her at the school in Honolulu."

I let that go by also. It was curiously as though she had to pay me back for having done her a favor.

Mrs. Perry laughed gaily. "She has a very rich uncle, the Honolulu one, not this one in San Francisco."

"Silas Underwood."

She nodded vigorously.

"There seem to be mysteries about her ancestors," I said cautiously, and wished I had not said it.

Mrs. Perry emitted the tinny laugh again. "Charley says that she is made ridicule at the school because of the mysterious ancestor!"

I felt outflanked by the clever Mrs. Perry, whose scent was jarring my senses.

"You had better go and find Lawyer Curtis," I said. "Before he goes out for dinner."

Her face became instantly solemn. She began slipping her gloves onto her tiny hands. "Yes! I must go!"

She was on her feet, forking her glove fingers into place. I rose, also. She patted my hand, smiling with her thin lips, eyes fixed on my face. "You must be careful," she said. "For she is very strong. Charley told me she killed a boy at the school with her strong . . . arms!"

And she was gone with a flip of her black skirt out the door and the trotting tap of her boots on the tiles, leaving me to sink into my chair again in a waft of depression.

CHAPTER 19

ZIGZAG, v.t. To move forward uncertainly, from side to side, as one carrying the white man's burden.

— *The Devil's Dictionary*

WEDNESDAY, JANUARY 21, 1891

Later that day I rode with Bierce in a hack headed out Van Ness Avenue, toward the new mansions there. Hooves crackling on the stones, the horse swung off the street under a porte cochere, where a dark-skinned footman in a maroon uniform hurried out to help us down. In a marble entry a grand portrait of the island sugar magnate, father of Aaron Underwood, gazed down upon us, a spade-bearded old man with white locks combed over his forehead. The belong-him man.

We were ushered into a big room with striped wallpaper and a high ceiling with a central fancy boss. Aaron Underwood had risen from a wing chair across the room.

Beside a marble fireplace a woman reclined in a wheeled chaise longue, the mother (I guessed) of the boy around the corner sprawled in his own special chair in his exile. This woman was supposed to be near death, after which her husband wished to replace her with his father's ward, the beautiful Haunani Brown. In this it seemed he was in contention with his own father, who ran him, unless that was another obsession of Haunani's.

Mrs. Underwood's chalky petulant face, under a white mobcap, regarded Bierce and me with hostility. Aaron Underwood approached to shake hands. Edward Berowne rose from the chair beyond the hearth from Mrs. Underwood's, groomed and corpulent.

"Mr. Underwood," Bierce said. "I am sorry to say that I must abandon my search. I have not found the princess Leileiha, and I do not wish to pursue this effort any longer."

"I am sorry to hear that," Aaron Underwood said.

Bierce dusted his hands together.

Aaron seemed ready to protest further, when his wife interrupted: "A woman should be allowed to disappear when that is her wish!" she said in a harsh voice like a parrot's squawk. "No doubt she has her reasons."

"Which reason cannot fathom," Bierce said with a bow.

Berowne leaned forward to shake hands. He smelled of barbershop lotions. "My niece and her friend Mr. Grady are socializing with young Walter Underwood next door. I came along with them to p-p-pay my respects here."

Aaron introduced us to his wife.

"The infamous disrespecter of the female gender, I believe, Mr. Bierce."

Bierce inclined his head again, toward her. "It is my misfortune to be regarded in that light, madam."

"And this is Mr. Redmond from the *Chronicle*, whose work I have also read. Who is an admirer of our Haunani Brown, I believe."

"That is true," I said. I proffered a smile that felt like a scar.

"We have just been hearing of the superior qualities of her suitor," Mrs. Underwood said, while Berowne retreated to his chair with his raised hands of gift-giving.

"His name is Albert Grady," he said. "He is a young man who has important lumber interests on the northern coast."

Aaron's eyes fixed on my face, on a point on my left cheek, precisely. His wife's head had sunk back onto her pillows. Her lips were unhealthily red in her white face.

"Lumber interests!" she muttered. "Well, then, Haunani will marry this magnate and spend the rest of her life lumbering among the redwood groves of Mendocino County. So much for one's hopes and dreams, Aaron!"

Aaron busied himself ushering Bierce and me to chairs. In Mrs. Underwood's presence I had the uneasiness of the company of a drunk who might throw a chamberpot at any moment.

"Lydia Kukui has a friend on the Palace staff, the fire marshal," Aaron said. "He has been making enquiries through a wide acquaintance in the city Fire Department. I haven't heard from her; she has been much occupied. David Kalakaua is very low. He cannot live more than a day or two, Dr. Sawyer tells me. His liver—"

"David should have been more considerate of his liver," Mrs. Underwood said. "The Merrie Monarch is paying for his merriment. Are you a respecter of livers, Mr. Bierce?"

"I am, madam," Bierce said.

"I am a disrespecter of high-livers," Mrs. Underwood said, raising her head from her pillows again. "Not having been granted the blessing of much living at all."

"Now, Gwendolyn."

"If debts are owed, Mr. Bierce, Mr. Redmond, a mighty debt is owed me by the Lord of heaven."

"Madam, I have seen nothing in our existence that makes me believe that the Lord of heaven recognizes His debts," Bierce said. He seemed to enjoy this difficult woman.

"I will not confront Him on His debts soon enough to please my husband."

"Ah, Gwen," Berowne protested. "This is very p-p-perverse!"

I could feel on my face the stiff smile of pretence that this woman did not mean what she was saying. Underwood must have been through this many times.

Mrs. Underwood continued: "This meeting has the elements of a literary salon. We have with us a famous poet and a famous critic of female poets. And a young journalist."

Bierce bowed his head to her.

Tea was wheeled in on a cart by a homely young Irish woman in a black dress and white crisp apron, and there was some respite from Mrs. Underwood's bile while tea was served.

"So it appears that the sister of David Kalakaua will become queen," she said. "Will the remains be transported back to the Islands on a naval vessel?"

"The cruiser *Charleston*, flagship of Admiral Green."

"Who will accompany the remains?" Mrs. Underwood asked.

Her husband named names.

"Miss Brown?" Bierce asked.

"I b-b-believe not," Berowne said quickly.

"The demeanor of that young person has been affected by her uncertainty about her parentage," Mrs. Underwood said in her harsh voice. "William never told her the truth, of course. Nor you, Edward."

Berowne spoke up strongly. "I have followed William's wishes in the matter."

"How often truth is our undoing," Mrs. Underwood said. "We take our comfort from lies, as does that charming young person, with whom, for some reason, I am unable to sympathize."

"That will do, Gwen," Aaron said, but now his wife had built up a different head of steam: "No doubt my husband's esteemed father is en route to the mainland on his quarterly visit, Mr. Bierce. I can feel the quivering in my bones, like Marines preparing for a naval bombardment. Silas has left his godforsaken acres on Maui and is in transit gloria mundi."

" 'Godforsaken' is a word that should be expunged from your vocabulary," Aaron said. "God does not forsake."

"I, who have been forsaken, may argue the point."

Berowne, his big bland face livid with embarrassment, gazed helplessly at Underwood, who turned to Bierce.

"But haven't you anything you can tell us, Mr. Bierce? Surely some progress has been made."

"No, sir; I can report no progress. The princess has covered her tracks too well."

"This is very disappointing," Aaron said.

"It is also disappointing to me that I have failed."

It was clear that Mrs. Underwood and her husband knew the secret of Haunani's heritage. So Silas must also, which seemed to give the belong-him man, who was en route, an advantage that made me fearful.

All at once Mrs. Underwood laid her head back on its cushion, eyes tightly closed, lips on the pout. Aaron sighed and said, "Gentlemen, if you will pardon us . . ."

He accompanied us to the door, Berowne had also risen and was gathering himself to depart. In the entryway Underwood drew me aside. Gazing past me as he spoke, he said in a low voice, "Please accept my apologies for my rudeness in the past. It concerned a matter in which considerable emotion was invested."

I shook his hand.

Outside Bierce said, "That woman engaged my sympathies. Her husband is waiting for her to die of her affliction so he can marry a younger woman. That seems to me indeed a godforsaken state.

"She seems to know the secret of the heritage of your friend, Miss Brown," he continued. "Perhaps you should find a means to ingratiate yourself to her, in order to pursue that secret."

"I believe I will abandon pursuing it," I said. "For Miss Brown has found an appropriate suitor."

Bierce speculated on the involvement of Charles Perry. "There is a fellow who would well serve Regan's purposes," he said. "But Pusey has him incarcerated."

———

In our hack I asked to be let off at the adjacent Underwood establishment, for I wished to see Haunani with Walter Underwood, and to gaze upon her proper suitor. Mrs. Mulberry directed me into the parlor.

Haunani had drawn up a chair beside Walter's patent chair. Her light-brown hair was piled complicatedly high. Walter's arms were in motion as though he was explaining a baseball game to her. In a chair by the fireplace a big man sat with his legs crossed. His black hair was brushed straight back like porcupine quills, and his florid high-nosed face watched me enter. The brindle cat lay on his knee, and his hand mechanically scratched the animal's chin and ears.

Haunani hurried to me, taking me by both hands and tugging me to her proper suitor, the wealthy lumberman Albert Grady, who now rose to his feet, dumping the cat.

"How do you do, sir?" he said in his deep voice. "I have heard a lot about you from Nani."

"And I you, sir," I said. I shook a big, callused hand. After some conversation about the weather, I excused myself to go to Walter. The boy writhed up at me, grinning with delight. I grasped a hand that would have passed Bierce's handshake test with a higher mark than Grady's. Haunani and her Albert stood together watching me. He was taller than she was by a half-inch.

"A room full of company, Walter," I said.

He stammered that it was good company.

"Haunani is always good company," I said in a lowered voice.

He giggled and jerked his head toward Albert Grady.

"New . . . friend!"

"Too bad for us," I said. He gripped my hand again in his strong hand.

Haunani came toward us, and she and Walter started a game with much laughter, shaking their hands twice and then producing a fist, a palm, or two fingers. Haunani sometimes chanted a phrase that sounded like "Chung gon see phat!" and Walter would get out "Chung!" all with peals of laughter.

"What's that they are doing?" Grady wanted to know. When he was seated again, the cat jumped back into his lap.

"It's a game I've seen in Chinatown. Paper wraps rock, rock breaks scissors, scissors cut paper."

"Chinks!" Grady said. "I believe they should send those coolies back to China, that's what I believe."

"Charles Crocker found them useful when he was building railroad."

"Should have shipped them home afterwards."

"Sandlotter sentiments," I said, before I could stop myself. I realized that I would dispute almost any opinion that Albert Grady gave utterance.

"I go along with the workingman," he said. "I have got good friends amongst those fellows."

I expressed interest in the logging industry on the Mendo-cino coast and received a full report.

"I've been working like a mule," Grady told me. "If you want something done right you have to do it yourself, but now I have a dependable fellow or two. I hope to spend more time in the City. I don't mind telling you that pretty lady over there makes things in the City look a good bit sweeter."

I said I was sure that that was true.

"Like to get to know some of the folks down here now I have made a stake. Get myself a house, put on some matinees, levees and such." The cat stretched her neck to look up at him lovingly.

"Yes," I said.

"I have never met a poetry person like her uncle before. Him and me get along just fine."

"He is a well-connected poet," I said, watching Haunani with Walter Underwood. I had never seen this side of her be-fore, a total attention to Walter. She loved that boy and was the recipient of his love. I felt a curious weakening of my neck muscles to realize the strength of it.

"I'd like to know who it is left a black stone for me in my box at the hotel," Grady grumbled to me.

Kanekoa!

And so it was Haunani who was the *kahuna*'s focus.

"Was there a piece of paper with it?" I asked.

He looked at me in surprise. He had shoved the cat from his lap, and she wove figure eights around his leg, purring.

"Matter of fact there was. Piece in the *Alta California* about a deal I'd made on some redwood timber."

"Mysterious," I said.

Haunani strode from the room to ask Mrs. Mulberry to bring tea and cookies. There was some moving of chairs and a little table so we could be with Walter. Haunani's warm brown arms and hands at work, the moving swell of her bosom, were a delight to observe.

After tea she engaged in another game with Walter, this one involving drawings on folded pieces of paper, and more laughter. And I realized that the games had been planned to help Walter to control the involuntary jerking of his arms and hands.

When I left Haunani came to the door with me. She grasped my hand and squeezed it and let it drop. "I am glad you came, Tom."

"I wish I was a *miliona*," I said.

"Yes!" she said, smiling brilliantly with her full lips, with her beautiful blue eyes.

———

Starting up the steps to my rooms I could see the edge of paper on the top step. Another step and I saw the rock. I stopped where I stood with electric shocks running along my nerves. Slowly I moved up to the top step, where a pebble the size of a pigeon egg rested on the clipping of my short piece on King Kalakaua that had been published yesterday in the *Chronicle*.

My stone might be a warning, but it was not volcanic or even Hawaiian, like the one Grady had complained of receiving, or the one I had appropriated in the basement room.

As I tossed the stone away and crumpled the newsprint into my pocket, I felt a twinge of guilt that I had not warned Albert Grady of the *kahuna*, who seemed to be watching, guarding, stalking Haunani for his master Silas Underwood.

CHAPTER 20

—the mad race run
Through to the end; the golden goal
Attained and found to be a hole!
    — The Devil's Dictionary

THURSDAY, JANUARY 22, 1891

When I woke at first light to gaze at the gray blank of the window, with the ring of the window shade swaying slightly like a hangman's noose, something was changed.

The royal suspiration that had breathed through San Francisco's streets for these last weeks was stilled.

King Kalakaua was dead.

He had in fact died yesterday. His death was plastered in black headlines in the morning *Chronicle*, which I picked up on my way to breakfast.

THE KING IS DEAD

DAVID KALAKAUA, MONARCH OF
HAWAII, PASSES AWAY

Princess Liliuokalani Is the Legal
Successor to the Hawaiian Throne

The United States Cruiser Charleston *Will Sail To-morrow for Honolulu*
With the King's Remains—A Military Funeral to be Held in This City—
California Commandery, Knights Templar, Will Act as a Special Guard of
Honor—Disturbance on the Islands Not Anticipated.

King Kalakaua of the Hawaiian Islands died at the Palace Hotel yesterday at 2:30 P.M. of uremia, arising in the course of Bright's disease. It had been well recognized during the previous night that the case was hopeless, and the only wonder expressed by the attendant physicians was that he had not passed away in the hours of the forenoon. Twice during the morning the action of the heart was momentarily suspended. When death actually came, it was preceded by three cessations of the heart's action, the first of which occured at 2:23 and led the bystanders to believe that the struggle was over. The silence lasted fully fifteen seconds, when the king gasped and the death agony was resumed. The second interruption of respiration, however, being noticeably weaker. After the third interval of silence, the movements of the chest became very slight indeed, and the king heaved a deep sigh. When the fourth cessation came, precisely at 2:30, the tongue protruded between the lips and the eyes were closed. An instant later the lids were very slowly raised, but fell on the instant, and that indescribable change passed over the features which men have learned from all time to associate with the presence of the Angel of Death.

The account of the king's death was written by James Mc-Candless with considerably more attention to heart rates and respiration than seemed to me to be called for. My own researches on Hawaii and King Kalakaua had been used as follow-up, with the principal events of his reign, the new Constitution of 1887, the succession, and opinions on the reciprocity treaty and the Pearl Harbor leases.

I had never met the Merrie Monarch, never even seen him, but his labored breathing had become a presence in my life. And he would continue to be so.

On the roof of the Palace Hotel on Market Street, the Hawaiian flag flew at half-mast.

The account of the death in William Randolph Hearst's *Examiner* was very different from that in the *Chronicle*, with a quarter-page cut of the last photograph made of the seated king, plump, dark, with a tricorn of mustache and beard, in an eight-button double-breasted jacket:

A KING'S DEATHBED

HOW KALAKAUA, MONARCH OF THE HAWAIIAN ISLANDS, PASSED AWAY

DEATH FREE FROM PAIN.

THE WILD GRIEF OF KALAUA, THE HANDMAIDEN

WHAT THE RULER'S DEATH MEANS

His End Was Peaceful — He Passed Away Surrounded by Friends, Amid the Tears of His Loving Handmaiden Kalaua — The Church of England Service for the Dying read During His Last Moments — A Grand Civic and Mil-

itary Pageant Will Be Held in San Francisco today, When His Embalmed Body Will Be Escorted to the Charleston *for Removal to the Islands.*

The king of the Hawaiian Islands is dead, and a queen will reign over that beautiful land.

Through the watches of the early morning yesterday a man knelt at the bedside of David Kalakaua crying unto the Lord to look graciously upon the dying king and grant him a longer continuance on earth. Near the clergyman leaned Kalaua, the young Kanaka girl who has attended the king since she was a child. It is the custom of the Hawaiian chiefs, since the times beyond traditions, to be attended by a maiden who shall minister to them in illness.

Kalaua was clad in a dull gown that fitted her figure loosely, and she passed her hands softly and swiftly over the chest and limbs of her chief, as is the native manner of massage. This is one of the Kanaka customs, and when it was called to the attention of Drs. Sawyer and Taylor they said it would do no harm, and that there was good in it.

The girl murmured tender words in her native tongue as she continued in her labor of love. There was nothing of grief or despair in her tones, but only the melancholy of hope against fate. . . .

Here there was another cut of the king on his deathbed with its high carved bedstead, and the clergyman and Kalaua kneeling beside it.

Six Negro porters, followed by an honor guard, carried the casket down the main stairway of the Palace Hotel to the Jessie Street entrance, where it was loaded onto a funeral carriage and borne to Trinity Episcopal Church at Post and Powell. There the crowds were so large, men in plug hats and soft caps, and women in fancy millinery, so jammed together that it required fifty sweating policemen to allow the mourners to follow the casket into the church.

I stood in the crowd watching for Kanekoa, and observing the men of the royal entourage, Aaron Underwood, Major Baker, and the frail chaplain, out of the hospital for this funeral service at a church which was not even his denomination, Charles Perry with his skinny wife on his arm, out of jail for the same occasion, and Haunani Brown escorted by her uncle and the top-hatted Albert Grady. Haunani was monumental in black with a high complicated black hat almost as tall as Grady's topper. They disappeared into the maw of the church, with Grady halting a step to let Haunani and Berowne precede him into the inner dark.

I had a glimpse of Alexander Honomoku speaking with the black-clad Kalaua, and a stout, veiled young woman that I did not then realize was Princess Leileiha.

After the funeral the crowd followed the official cortege with its Marine guard to the waterfront, where the gleaming white *Charleston* was docked, preparatory to its voyage to Hawaii.

I was feeling that pleasant slow-moving post-ballgame tiredness as I stepped inside the dimness of the chancel of the church. There were a few people there, a priest hurrying past. Albert Grady stood with his hat in his hands and his long legs spread, gazing down the aisle at the candle-blazing white and gold of the altar.

Haunani and the veiled young woman I had seen earlier stood close together in conversation in the right-hand shadows, and I realized that it was the princess, come to her king's funeral service.

I started to move away to leave them alone, as Grady had done, but I wavered and halted. Too much had gone past. I joined them.

"Please introduce me to your friend," I said to Haunani.

She swung toward me big-eyed, and complied. The princess had a sweet voice.

"How do you do, Mr. Redmond. So you have found me."

I said I had only found her when I had stopped looking. I couldn't tell in the dimness whether Haunani was pleased or displeased by my presence. The princess, who was a head shorter, stood with her hands clasped together at her waist.

"I am aware of your affliction, madam," I said. "I am terribly sorry."

"Thank you," she whispered. "I will no longer seek to conceal it."

"I have told her that Andrew Akua is dead," Haunani said. "They were very close. They had known each other all her life. It was what has caused her to change her mind."

"I hope your Mr. Bierce will turn his talents to that terrible business," the princess whispered.

There was a rapid thud of approaching footsteps on the stones, and Honomoku swooped past me. Haunani moved beside me, so we were like two couples in a ballroom waiting for the music to begin. Honomoku spoke to the princess as though they had been interrupted in a previous conversation.

"It is not the end, my darling! I will go with you! We will live our lives together!"

"I cannot go there!" She unclasped her gloved hands to press them to her cheeks.

"Listen, my darling! Of course we will go there. You will go there, as is proper and the law, and I will be with you always. David has died and Liliuokalani is queen. And I am free! I will be with you! I will never leave you!"

"Ah, Nani, what can I do with him?" the princess wailed.

"You must accept what he offers you, Leilei!"

Honomoku embraced the princess while she wept. Haunani frowned at me through her tears. Albert Grady had swung around to watch us.

"Leave us now!" Haunani said to me. But as I turned away she caught my arm.

"There is a memorial occasion for David Kalakaua at my uncle's house this afternoon," she said. "Please come."

———

I discovered Bierce in the third saloon I looked into, and told him that the princess Leileiha had been found.

"So now I, at least, am quit of these emotional and overly dramatic islanders," he said. "I wish I had never allowed myself to be recruited to this business, and I have no sense that it has concluded well."

I told him of my invitation to a memorial occasion at Berowne's house. I wondered if the *kahuna*, Kanekoa, might show up also.

Bierce only groaned.

CHAPTER 21

THURSDAY, JANUARY 22, 1891

On the veranda of Berowne's house I could hear the flatted syllables of a chant, and through the window I saw Haunani dancing. I slipped inside. Charles Perry danced beside her, copying her motions. He was in his shirtsleeves, bare-legged with a dark cloth bound around his hips. Haunani wore an ankle-length grass skirt. Her knees protruded through the strands in her steps. Her arms twined and circled above her head. Her bare feet patted. She was chanting.

There was a sweetish burning stink to the room from two slab-sided candles on a sideboard.

Albert Grady sat watching Haunani from a low chair. On the settee was Berowne, one hand patting the arm of his chair in Haunani's rhythm. I couldn't keep my eyes from Haunani, her knees appearing and disappearing, the sway of her hips, the lithe waist, the fine bosom in a white blouse that exposed her golden arms. Sweat gleamed on her face and neck. Her voice was low and harsh. Perry sometimes chanted with her, swaying with her. Haunani's eyes fixed on me, but not as though she saw me. The solemnity of the occasion was as taut as cable on the strain.

I slipped farther inside to seat myself beside Berowne.

"They are dancing David Kalakaua's ancestry," he whispered to me behind his hand. Grady's face jerked toward us at the sound of Berowne's voice. His black hair was brushed back in a pompadour, his lips sagged open.

The dance continued. The intensity that I felt gradually faded to a lassitude in the repetitive postures and sounds. Haunani's movements now seemed uncertain.

I heard a gasp.

A man had appeared out of the wing of the house. It was Kanekoa, black-clad, his dark malevolent face with its fringe of graying curls peering from one to the other of us.

He plucked from a low table an onyx candle holder and smashed it into his open mouth.

Berowne sucked in his breath. The muscles in the backs of my legs crawled at the sight of bright blood glistening on the *kahuna*'s chin. His face was set in a bloody grimace. Haunani and Perry had halted their dance to stand awkwardly together like two children humiliated by a teacher.

Berowne continued to gaze at Haunani, as though it was dangerous even to glance at Kanekoa. Haunani's eyes showed their whites. Perry's lips puffed out as he edged away from the newcomer.

The *kahuna* took up the chant in a shriller, penetrating voice. Blood from his mouth dripped from his chin.

Perry slipped away to stand beside his wife. Cupped in her big chair, her dark-red hair fitting her head like a cap, she propped her chin on her hands as she stared at Kanekoa's bloody mouth.

Haunani's bare feet whispered on the floor as she retreated across the room. Her eyes rolled toward Kanekoa. She made herself small, standing leaning forward a little, a knee show-ing between the strands of her skirt, her face grimly anxious. The *kahuna*'s chant continued. I watched his malicious snout-like features with his cap of graying curls, his hard, short body. He did not seem conscious of anyone else in the room. He swiped a hand at the blood on his chin.

He finished on a sustained note, straightened motionless for a moment while he gazed around the room again. His eyes fixed on me and passed on. He dabbed at the blood again. Then he was gone out the veranda door.

The relief in the room was like an intolerable weight removed.

It seemed to me that Kanekoa had come here because his king was being celebrated, had performed the genealogical chant as he deemed correct, and departed.

"My God!" Berowne said.

Perry and his wife had their heads together. Haunani slumped into a chair.

My muscles ached with tension.

"That Hawaiian fellow!" Grady marvelled. "He took that candlestick on the table there and knocked a tooth out, cool as you please!"

"That is customary when a king dies," Berowne said. His voice shook before he got control of it. "When the catafalque arrives in Honolulu many teeth will b-b-be knocked out, hair torn, faces scratched. Hawaiians take their grief seri-ously."

"Don't just *talk*!" Haunani said in a stifled voice. She rose to stand beside Grady, taking his arm and pressing against him in a movement I knew too well.

Mrs. Perry said in her shrill voice, "So that is Hawaii!"

"Yes, Marianne," Haunani said, turning toward her. Perry spoke to Haunani in Hawaiian.

"I did not know David Kalakaua's name chant back to the *Kumulipo*," she replied. "*He* knew it. I shame!"

"No shame, Nani!" Perry said.

Grady gazed at him with an expression of dislike.

"Lapidus Kanekoa knew I did not," she said. "I do not even know my own!" she said.

I remembered Perry at the funeral telling me that Hawaiian answers lay in the past.

"What was he doing here?" Grady demanded.

"He was David's *lapa-au*," Perry said.

"He is more than that," I said.

"He observes the stars and foretells good and evil," he said with a shrug.

"More than that," I said again.

"Tom," Haunani said in a low voice. Her face was lightless.

"Uncle Sugar is involved," Perry said. "Mark my words!"

"Who was that bird, anyway? What are you talking about?" Grady wanted to know.

"He is what is called a *kahuna*," Berowne said. "He was a native medical p-p-practitioner for the king, but, as Tom says, he is a good deal more than that. He is a scary fellow."

He took my arm and escorted me out on the veranda where in the clear winter air Alcatraz floated just off North Beach.

"It was as though he knew exactly what was happening here," Berowne said. "Haunani had undertaken to chant David's heritage, and when she faltered, he appeared."

He brushed a hand over the neat part that bisected his head. "David is dead," he said. "The volcano is in eruption. Chaos stalks the islands. I wonder if that fellow is looking for a sacrificial victim."

"How, sacrificial?" I demanded.

"It is a violent religion, of which he is an emissary. Ritual and sacrifice assumed essential roles in the old religions that existed before effective judicial systems. Sacrifice was the old Hawaiian way of directing a climate of violence into acceptable channels."

Perry stalked out onto the veranda to join us. He wore an expression of anger and anxiety like a fierce pout.

"The death of a king calls for violence," Berowne said. "You saw that fellow knock his tooth out, Charley."

"If that stink bird knocked his brains out instead of just a tooth I'd feel a lot better," Perry said.

"Let me say something else," Berowne said, looking into my eyes with his pale blue ones. "In the matter of sacrifice there must b-b-be a social link missing in the selection of a victim. He must b-b-be an outsider of some kind. So there can b-b-be no recourse of vengeance from the victim's family."

"A young warrior!" Perry said, which seemed to refer to something of which I was not aware.

Berowne gave a nervous chuckle.

"Judge Akua was an old warrior," I said. "And no outsider."

They both stared at me. Berowne licked his lips.

"Nevertheless—" Berowne started, and stopped.

Perry said, "It is true you have had some experience in these matters, Edward." There was insinuation in his voice.

Berowne showed his teeth in a smile.

Inside I could see Haunani sitting on the settee close beside Albert Grady. Their togetherness made me want to inform Grady that his black stone had been the curse of Kanekoa, for Haunani to explain.

I realized that poison remained in the room.

Marianne Perry stood with her white knots of fists clenched before her bosom, staring out at me.

I said to Perry, "What did your wife mean, Haunani killed someone with her strong arms?"

Berowne's big face paled.

"It was at the school," Perry said. "Two boys jumped her. She does not hesitate to speak her mind in certain matters. Sometimes boys would take after her, beat her up. She fought back."

"Rape?" I asked.

"Nothing like that. Just pummel her about. She had a headlock on one of them when they fell in an awkward way. His neck was broken."

With her strong arms. *You no mess wid me!*

"It was a b-b-boy named Joshua Kawanakai," Berowne said.

"A young warrior!" I said. Both of them looked startled.

I glanced in the door at Haunani and Grady again. Now it seemed to me that although they were seated together their closeness was misleading, for there was a sense of noncommunication rather than silence, of thoughts that were not of each other.

Charley Perry was regarding them also. In his irritatingly smug tone, he said, "Is Nani's Mendocino lumber magnate the gentleman who will make her happy forever, do you think, Journalist?"

I said she had my best wishes, what about his?

Just then Grady rose to his feet, Haunani also. Alexander Honomoku had entered. He approached them, heavy-bodied and heavy-footed. He held by the arm the elegantly dressed and veiled woman who was the princess Leileiha.

Berowne and Perry hurried back inside. I followed more slowly.

"The *Charleston* departs at four o'clock," Honomoku announced. "Leilei and I are returning to Hawaii with our king."

Haunani embraced the princess.

"Charley, are you coming?" Alexander said. He seemed to exert a force I had not felt in him before.

"There is nothing for you there, Charley!" Marianne Perry cried.

"Yes, I will come," Perry said. He stood beside Honomoku as though they were warriors at the gate. "Will you not come with me, my dear?" he said to his wife.

"*No!*"

"You see that I must go!"

She turned her back.

"It is the hour when Hawaiians must stand together!" Honomoku said. "God Save the Queen!"

Grimacing at his wife's back, Perry raised a hand as though it contained a sword.

"Nani?"

"My place is here," Haunani said, stepping away from the princess. She struck a posture at Grady's side, who looked puzzled and irritated.

Bierce would have detested this scene, "incarnate with lachrymosity and slavering with sentiment," everyone immobilized in his or her pose like some children's game.

"The *Charleston* departs in an hour!" Honomoku said again. "Come, Leilei! Come, who is coming!"

He took the princess's arm again, and swung toward the door. Perry followed them, retrieving his hat from the hat stand. He made a gesture of hopelessness to his wife, who still faced away from him.

Haunani came to me as though I needed to be placated, or to prepare me for bad news. She directed me out onto the veranda.

"Will Honomoku go with the princess to the leper colony?" I asked her.

"He will!" She nodded vigorously. "He will stay with her until she dies. I have been wrong about Alexander!"

I asked about the Reverend Prout.

"He has returned to the hospital," she said. "He is safe there."

"What do you mean?"

"There is a poison that is known on Maui," she said, chin up. "It is a seaweed from Hana. It is very deadly. Lapidus Kanekoa is from Maui."

As everyone but Lydia Kukui seemed to be.

"Why would Kanekoa poison Jonathan Prout?"

"Why does he do anything? Why would he put a stone in Albert's box at the hotel?"

"He also put one on my top step," I said.

She hissed.

I said slowly, "It appears that Kanekoa is in the City to attend the king because of his expertise in ancient Hawaiian medicine. The stone he presented to me may be a warning because of the long piece I've been writing about the king. But what has Albert Grady to do with anything but *you*?"

"I don't know!" she murmured, hands to her cheeks.

"Tell me," I said. "How could he give me a headache at fifty feet away?"

"He is a *kahuna ana-ana*!"

"And you believe in his power?"

"Yes, Tom." Her brilliant eyes flashed at me. "Don't you?"

She moved toward the railing with a rustle of her grass skirt. It was chilly in the shadow and she wrapped her arms around herself.

"Tom," she said.

"Yes?"

"I'm going to marry Albert." She leaned against the rail, shivering in her grass skirt and thin blouse, gazing out at the bay.

There was a sudden intensity in her posture as she watched

a white steam yacht glide past Alcatraz. It was as though she had forgotten me and her marriage to Albert Grady.

She pointed. "It is the *Haleakala*!" she whispered. "Uncle Silas has come!"

She hurried back inside with the news.

———

"Please take me back to my hotel, Mr. Redmon'," Marianne Perry said to me, when the *Charleston* contingent had gone. Her hard little face was stained with tears and streaked with pale female powders.

I walked down the hill into North Beach with her hand on my arm. Occasionally she patted her face with her handkerchief. She would be leaving on the train tomorrow morning, bound for New York and by steamer to Paris.

"I am all alone in this city," she said. "Who will entertain Marianne this lonely evening?" To which I did not respond. In her petulance Mrs. Perry had reminded me of my wife in her long grieving.

In North Beach I helped her into a hack bound for her hotel. "Good-bye, Mr. Redmon'," she said, and gazed straight ahead with her taut face as the hack bore her away.

The guilt that I had disappointed her was not as strong as the relief that settled over me.

———

In my room I heard the distant guns of Fort Point saluting the departure for Honolulu of the *Charleston*, which must have passed the arriving steam yacht *Haleakala* in San Francisco Bay.

CHAPTER 22

CREDITOR, n. One of a tribe of savages dwelling beyond the Financial Straits and dreaded for their desolating incursions.
— *The Devil's Dictionary*

FRIDAY, JANUARY 23, 1891

I was with Bierce at the *Examiner* when Charles Perry stalked into the office. He carried his hat in one hand and moved in his toe-stretching affected pace like an official in a ceremony. He wore a black cutaway with a black armband.

I was so startled to see him the legs of my chair screeched on the floor as I shoved it back to rise.

"My wife must be on the train, but where did she spend last night?" he demanded. He jutted his jaw at Bierce and me.

"I thought you had sailed on the *Charleston*!" I said.

"There was no accomodation for Charles Perry," he said in an offended tone. "Others, yes. Do you know the whereabouts of my wife?" he said to Bierce. "You who are the locator of missing people."

Bierce knew nothing.

I said I had left Berowne's with Mrs. Perry and put her in a hack bound for her hotel. She had said she was leaving on the morning train.

"She had departed from the hotel when I returned." He sank into the chair Bierce had produced for him. The *Examiner* clamor racketed in the hallways. Perry was not his usual cocky self, sagging in his chair, long-faced.

"Alexander has found his princess and I have lost mine," he said dramatically.

Bierce had seated himself with his fingertips tented together. The skull observed the scene from his desk.

I was thankful beyond measure that I had not responded to hints that I should entertain Mrs. Perry on her last night in San Francisco.

"My wife is not a princess, you understand," Perry went on. "But she is well-born. Her uncle is a marquis! In France she has fences without end to mend. And in Hawaii I have fences to mend." He spread his hands sadly, palms up. "Liliuokalani does not like the red shirts of the Diamond Head Rifles!"

"Will you return to Hawaii?" Bierce wanted to know, squinting at him.

"I must return! I have friends and family there. I must make a living. I am not a rich man. That also was discouraging to my wife, you see."

He laughed hollowly and said, "There was accomodation aboard the *Charleston* for Lydia Kukui, but not for Charles Perry. So I sailed alongside on the tugboat to bid my farewells, and who should we encounter?"

I knew whom he had encountered.

"Uncle Sugar! Of course he did not know that the corpse of David Kalakaua was aboard the *Charleston*. It was Charles Perry who hailed the *Haleakala* and so informed him. The *Ona Miliona* grieved hard! So now he is here."

He looked down at his soft hat in his lap, punching new dents in the crown with the flat of his hand. No doubt his wife had found someone else to entertain her on her last night in San Francisco.

"Mr. Bierce, the police of this city were so stupid as to arrest me for the murder of Andrew Akua."

"And released you."

"Andrew Akua was my father's friend. More than friend. I loved that old fellow!"

Bierce stirred uncomfortably.

"He was high counsellor," Perry went on. "He was *alii* of the highest—he was of the old royalty! He was the enemy of *Ona Miliona*! He wanted David Kalakaua out of that old badger's grip. Uncle Sugar had lent too much money to the kingdom. He has too much power."

"Are you saying that Silas Underwood should be suspected in the murder of Judge Akua? He was not in San Francisco."

"He is here now, as I can attest. And there are those who will do his bidding."

"The *kahuna* Kanekoa," I said,

Perry sat up straighter in his chair. "You have seen him at Edward Berowne's!" he said to me. "See how he brings fear. All are fearful. It is his weapon!"

"Akua was fearful when we saw him last," Bierce said.

"Andrew Akua was a proponent of the London loan!"

Bierce said, "The London loan would entail a lien on the income of the nation, and the danger of Hawaii becoming another Egypt. It is not in danger of becoming the property of Silas Underwood."

Perry raised his chin and gazed back at Bierce. "One may not be certain of that. Uncle Sugar is acquiring much land on Maui. The plains of Mauikai!"

"To which Princess Leileiha objects, as well as Judge Akua."

"As she should! She will inherit a thousand acres there!"

I said, "How do you stand on the London loan?"

"I stand with Andrew Akua!"

"And Queen Liliuokalani?"

"The same!"

"And what is it you wish of me, sir?" Bierce asked.

"If you could discover the murderer of Andrew Akua, and the reason he was murdered, as you have searched for the whereabouts of Princess Leilei—"

"I failed in that!" Bierce said quickly. And he said, "Mr. Perry, do you believe that Silas Underwood ordered this man Kanekoa to murder Judge Akua?"

Perry sat silent as though it were a decision of great importance for him to make. He said, "No, Mr. Bierce, I cannot believe that."

"Tell me," Bierce said. "What is the position of Aaron Underwood in regards to his father?"

"It is well known," Perry said grimly, "that Aaron Underwood can only hawk when permission comes from Honolulu to spit."

"Could his son then be employed in such a matter?"

"Ah, no," Perry said, shaking his head. "Not good Aaron. No, he would do nothing illegal, bad, wrong, ever!"

"Tell me," Bierce said again. "When William Brown was stricken with an illness, and he and Miss Brown moved to Honolulu to reside with Silas Underwood, to whom was his plantation sold?"

"To *Ona Miliona*."

"Your relation with old Underwood is one of enmity?"

"I confess it, sir!" Perry took a deep breath and said, "I repeat my request!"

"I will think about it, Mr. Perry."

Perry rose and cracked his heels together with a brisk bow, very military.

"I must believe my wife is on the train crossing this continent," he said. He shook hands with Bierce and with me. His heels tapped away down the corridor.

"I think," Bierce said, "I would just as lief conduct a search for a diamondback in a snake pit."

———

I had been working on a long piece for the *California Monthly*, entitled "King Calico," on Hawaiian history and politics related to the death of Kalakaua, based on the background material I had furnished the *Chronicle*. That evening I was typing on my Remington, the stalks of the keys whacking forward against the paper on the platen. It was a sound pleasing to me, of creation and production. The completed pages were stacked by my left elbow. The green glass shade of my lamp threw its warm oblong of light on my desk and the typewriter. After each page I sipped from my mug of cold coffee to reward myself, and then went back to work again. I was, however, feeling an unaccustomed fatigue, and making more typing errors than usual.

A headache like a band of pain crept by increments into my skull, increasing until I gasped.

Fear constricted my chest.

Kanekoa loomed in the casement. The net curtains drifted around him like scarves in a breath of air through the window. He crouched there lithely, watching me with his hard dark face full of its queer impersonal malice.

The headache was like a crown of pain.

I struggled to my feet, thrusting with my arms on the arms of my chair, straining my legs against the terrific weight. When I started toward him, I fell full length forward. I seemed to fall for a long time. My arms would not rise to break the crash, which shuddered along my frame. Stretched on the rug, I managed to turn on my side to watch him as he stepped past me. He wore black boots and trousers, and a black sweater. His spray of white curls gleamed in the lamplight like a silver halo as he seated himself at my desk.

I could hear someone groaning. The sound was bubbling from my own paralyzed lips. He paid me no attention, craning his neck to read the words on the sheet of paper on the platen.

He tore the sheet out of the typewriter, crumpled it and dropped it into the metal wastebasket. He discovered the stack of completed manuscript and read the first two pages before crumpling them all and tossing them into the wastebasket.

Paying no attention to me the while, he looked through the drawers of the desk, and swung around to open drawers of the oak file cabinet and peer into them.

As he might have gone through Judge Akua's papers, to burn the packet of them on the grate.

My headache seemed to throb in long cycle, unbearable, then a little less unbearable, when my groans subsided.

I watched him as he took from my bureau a leather cardcase that Haunani had left. He slipped it into his pocket. I tried to protest, for it would give him power over her! No sound would come.

He moved back to bend over the wastebasket. A match flared. He bent to apply the match to the crumples of paper in the wastebasket. A flame flickered. Someone was sibilantly murmuring, "Don't—don't—" Flames in the wastebasket flared up.

In two steps he was through the window behind my head and gone. *How had he managed to climb to that second story window?*

Staring at the flames leaping from the wastebasket, I could see the room in flames, the building, Sacramento Street in flames, the city burning, I could hear the clang of the fire bells, the shouts of the fireman and the galloping hooves as the pumpers and the hose rigs arrived, the high sprays of water arcing upward, hopelessly. I saw the flames dancing above the hills, Nob Hill, Russian and Telegraph, a lacework of fire against the night sky.

Signora Sotopietro so fat and crippled next door!

I dragged myself with enormous effort an inch toward the flaming metal basket, another inch. Groaning like breaking timbers I managed to push to my knees. I reached the desk and flung the contents of the coffee mug into the flames. They leaped up more vigorously. I could smell the stink of hot metal.

I grasped the wastebasket in both hands and inverted it. I breathed smoke. The headache had subsided. I scrambled to my feet and staggered to seat myself in my desk chair. When I turned the wastebasket back right side up there was only smoke. My scorched palms ached.

I leaned back in my chair panting and staring at the open window with the net curtains rippling in a breeze I could not feel.

Judge Akua had been brained with a blunt instrument and his rooms set afire, I had been metaphorically brained by malevolent *kahuna* power and a fire set that would have consumed me and my rooms.

I sat staring down at the red blotches of my scorched palms.

You no mess wid him!

He had tried to kill me twice.

CHAPTER 23

OBSESSED, pp. Vexed by an evil spirit, like the Gadarene swine and other critics.

— *The Devil's Dictionary*

SATURDAY, JANUARY 24, 1891

At breakfast I rubbed butter into the burns on my palms. Last night could have been a nightmare except for my burns, and my incinerated manuscript. The piece was easy enough to rewrite.

———

I was reluctant to speak of my humiliation lying helpless on the floor groaning while Kanekoa burned my manuscript, but in Bierce's office he asked me what I had done to my hands and I told him.

Pusey arrived. "Mr. Bierce, you have got to tell me what is going on with you and that pack of Kanakas."

"They have departed on the *Charleston* for Honolulu," Bierce said. "I was employed to discover the whereabouts of the princess Leileiha, but she discovered herself. That is all there is to it, Captain."

"This old fellow that got coshed."

"That is not my business."

"Oh, I think it is," Pusey said. "I do think it is. Tell you why. Here is Mr. Charles Perry complaining his wife's disappeared on him. Supposed to took the train for New York on Friday, but the ticket fellow there at the ferry has no recollection. And Mr. Redmond here the last to see her."

I blew out my breath in a long sigh.

"Looks like your hands have got some burns there, Mr. Redmond," Pusey said.

"I had to put out a fire," I said.

"So."

Bierce watched us with his fingers steepled together.

"Fellow broke into my room and knocked me out and set fire to the place."

"Sounds like somebody coshing the old judge. Who was it?"

"Name is Lapidus Kanekoa. He is a Hawaiian witch doctor who was treating the king."

"Making a complaint?"

"Not at this time."

Bierce opened his desk drawer against his belly and took out the charred menu. He presented this to Pusey.

"Found with some burned papers in Akua's fireplace."

Pusey frowned at the card. I saw his lips frame the word "jongleurs" but he did not say it aloud. When he looked up there was a queer widened innocence in his eyes.

"What's EC–4?"

I said it might refer to Engine Company #4.

"What's PO–8?"

I didn't know.

"What's this other thing, clock hands?"

I didn't know that, either. Bierce was looking smug.

"Are you sure you don't recognize it, Captain?"

"I purely don't!"

"It's a clue," Bierce said. "I just don't know what it's a clue *to*."

"I'm taking this as evidence," Pusey said, and pocketed it.

"Now, Mr. Redmond," he said. "I can find out if Mrs. Perry is on that train, but it will take some doing. Now: just what do you know of her proceedings?"

"We walked down the hill together after Edward Berowne's party. I put her in a hack to her hotel. She told me she would be taking the train in the morning."

"Well, we will see about that. Where is this witch doctor at?"

I didn't know.

When the chief of detectives had gone, Bierce said, "That vat of corruption hopes that I will pull his chestnuts out of the fire. Could you decide if he had seen that menu before?"

"Something."

"I detect a slight stench of blackmail, Tom," Bierce said.

———

Bierce and I had supper together, and at his invitation I accompanied him to the Schiller Hall for the woman's suffrage program that had been advertised on the hoardings and in drugstore windows for the last two weeks. Rose Blessing Hansen was the first speaker.

I had worries of my own about women; whether Marianne Perry was on the train for New York, how Silas Underwood's arrival would complicate Haunani's decision to marry Albert Grady, and the plight of the princess Leileiha.

———

"You know my feelings about the inferior gender," Bierce said to me, a little too loudly for comfort, as we made our way through the crowd of pleasantly odiferous, big-hatted and bonneted females in the lobby.

He continued when we were seated: "Certainly homage is

paid them, deserved or not. The chivalrous man pays his taxes with alacrity. Although the ladies may have a higher conception of what is due them than the man would concede.

"Rose Hansen has many qualities to admire, and few that irritate," he went on. "She is outspoken on the subject of women's rights and women's wrongs, and I must admit that in all fairness she has brought me to some interest in the matter."

He exchanged glares with a large woman in the seat ahead of him.

"I went to call on Mrs. Underwood, to see if I could elicit information about your Miss Brown's heritage," he said. "But she was 'not at home' to me. Her husband says she has taken a turn for the worse."

The echoing hall with its high decorated ceiling was filling with members of the inferior gender in their hundreds, seating themselves with much disposition of wraps and handbags. The dais was covered with red cloth, its lectern looming over the audience. The women regarded Bierce and me with interest, but they were not friendly. We sat on the aisle for a quick exit once Bierce's Rose had finished. Arrangements had been made for us to meet her after she had retired from the dais.

Her topic was women through the centuries. I thought she was impressive, her tone generally light, heavier when solemnity was called for. She was an attractive figure at the podium, with her flyaway hair, her pretty face and neck and a blocky costume of gold and brown which concealed her figure except for her thin arms. Her active hands danced about her words.

I sneaked a sideways glance at Bierce, who was watching her indulgently.

She was not speaking in a trance tonight, but instead was bright and alert. Her words concerned queens wicked and wise, courtesans who determined the actions of royal lovers, women entrusted with power who had conducted themselves in exemplary fashion. She began by extolling Mary Wollstonecraft, the founder of the woman's movement; she cited the accomplishments of the female rulers in history, Cleopatra, Semiramis, Arsinoe, and Queen Elizabeth; she mentioned the misdemeanors and felonies of the wife of Marcus Aurelius; she discussed Mary Queen of Scots in disapproving terms; and she praised Elizabeth Cady Stanton, Susan B. Anthony, and the president of the San Francisco Ladies League in complimentary phrases. She brought the history of womankind up to our own time, and finished to enthusiastic applause, after which she made her way back to the recesses of the stage at her sidling hesitant gait, and disappeared.

Clapping with the women around us, Bierce said, "I do consider her speech shallow in content, but charming in delivery. Let us go to meet her and toast her success. I know she has been much occupied by her speech tonight."

We departed as a large lady with a powerful bosom replaced Rose Hansen at the podium.

We waited outside a side door of the hall like stagedoor admirers, until Rose Hansen, wearing a heavy wrap and her masculine soft hat, came out to join us.

———

Mrs. Hansen was the only lady in our section of the male alcoholic clamor of Saturday night in the Crystal Palace saloon, object of many glances, for she was very pretty tonight, smoothing her high planes of hair, and bending her neck to touch the tip of her cigarette to the match Bierce had lit for her.

We congratulated her on her speech. I thought Bierce's praise genuine, beneath a gloss of sarcasm.

"Thank you, friends," Rose Hansen said, her face wreathed in smoke from her cigarette. She picked a shred of tobacco from her lip. "I was very nervous," she said to Bierce.

"You did not show it, my dear."

"And were you persuaded to our cause, Mr. Redmond?" she enquired.

"Powerfully," I said.

"Ah, but successfully, sir?"

Bierce laughed.

Champagne was brought, poured, and Mrs. Hansen toasted. Her face was pink with pleasure as she touched her glass to Bierce's and mine.

"I do understand," she said to Bierce, "how you might scorn both the Christian religion and the female gender."

"How is that, my dear?" Bierce said.

She tapped the ash from her cigarette into the saucer provided. "Because our gender has made such perfect Christians. Poor in spirit, sickly, passive, self-denying, good at giving things up and producing progeny every ten months, including the final strength to make a good death and cause no trouble. All those Christian virtues, of which the movement is trying to rid the nation."

"You did not mention this in your splendid speech," Bierce said.

"I was instructed to begin the night's proceedings on an uplifting note."

I saw that she had managed to finish her champagne without appearing to do so.

I said, "Has Bierce told you that we are faced with a sorcerer?"

She laid a hand to her throat. "Can this be true?"

"A Hawaiian sorcerer who has the power to induce paralyzing headaches, and perhaps more than that."

"There are people who have peculiar powers," Mrs. Hansen said solemnly. "Heaven knows, I have seen such."

"Frauds," Bierce said.

"I think not all. I knew a man who emanated a heat so profound you would feel yourself seared by the touch of his hand. It was claimed to be a healing hand. I thought it diabolical. Another who was able to stop a watch by staring at the face. These I thought were real manifestations."

"Of what, my dear?" Bierce said, leaning toward her.

"I don't know, Ambrose. Spirits? Sorcery?"

She scrubbed out her cigarette and held up her glass as the waiter approached again. He filled the glasses. Another bottle was ordered. There was a great deal of movement along the bar. Men circulated past for a glimpse of Mrs. Hansen.

Bierce said, "You have told me that in your own career it became a necessity to perform such tricks."

She compressed her lips into a tight line. Her cool eyes flashed to mine, and down to the tabletop. "There are many tricks," she said. "There is a class of men, such as the magician Houdini, who devote themselves to exposing the women who have been connived into dishonesty. It is simply a part of the male conspiracy against female efforts to rise out of the slavery of Christian martyrhood to which men would confine them."

"And you were one of these connived women."

"You are well aware of that, Ambrose," she said with some heat. "I have confessed all my sins to you."

Of course they were intimate. Bierce's female acquaintances were most often wealthy and attractive Nob Hill and Pacific Heights matrons, widows, and divorcees, and young female poet acolytes. This was certainly a different kind of attachment.

"Mrs. Hansen," I said. "You must have had some experience with persons with peculiar powers used malevolently. How would you deal with such a one?"

She considered me thoughtfully. I saw that she had again managed to absorb her portion of champagne.

"I think," she said, "that a part of the powers are an acceptance of them by someone like yourself. I would recommend to you the skepticism that Ambrose so bravely displays."

When she saw that I was not satisfied, her forehead wrinkled prettily.

"I think," she said, "that men, or women, who have such powers, or appear to, are very suggestible themselves. If there could be found some way of appearing to confront them with a similar or stronger, or more mysterious power, they would be terrified of it."

I tried to think how this might be accomplished with Kanekoa, for I knew I was not finished with him. Mammy Pleasant had offered her assistance, but I didn't know how to take advantage of it.

"That is good advice, Rose," Bierce said. "But it resembles the old dilemma of belling the cat."

"I would consider engaging the powers of Mrs. Pleasant," she said, smiling vaguely. Her speech had become blurred. She herself looked blurred, as though her features had thickened.

"I think you must take me home, Ambrose," she said in a whisper.

———

When I returned to Sacramento Street the white bundle that was Haunani was propped on the top step, rising as I mounted toward her. Inside, when I started to light the lamp, she whispered, "No, please, no light."

We stood clasped in each others' arms. She was shivering.

She pulled away to seat herself on the arm of the easy chair. In the darkness I could make out that her hands were clasped together as though in prayer.

"He says I must come back with him," she said.

I knew who she meant.

"Why?"

"To be his wife. He has a plan—it is a crazy plan! He is building a palace on Maui. He thinks Liliuokalani will . . . I don't know what he thinks! He has a plan for the loan which as you know they are renegotiating. Tom, he is *pupule*, he is insane! But he says I must come!

"We owe him so much," she went on. "My father and I. He was so good to us. He saved us from . . . I don't know what. I owe him everything I am. He says I must do as he says!"

"Must you?"

"I told him I would not," she said.

"What did he say, then?"

"Nothing," she whispered, "Just—nothing. Just—I am to think what it means that I have refused him. But Tom, I will not go back! You know, I left Honolulu because I saw that this was coming."

"And you will marry Albert Grady?"

"I don't know!"

She had told me once that Princess Leileiha would not go home. When I thought of that ancient magnate, like some lusting Zeus carrying her back to Hawaii my heart seemed to slow, so that I could feel the individual beats like a tapping on a wall. Underwood's powers, and his desires, seemed so much greater than mine that I felt diminished. We made *panipani*.

I whispered to her, "I will not let him take you back!"

She murmured something. I buried my face in her bosom. I thought she would not marry Albert Grady.

"He says I must learn to chant the names of the kings of Maui," she said.

CHAPTER 24

PREDESTINATION, n. The doctrine that all things occur according to programme. This doctrine should not be confused with that of foreordination, which means that all things are programmed, but does not affirm their occurrence, that being only an implication from other doctrines by which this is entailed. The difference is great enough to have deluged Christianity with ink, to say nothing of gore. With the distinction of the two doctrines kept well in mind, and a reverent belief in both, one may hope to escape perdition if spared.

— *The Devil's Dictionary*

SUNDAY, JANUARY 25, 1891

Over breakfast ham and eggs, I turned to "Prattle" in the *Examiner*.

Bierce's first item was critical of the governor for appointing a crony to the Supreme Court:

"Take him, gentlemen of the Republican Party; he is all yours—he and the fragrance of him. His appointment takes high rank among the rare and shining examples of fraternal consideration."

There followed some brag about *Examiner*:

"A newspaper reporter rarely obtains the privilege of traveling on a man-of-war. The *Examiner*, however, has a representative on the *Charleston* in the person of Harry Bellamy. While this is probably a matter of personal gratification to young Mr. Hearst, the reading public has reason for satisfaction. It secures a thoroughly adequate account of an historic event. The scene in Honolulu will be memorable. To picture in graphic prose the ardent and extravagant grief of the Islanders when they realize their king is dead, and to tell, with spirit and pathos, of the funeral ceremonies, are tasks that might engage worthily the most gifted pen in the world. Mr. Bellamy has an admirable opportunity and will undoubtedly make a record. His account of the death scene was an excellent piece of work, particularly when it is considered it was written at lightning speed, with no thought or opportunity to revise."

———

The opinion among my colleagues at the *Chronicle* was that Bellamy's description of the death of Kalakaua, with its farcical focus on the handmaiden Kalaua, was *Examiner* trash at its most extravagant. Willie Hearst had named his father's newspaper "The Monarch of the Dailies," and his order to his staff was that readers were to be impelled to exclaim "Gee whiz!" at the sight of the front page, "Holy Moses!" at the second, and "Gosh almighty!" when they turned to the third. *Examiner* disregard for facts was often shocking.

I had never criticized Bierce's employer to him, for I considered my friend's well-known contempt for his profession to be a criticism in itself. But when I reread the piece on Bellamy, I discovered that it was not so fulsome as I had first thought. Bellamy's account of the arrival of the *Charleston* in Honolulu would be "thoroughly adequate," he would undoubtedly make a "record." His account of the death scene was excellent considering that "it was written at lightning speed" and not revised.

So Ambrose Bierce was not as content as he might pretend with the Monarch of the Dailies and his employer, young Mr. Hearst, who was presently in Egypt collecting mummies.

———

Parris, Frank, and I had a spirited game of catch in the park, after which I repaired to the Sacramento Street baths for a soak and scrub.

———

The latest event at Berowne's was a welcoming soiree for Silas Underwood. I had arrived early in order to see Haunani alone.

She sat on the settee with her lace handkerchief pressed to her mouth, her teary blue eyes gazing at me over it.

"Albert is hurt!" she wailed. "His leg is broken. A log has fallen on him."

I said I was sorry.

"It is Lapidus Kanekoa!" she said.

In San Francisco? Bierce had asked. Now up on the Mendocino coast? I had not told her of my own latest encounter with the *kahuna*.

"What has happened with Silas Underwood?"

"I have not seen him again. He will be here today, of course."

"Is he residing with Aaron?"

"He stays on the *Haleakala*."

"What had your father done that there was a curse?" I asked.

"*Hala*," she said. "Offense. He had built the foundation of the mill in Hana with stones from a *heiau*."

"A grave?"

"An altar. And there was the death of Judge Akua's son. After that my father kept getting sicker."

"Like Prout."

"Yes."

The *kahuna* had her card case. Did he also have something of Grady's?

"Could Grady's accident have been because of you?"

She closed her eyes.

"What have you done to . . . *offend*?"

"To think I could leave Hawaii forever," she said, looking down at her hands.

Just then Berowne bustled inside, removing his hat to hang it on a hook. "I'm late!" he said. "Chang must be frantic."

———

There was not much of the San Francisco Hawaiian colony left for this affair, but Chaplain Prout was on hand, as were Mr. Regan and Aaron Underwood. There were the usual poets, and some society swells. Charles Perry did not appear, so I assumed that he had found his wife.

The sugar magnate, arriving a half-hour after his son, stamped inside in a great bustle of divesting himself of top hat and overcoat, embracing Berowne, and swinging his arms to greet the assembled. He rather resembled Saint Nick, a tall, white-headed, spade-bearded old satyr in a fine black broad-cloth suit, with a kind of smarmy, sarcastic smile graven on his ugly face, and a big laugh that rattled Berowne's Chinese artifacts.

Uncle Sugar was accompanied by a natty little gent with center-parted hair, who absented himself onto the veranda.

Silas Underwood shook my hand, gazing at me with bright eyes. "How-do, sir."

I regarded him through a red mist of hatred.

He trumpeted to the other guests, "It is my great sorrow that I did not arrive in San Francisco to bid my old friend David Kalakaua farewell. Hawaii has had a great loss! God bless the queen!"

A toast was drunk.

Haunani kept herself across the room from Silas, curtseying once when she met his gaze. She wore a form-fitting dress of pale water-silk that set off her complexion, although her face looked strained. It became a kind of three-cornered dance, with Haunani avoiding both Underwoods, and me as well, and the father ignoring his son. His great laugh resounded regularly. It had a peculiar progression, as though he was sounding out the vowels in order. The small crowd in the room formed into a series of eddies around him. I had to admit that Silas Underwood presented an amiable face.

Haunani avoided me.

"Looking up at that mountain do make a person realize the size of himself," I heard the old man saying. He had a habit of swiping his big flat hands together, as though dismissing a subject. "Look up at old Haleakala every morning!" he said with the big laugh, who was building a castle on the plains of Mauikai, on the Island of Maui.

He forged toward Haunani who moved away from him. Aaron sidled and backtracked, always with an eye for Haunani. It might have been comical if I had not been in a fit of rage.

Once in our motions I confronted Aaron. "Good evening, Redmond," he said, gazing past me.

"What will happen when the music stops?" I said.

He looked dimly amused.

Chang circulated with plates of Chinese delicacies. A bartender poured from bottles of Veuve Cliquot. A lady in a blue gown played Berowne's Chickering with a great deal of arm motion and glittering bracelets.

Berowne read a new poem. Two young men and a palely pretty young woman also read their verse. I managed to reach a position near Haunani, and replenished her cup of champagne punch. She slipped on away. Out the windows steamers, scows and sailing vessels passed each other on their routes past Alcatraz. Tall displays of sails gleamed in the afternoon sun. The guest of honor conferred with various groupings of the other guests. His vowelly laugh sounded at regular intervals.

In a conversational lull, he called to Haunani, "The *Hally* will be leaving any day, Missy. Will you be coming along?"

Every eye turned her way. She shook her head as though she didn't trust herself to speak. "No, I will not, Uncle Silas," she said. "I am enjoying my visit to the Mainland."

"You are an Island girl, Missy!" The big laugh rumbled through the guests.

"You remind her now, Arnie! I want to see her aboard the *Hally*!"

Aaron stood staring back at his father with his lips sucked flat. He did not reply.

Silas Underwood shone his sneering Saint Nick countenance around, brushing his hands together, and turned to speak with Berowne. The little center-parted gent appeared as though from a trapdoor with his coat and hat, and Uncle Sugar tramped on out the door making a mechanical saluting motion, his grin preceding him like the cowcatcher of a locomotive.

The relief was instantaneous. Some color appeared in Haunani's cheeks. Even Berowne appeared relieved. Aaron stood against the far wall with his hands at his sides. His eyes met mine for a moment. The tone of the party changed to one of mild revelry.

I took a stroll outside. A hired hack was drawn up directly in front of the house, top up, the little attendant up on the seat, twin headlamps on gooseneck iron rods glaring. Inside I could see a shadowy Silas Underwood sitting stiffly upright, hands folded on his lap, grim-faced and staring straight ahead.

Breathing hard, I retreated inside to join Haunani, who this time did not slip away, and just then grasped my arm with a hand hard as an ice tong.

Kanekoa had come out of the bedroom wing, where a Chinese screen half blocked the door. He wore a tight black jacket over a white singlet, and black trousers. His face was dark as ebony beneath his silvering cap of curls.

He flexed his wrist at Haunani.

"Hele mai!" he commanded. He moved toward her at his predator's shuffle.

"A-ole!" she cried, retreating from him.

"Kanekoa!" Aaron said.

The *kahuna* made a slashing motion with his hand, dismissing Aaron. Prout stepped away from the company of the young poets, stooped and gray-faced. He was holding up a small wooden cross.

He muttered what must have been a Protestant incantation.

Kanekoa cuffed the cross out of his hands with another slash of his arm.

"Come!" he cried at Haunani.

Bierce had appeared in the doorway as if on cue. With him was an old woman wearing a dark cloak, a dark poke bonnet. From the bonnet a wrinkled dark face glared past Bierce, who stepped aside.

Mammy Pleasant faced the *kahuna*.

She stooped with a quick motion to snatch up the cross. She held it upside down, thrust toward the *kahuna*. She spoke in a high raspy voice a language I didn't understand, maybe French.

Kanekoa retreated a step, shoulders hunched. When she advanced a step, he retreated again.

Then, moving swiftly, he circled past her and was gone.

My breath started again.

Bierce guided Mammy Pleasant to a chair, where she sat straight-backed.

Haunani said, "He came out of my room!"

She hurried past the Chinese screen. In a moment she shrilled my name. I ran to her.

Her room was a small one with an open window facing Russian Hill, a bed with a neat coverlet, a chest of drawers with two high hooks from which hung collections of necklaces. On the bed was the white-eyed figurine of dark polished wood.

Haunani stared at it with an expression shockingly like that of the statuette. I caught her in my arms.

Faces looked in the door at us. Aaron forced his way inside. Haunani was shaking as though she would come apart. Suddenly Mammy Pleasant was with us.

She snatched up the statuette, and turned it to reveal a rectangular hole in the back. From this she extracted a loop of darkened leather which she tossed to me. It was the sweatband from my hat. She also brought out Haunani's leather card case, which she set aside. Then she jerked the coverlet from the bed and wrapped the obscene object in it.

"It cannot touch you now!" she said in her harsh voice, to Haunani, and to me.

————

When Bierce had taken San Francisco's triumphant Voodoo Queen away, along with the wooden figurine, Haunani and I stood together on the veranda. She leaned against me, staring out at the bay.

"Silas Underwood was outside in a hack," I said.

She didn't respond, but I could feel her tension.

"Kanekoa was to bring you to him."

"Yes," she whispered.

We were silent for a time. "Do you know how hard it is to say no?" she said.

"You are strong," I said.

"Strong," she said, pressing against me.

Aaron watched from inside the house.

MONDAY, JANUARY 26, 1891

My friend Jim Mattison at the Port offices knew the *Haleakala* well. Silas Underwood's yacht docked at the American-Hawaiian Sugar Company refinery on the eastern shore of the bay, but sent a daily boat to Robinson's Wharf in the City for supplies.

———

There were three telephones at the Chronicle Building, and Berowne took advantage of his social and literary position to telephone me at the publisher's personal number. Mike De Young's secretary Miss Bentley called me to the telephone. Berowne was hysterical.

"Thomas! Haunani has disappeared! She would not do this, she always lets me know if she is going out. She was not dressed for going out! You know, that *kahuna* fellow tried to make her leave with him last night. It is Silas Underwood, surely! I don't know what to do!"

"Call Sergeant Willsey at Central Station to look for her at Robinson's Wharf. I'm going there."

The day had turned cold. My overcoat hung on its hook. When I put it on I was startled to feel the hard lump of the volcanic rock like a fist in the pocket.

I hustled a hack down to the waterfront. Robinson's was off East Street between Jackson and Pacific, a complex of wharfage thrust out into the bay against the high thicket of masts and spars. Panting, I sprinted along the paving stones, and cut out onto Robinson's Wharf, looking for a small boat. Goat Island loomed in the bay. There was a bustling traffic of scows and barges, and the ferry heading out from the Alameda Wharf. The air was heavy with the waterfront stink of rotting fish, tar, and sewage.

I saw them, a wharf away, two men and a large woman who looked boneless in her brown dress, her legs only half carrying her sagging along with the men, one of them surely Kanekoa, the other a burly fellow in a mate's cap. They were fifty feet away across a slash of gray water. Haunani's brown face was turned toward me.

"*Kanekoa!*" I shouted.

The struggling threesome halted. Kanekoa unhanded Haunani and leaned forward toward me with his hands on his knees, as though projecting a headache. I took the stone from my pocket. With my fist gripping its smooth surface I stretched back, and hurled it.

I could follow its flight only part way. Kanekoa sat down. He toppled over backward. I started the run back to East Street and around to the next dock.

Mate's cap had almost lost Haunani, who sagged to the planking. He tried to lift and walk her on out the pier, but the process was impossible without Kanekoa. He ducked and almost lost her again as I faked another throw.

I trotted after them.

Kanekoa was a dead *kahuna*. His forehead was collapsed like crumpled brown pasteboard, square in the middle, like Judge Akua's caved-in forehead, his mouth gaping open to show the space of the tooth he had knocked out, and a splash of blood down his nose and cheek. I'd given him a worse headache than he'd given me.

Ahead of me the mate had let Haunani collapse to the planking. He produced a revolver, and aimed it at me. He had a side-whiskered face twisted like a worried rat.

"Stand off!"

He was not going to be able to hold the revolver aimed and hoist Haunani to her feet.

All at once he swung around and lit out along the wharf, his boots whacking on the splintery wood. I followed him until I could see where he was bound, a twenty-foot sailer with a blue band around the hull. He fell into it, unhitched, and began rowing like a madman, peering at me over his shoulder.

I trotted back to bend over Haunani. She stank of choloroform. Her eyes gazed up at me blearily, like Rose Hansen after an excess of champagne at the Crystal Palace saloon.

She was very heavy, but she managed to help as I lifted her. She whispered my name, her strong arms around me.

Sergeant Willsey strode toward us on the dock. Farther back was a patrolman, looking down at Kanekoa's sprawled body.

Willsey wanted to know where was the picnic.

"They were going to take her to Silas Underwood's yacht." I pointed out the sailer, which had its sail raised and was slanting away into the gray bay.

Haunani detached herself to stand by herself, swaying. She stroked at her hair.

"Chloroform," Jack Willsey said, sniffing. "Who's that dead *kanaka* back along the dock, Tom?"

"Name of Kanekoa," I said.

"What happened to him?"

Haunani's blue eyes were fixed on mine. "Tom . . ." she started, in a thick voice, swaying so that I took hold of her arm.

"Looks like he took a cosh," I said to Willsey.

"Tom . . ." Haunani whispered.

Berowne had arrived, frightened and pale, to carry her away in a hack.

CHAPTER 25

FOREORDINATION, n. This looks like an easy word to define, but when I consider that pious and learned theologians have spent long lives in explaining it, and written libraries to explain their explanations; when I remember that nations have been divided and bloody battles caused by the difference between foreordination and predestination, and that millions of treasure have been expended in the effort to prove and disprove its compatibility with freedom of the will and the efficacy of prayer, praise, and a religious life—recalling these awful facts in the history of the word, I stand appalled before the mighty problem of its signification, abase my spiritual eyes, fearing to contemplate its portentous magnitude, reverently uncover and humbly refer it to his Eminence Cardinal Gibbon and His Grace Bishop Potter.

— The Devil's Dictionary

MONDAY, JANUARY 26, 1891

In his office, leaning back in his chair looking pleased with himself, Bierce said to me, "Rose Hansen and Mammy Pleasant are, not surprisingly, well acquainted. Rose's parents were also active in the abolitionist movement. Being stoned as abolitionists makes for a considerable bond. I enlisted Mammy Pleasant's help against the Hawaiian sorcerer, and the timing turned out to be quite perfect."

I congratulated him.

"It appeared that Silas Underwood meant to carry your Miss Brown back to Hawaii on the *Haleakala*?"

"He tried to have her carried off by force this morning," I said, and told him what had happened.

Finger to his chin, he said, "It seems that personage knows how to get what he wants. Or he is simply mad."

It was what Haunani had said also.

———

I was at the *Chronicle* when the urchin from the Rincon Messenger Service appeared with a note from Bierce. We were invited to dinner aboard the *Haleakala*, which would come across the bay to Robinson's Wharf that evening. I felt a flash of chill to think that revenge for the death of Kanekoa was planned.

———

I told Bierce my fears in the hack headed for the docks. I had killed Silas Underwood's pet *kahuna* with a lucky throw to second. It did not seem a promising subject for dinner conversation.

"I have informed Captain Pusey of our whereabouts," Bierce said. "And I will inform Mr. Underwood of *that*."

"What can he want of us?"

"That's what we will find out."

———

Aaron Underwood, wearing a top hat, strode toward us when we arrived at the wharf, and directed us along to where the *Haleakala* was moored, like a great white wedding cake with masts thrusting into the overhead darkness. The steam engine throbbed like a pulse I could feel through my shoe leather as we came aboard up a slant of gangway.

Silas Underwood met us in the cabin, so tall that his head was canted under the low overhead, his face contorted in his sneering grin of welcome. Hands were shaken all around.

"Welcome aboard the *Hally*, Mr. Bierce. Mr. Redmond."
Aaron stood a little diffidently to one side, hat in hand. Silas
Underwood swiped his big hands together. Maybe he had not
yet heard of the death of Kanekoa.

"Arnie, we must give these gentlemen the tour of my hum-
ble a-boat!" He laughed at his joke. I was more nervous than I
wished to be.

We inspected cabins, and looked into the engine room
where the great steam engine purred and throbbed. Trailing
along a passageway, I encountered the center-parted attendant, who, smiling and nodding, flattened himself against a
bulkhead to let us by. Silas introduced him as Mr. Barley.

Lastly we were shown into the dining cabin, where the
table gleamed with napery, cutlery, water glasses and china
service plates. We were seated, Silas Underwood at the head,
Aaron opposite him, Bierce opposite me. Mr. Barley, in a
striped apron, brought in a steaming platter. The dinner
plates bore a crest, a potato shape with a small head circled
with a ring of gold, maybe a crown.

"May we have grace, Arnie?" Silas boomed, swiping his
hands together. "We must thank the good Lord for this
repast!"

Arnie bowed his head. Bierce did not. He did not think the
Lord deserved thanks for the botchwork world He had
created.

"Bless, Lord, this food for our use and thus for Thy service," Arnie intoned. "Defend us from evil and its usages,
from the pride of the will and the lusts of the body, bless us
with filial, paternal and heavenly love. For Jesus Christ's sake,
Amen."

"A little preachy for my taste, my boy!" Silas said. Sometimes his grin reminded me of those Chinese gods to be seen in

Mandarin restaurants, that were either evil or defenders against evil.

"We are of missionary stock, Mr. Bierce," he continued. "Preaching seems embedded in the bone."

"California has its own brand of galloping malignant Christianity that may soon drown us in bosh," Bierce said.

The Underwoods glanced at each other; they were Christians.

"And you, Mr. Redmond," Silas said, serving and passing. "Of what religion, sir?"

"Roman Catholic, Mr. Underwood."

"A Papist, my goodness! Aboard the *Hally*!" The big laugh sounded a little strained.

"And you are a historian of the War Between the States, Mr. Bierce?"

"Not a historian, sir. History is an account mostly false, of events mostly unimportant. I am a writer of short stories that I hope are important, and of journalism that I am certain is not."

We were imbibing some kind of stew with a Chinese ginger flavor, heaped onto an unfamiliar brand of potato.

"Breadfruit," Aaron said. "A Hawaiian staple."

"And a detective, I understand," Silas said to Bierce.

"No doubt your son has informed you of my latest failure in that presumption."

"The matter of the unfortunate princess Leileiha," Silas said, loading his fork and planting it in his mouth with gusto. He winked at me. "And you are his assistant and strong right arm, Mr. Redmond?"

"Yes, sir," I said.

"My son spends his days in the company of lawyers," Silas said mysteriously. "What a damnable waste of days it is!"

Aaron's face hardened, but he did not respond.

Dinner proceeded. Bierce chose to discourse on the bravery of the Confederate soldiery in the late war, and wondered if he had fought on the right side in a conflict generated by knaves and fought by fools.

And he said, "So you have brought this breadfruit from Hawaii, Mr. Underwood. And also a practitioner of the black arts. To attend the king, I believe."

"Yes, poor fellow. Dead in a tragic accident this morning on these very docks." With a fierce smile, and a swipe of his hands, Silas looked from Bierce to me.

"In an effort to kidnap Miss Haunani Brown, as I understand it."

"That is all an unfortunate misunderstanding, sir. Poor Lapidus was suffering from terrible grief because of his failure to preserve David Kalakaua's life. Not responsible for his actions, I would swear."

He picked up his little bell and tinkled it, and Barley appeared to clear the table. Silas's eyes rested on me, his grin stiffening. Of course he knew that I had killed Kanekoa. This dinner was a charade.

"It is important to you that Miss Brown be transported back to Honolulu aboard the *Haleakala*," Bierce said. "Now why is that, sir?"

"Important to her!" Silas said. He slapped a hand down on the table, causing china and cutlery to jump. "Important to her health! Hawaiians do not fare well in the less salubrious climate of the Mainland, Mr. Bierce. Consider poor David, if you please!"

"Ah, Father, I—" Aaron started.

"Kindly do not interrupt, my boy. And now, Mr. Bierce, you and your assistant are playing detective again in the matter of the death of poor Andrew Akua?"

I had pondered why Bierce and I had been invited aboard the *Haleakala*: I thought this was the reason. Silas was bent forward, frowning at Bierce intently.

"No, we are not," Bierce said. "That is a police affair."

"Surely, sir, your self-esteem—"

"Self-esteem is always an erroneous appraisement," Bierce snapped, quoting himself.

Dessert was a sweet bread sauced with a golden syrup.

"Pineapple, brought from the Islands also," Aaron said.

"Ah, your chef is handy with a Sally Lunn!" Bierce said, with a raised eyebrow at me.

"Very handy with all provender, Liu," Silas said.

I said, "I wonder at the crest on your dinnerware, Mr. Underwood. Is it a Hawaiian god?"

Silas ran through the vowels of the big laugh. "A wrong assessment, sir! That is the outline of a royal tortoise of Maui. Very few of them left now! As you see, I have taken it for my personal crest. It will be all yours some day, my boy!" he said to Aaron. "Unless other heirs of my blood and bone appear!"

Aaron looked even more uncomfortable than his habitual expression.

Silas Underwood become less and less cheerful and smiling as dinner progressed to port and cigars.

"You could light my cigar for me, my boy," he said to Aaron. "Your lawyers would allow you to do that much for your beloved father, wouldn't they?"

And Aaron rose to the command.

———

When Bierce and I had separated from Aaron in the stink of the docks, Bierce said, "I believe I have heard that one of the peculiarities of the Sandwich Islands is the total absence of reptiles. That would include tortoises."

"I think that shape may be the outline of the Island of Maui," I said.

"With a crowned head," Bierce said.

"He is building a palace on Maui."

"It is simply megalomania," Bierce said.

"Miss Brown says he told her she must learn the names of the kings of Maui. There is a chant, apparently."

Bierce said slowly, "Judge Akua was descended from the last king of Maui."

We stared at each other in the fetid darkness. I whistled for a hack.

CHAPTER 26

LONGANIMITY, n. The disposition to endure injury with meek forbearance while maturing a plan for revenge.
— *The Devil's Dictionary*

TUESDAY, JANUARY 27, 1891

Thumbtacked to the wall beside Bierce's desk was a sheet of paper on which he had made from memory a copy of the charred menu I had found on the grate in Judge Akua's rooms, two rabbit ears surmounting a convexity, the intertwined EC–4 and PO–8, and the handwritten "Jongleurs." At the bottom he had written "many pastries."

At the sound of footsteps in the hall he leaned back in his chair with a sigh.

Captain Pusey and Sergeant Willsey turned into the office. Pusey appropriated the chair beside the skull. Willsey stood spread-legged, hands clasped behind his back.

Pusey ceremoniously unfolded a square of newsprint. "I have had a complaint from Judge Thornton that you have employed mordacious libel toward his person, Mr. Bierce."

He read aloud, " 'Of all the pusilanimous juridical he-prostitutes of this City, Judge Oliver Thornton surely has suckled longest and deepest at the Southern Pacific teat. He displays his bullying severity by sentencing Irish lads suffering from one dram too many to terms in the juzgado, while the moneyed citizens enjoy their own recognizance.' "

Bierce did have a low opinion of most of the San Francisco judicial fraternity.

"Often, in the case of public officials, calumniation is complimentary," Bierce said.

Pusey showed his teeth, and refolded the clipping from "Prattle." He appeared to think he had begun the game with a winning trick. He squinted at the paper pinned to the wall beside Bierce's desk.

"That!" he said.

"You have the original, I believe, Captain Pusey."

Pusey showed his teeth.

"I have heard an old story that may interest you," Bierce said. "Back in the fifties, a play called *The Hunchback* was mounted at one of the downtown theaters. At one point an actor appeared on stage, arms raised, to declaim the line, 'What does this mean, my Lord?' At which a wag in the audience called out to a gust of laughter, 'Sidewheel steamer!' "

Pusey gaped at him.

"He was referring to the semaphore atop Telegraph Hill that used to announce the arrival of ships through the Golden Gate," Bierce said. "It operated for only a couple of years before an electromagnetic telegraph was installed, but long enough to give Telegraph Hill its name."

Pusey's arms jerked up like the rabbit ears in the drawing. "What's this, then?"

"A sloop of war," Bierce said.

"What's a sloop, exactly?" Willsey wanted to know.

"A sloop of war is any ship or schooner rigged out with cannons." Bierce produced a sheet of paper which he slid across the desk to Pusey, who accepted it reluctantly. I leaned toward him to read it.

The sheet was labeled "Marine Telegraph Signals." The figure for a sloop of war had indeed the configuration of the rabbit ears from the charred menu: a central pole with a kind of finial capping it, and two arms rather shorter than the ones in Bierce's drawing.

"What's a sloop of war got to do with anything?" Pusey demanded.

"What of EC–4, PO–8 and the quantity of bakery goods on a menu?" Bierce said. "And Jongleurs," he added after a moment.

Pusey pushed the sheet of signals back at him, and said, "I don't believe this takes us anywhere, Mr. Bierce." He turned ponderously in his chair to confront me.

"The point here, young fellow, is Mrs. Charles Perry, that is supposed to be on the UP headed for New York—ain't. Telegraphed Reno, telegraphed Salt Lake City. No Mrs. Charles Perry on that train."

"Maybe her maiden name—" I started.

"Not on the train, Mr. Redmond. Tell me again when you last saw this lady."

I told him again.

Bierce had propped his fingertips together. Captain Pusey presented me with another display of his fine teeth.

"Inquire about your whereabouts Thursday night, Redmond," he prodded me.

"I was in my rooms," I said.

Jack Willsey stirred and rearranged his arms.

"I believe nookie is a man's own bidness," Pusey said. "But what we have here is maybe murder. I have a hunch this French lady is going to turn up in the bay. And maybe it will be her husband we bring in, or maybe it will not be, if you take my meaning."

I took his meaning.

"Bad bidness, Mr. Redmond," Pusey said. He regarded me bleakly. "Now," he said. "Take another incident. Hay-wy-yan chap killed when yourself flung a rock at him, busted him right in the noodle. Dead as mackerel. Sergeant Willsey here can attest the young lady was being transported off against her will. Chloroform, et cetera. Mr. Redmond here before me is an expert baseball thrower. Looks like he is the hero of that bidness, but wait just a minute.

"There was another Hawaiian fellow, old fellow, that was killed ten days ago, exactly the same, busted right on the noggin. So what am I to make of that? First-rate police work, Mr. Redmond, is seeing two crimes exactly the same, and find the perpetrator of one and you have found the perp of the other."

"You favor coincidences, Captain Pusey?" Bierce said.

Pusey sucked on his teeth. "No, sir, I don't," he said. He counted off on his fingers: "The old Judge. Mrs. Perry that's disappeared. The Hay-wy-yan fellow you bashed with the rock."

"What has been the disposal of the kidnapper's body, Captain?" Bierce said.

"Claimed by Mr. Silas Underwood."

"Are there charges?"

"Under consideration," Pusey said.

I saw how this was going to go.

"I am going to have to lock you up on suspicion of murder, Mr. Redmond," Pusey said.

"Kanekoa?" I asked.

"Mrs. Charles Perry."

"This is unconscionable, Captain!" Bierce said, slapping a fist down on his desk. "There is no habeas corpus here! You are trying to engineer matters so that I am forced to solve these crimes for you."

"That's about right, Mr. Bierce," Pusey said cheerfully.

Bierce said, "I believe I will reconsider the implications of blackmail I notice in this menu, Captain."

They stared at each other. I saw a flash of hard malevolence in Pusey's face. He leaned back.

"Take him away and lock him up, Jack."

Willsey beckoned.

CHAPTER 27

PRISON, n. A place of punishment and rewards.
— The Devil's Dictionary

TUESDAY, JANUARY 27, 1891

The jail was off Broadway on Dupont Street. I was flattered to be ushered into what seemed to be the best cell, large, close to the jailer's counter and with an easy chair, a patent wooden platform rocker that creaked alarmingly. There was a tolerable amount of racket attendant upon incarceration, drunken yells, a clatter of metal cups and plates, the jailor's heavy tread in the corridor and the jangle of his hipload of keys. It sounded a good deal like the corridors of the *Examiner*, but not so cheerful, and it stank of carbolic and urine.

Ambrose Bierce was my first caller, very debonair in his tan suiting with a carnation in his lapel and shiny boots. Sunlight through the high window glinted on his graying fair hair and shaggy eyebrows. The jailor left him alone with me, though he may have taken up a listening post. Both Bierce and I knew why I was here; no need to discuss it.

I motioned him into the rocker, and sat on the cot.

"How is the food, Tom?" he inquired.

"I haven't had that pleasure yet."

"I will have delicacies sent in."

"How long am I to remain here?"

"I regret your incarceration, but I am not quite prepared to snare Captain Pusey, or to satisfy his demand.

"Mrs. Aaron Underwood is hospitalized with galloping consumption and near death," he added. "I had hoped to have occasion to discuss Miss Brown's parentage with her."

I felt again a mix of outrage and dread thinking of Haunani sinking into her obligation to Silas Underwood. I said, "I wish I understood why that unholy statuette was left on Haunani's bed."

"A summons," Bierce said. "A talisman to make a woman receptive to command.

"We know that King Kalakaua encouraged the ancient magic," he went on. "Which earlier kings had discouraged under the influence of the missionaries. We know that Silas Underwood agreed with Kalakaua about the old Hawaii. This was certainly a manifestation of such. I'm sure the old Hawaii has its powers."

I knew that it did.

Bierce proceeded to other news. "Mr. Regan has proffered this information: One of Silas Underwood's corporations has been endeavoring to purchase a huge acreage on the island of Maui. This sugar plantation will be the largest in the islands. A great deal of expensive irrigation will be installed. The purchase requires an act of the legislature, and much prodding and payment from Silas Underwood to the legislators. Princess Leileiha and others have objected, but the king long ago gave the acquisition his blessing.

"Title to the plains of Mauikai will make Silas Underwood by far the largest landowner on the island. He has been spurred into action by the threat of the monarchy refinancing its debt to him. It may be that he is prepared to turn a setback into an advantage."

"The crown over the map of Maui on the dinnerware," I said.

"Crowns and palaces," he said, nodding, and rose to depart.

———

Next came Haunani Brown, magnificent in blue. She followed the jailor down the corridor accompanied by the jangle of his keys and the determined crack of her bootheels.

When he had let her into the cell she embraced me, and covered my face with kisses. The jailor's eyes were large as he let himself out.

"What is this silly business?" Haunani enquired. "Is it Lapidus Kanekoa?"

I told her it was not. I settled her in the chair with her ungloved hands clasped together and her booted ankles neatly crossed. The chair creaked. Her blue eyes never left me.

"What did you do with Marianne Perry, Tom?" she whispered. "That mingy little thing! Did you give her a good dinner?"

"They say she has disappeared, and that I was the last person to see her. I'm sure I was not."

She closed her eyes for a moment. "It is over with Albert Grady," she said. "His old sweetheart is taking care of him in Mendocino."

I said I should say that I was sorry.

"There is no need to be sorry," Haunani said.

"You must tell me about Silas Underwood."

She looked down. She shook her head in silence.

"Silas Underwood is buying land on Maui," I said. "The dinner plates of the *Haleakala* are figured with an outline of Maui with a crown over the head. I heard your uncle asking about his palace. Underwood wants you in that palace. Does he think he can be king of Maui?"

"I don't know, Tom."

"Help me," I said.

"He gets what he wants," she whispered.

"What does he want?"

"I knew what he wants when I saw that *thing* on my bed. I have known it for long time. For a year. It is one of the reasons I have left Hawaii."

"Father and son," I said, and was sorry I had said it.

"Aaron is an honorable gentleman!" Haunani said fiercely.

"But why is the old man after you so suddenly?"

"Because I am young. Because he will live longer if he possesses someone young. Because when his wife died he began to look at me with new eyes. I don't know! Because David Kalakaua is dead. Because Liliuokalani is queen. Because they will try to get out of his debt. Because he is mad!"

She had taken a photograph from her reticule which she held in her two hands.

"What is the photograph?"

She held it up, and I stepped over to take it. Two men and a woman stood together before a rough stone wall, a palm tree bole slanting upward behind them, spiky flowers bending from the top of the wall. Lower down was the torso and head of a third man, his face blurred with motion. One of the standing men was clearly Edward Berowne when young. The other must be his brother William. The young woman wore a dress with a tight black bodice, and had a pale lock of hair wound at the side of her head in an unbecoming manner. On the bottom of the photograph was the handwritten word, "Jongleurs."

Haunani said, "I found it in a box in which Uncle keeps his cuff links."

On the back of the photograph was the name of the photographer. "P.S. Foss, Kahului, Maui."

"What is Jongleurs?" I said.

"It is what the plantation was called in the old days. Later it had a Hawaiian name, *Kalikimaka*, for Christmas."

"It is Edward Berowne and your father? Who is the woman?"

"I was told I had an Aunt Julia," Haunani said. "Their sister, from Virginia. She died soon after I was born. In Honolulu."

"Like your mother?"

"Yes."

"Who is the man with the blurred face?"

"I think he is Daniel Akua." She laid her hands to her cheeks in a familiar gesture. "They are trying to make me crazy," she said.

"Are there any other photographs? Letters, notes?"

She was shaking her head. "Help me!" she whispered.

"Anything!"

"Uncle Silas gets what he wants," Haunani said, a despair so profound in her whisper that I hurried across the cell to pull her from the chair into an embrace. She tucked her wet face into my neck, whimpering.

I could feel the stiff shape of the photograph in her hand as I held her.

———

When she left it was late morning. I looked out through the bars to see Charles Perry confronting me. His handsome chipmunk face was set and pale, his jaunty mustache wilted.

"The fat detective with the shiny teeth says you are suspected of killing Marianne," he said in a hard voice.

"He says she is not on the train," I said.

"You were the last to see her, he tells me."

I repeated my story of my farewell to Marianne Perry.

"The train leaves very early in the morning," Perry said. He moved a little closer to the bars, and a ray of light from the high window glinted in his eye.

"She had left our rooms in the hotel. She was not there when I came home."

"She was not with me," I said.

He looked young and sad, with no arrogance to him. He had lost his wife, and lost his political aspirations as well, and no doubt he had been humiliated when they would not accommodate him aboard the funeral ship; and now betrayed.

"She was in tears," I said. "She thought you had gone to Hawaii on the *Charleston*. She said she was alone in San Francisco." I stood facing him and didn't know what to do with my hands.

"I'm sorry," was all I could think to say.

"If she is not on the train there are reasons for it," he said. "Her family cut her off when she married me. She must go back and tell them she was mistaken. She has an inability ever to say she has been mistaken. It will be difficult for her to return to France."

"I'm sorry," I said again.

"She is very good at making new friends," Perry said. "I know my wife, you see. Why are you here, I wonder?"

"I think it is for other reasons."

"The *kahuna* is dead," he said. "Somebody hit him with a rock!"

"Yes."

"Good riddance, Journalist!"

He stood outside the bars, his round face sagging, his shoulders slumped.

"What will you do?" I asked.

"I will make my peace with the sugar *kahuna*," he said. "He will have a position for me in one of his businesses. He will always help an *alii* who is in difficulties. It makes him feel big in Hawaii to help *alii*. Or kings. Perhaps queens, also."

He turned half away, his hands sunk in his pockets. "He is here for the lawsuit," he said.

"What lawsuit is that?"

"There is contention between father and son. Uncle Sugar has levied a stock assessment of five dollars a share on the stock of Underwood and Company which controls American-Hawaiian Sugar. The stock is low just now, but will rise like an ascension balloon when the Reciprocity Treaty is signed. It is, of course, a manipulation to force the small investors out, and consolidate Uncle Sugar's profits. Aaron is suing him. He has lawyers! Where has he obtained the *huahua*?"

I said I didn't know that word.

"Testicles," Perry said.

He drifted away, becoming incorporeal in the dim light of the corridor, disembodied as he retreated, gone.

CHAPTER 28

DUTY, n. That which sternly impels us in the direction of profit, along the line of desire.

— *The Devil's Dictionary*

TUESDAY, JANUARY 27, 1891

My father, the Gent, appeared early in the afternoon, big-bellied, solid, and dependable in a cutaway with his black chin whiskers slashed with white like a skunk's pelt. Inside the cell we embraced, he patted my shoulder and offered me a cigar.

"Good deal of room for reflection in this place, son. In my time they didn't have such fine accomodations." He propped his thumbs in his vest. A heavy gold chain was draped over his corporation.

"I think I am in this particular cell so the sergeant down the way can listen for anything interesting said."

He applied himself to the platform rocker and crossed his legs. His job with the Southern Pacific was to distribute railroad loot among the legislators in Sacramento to ensure their loyalty to railroad needs. As my mother said, giving away money was a career he had practiced long before he began being paid for it.

"I know half a dozen lawyers that could get you out of here directly," he said.

I said that I was part of a theatrical event and didn't need to be set free just yet.

"I understand that," he said.

"How?" I wanted to know.

"Son, we have ways of keeping track of things up in Sacramento. We know what is going on down here in the evil City, and I keep a special ear open for anything happening to kin."

It was probably all the answer I was going to get.

"Miss Clara Best," he said.

"Pardon?"

"Attractive young lady named Clara Best. Claims to have made your acquaintance. There was a fire in the Royce Hotel up in Sacramento that I took a hand in helping the residents out, including Miss Best. Lost every stitch of clothing except what she had on! I was able to buy her dinner and help her get settled. Says you and Bierce thought you had saved her and another lady from a fate worse than death. That was the way she put it."

The *Guillermo Fierro.*

"A fate worse than death was the way she put it? Or we *thought* we had saved her?"

"Both, I expect," the Gent said, and blew smoke. A gauzy blue layer had already collected on the ceiling of the cell.

"There was a felonious minister named Simms or Slaney," I said. "Who had recruited Miss Best and a Mrs. Hansen to teach in a school in Buenos Aires. It appeared to be white slavery. Miss Best is a schoolteacher?"

"I'd doubt that," my father said. "No better than she should be, I'd say."

"So we did not save them," I said.

"What *she* said. This Slaney sounds like a bad egg to me."

I told him what I knew of Reuben Slaney.

"Confidence tricks," he said, nodding. "Ladies' man, all right. Confidencing ladies out of their savings. He was the fancy man of this Mrs. Hansen, Miss Best says. Women go crazy over him, like catnip. The three of them was headed for Buenos Aires to do séance performances. Mrs. Hansen is a famous medium, Miss Best said. The three of them was going to make their fortunes in Buenos Aires doing materializing spirits sort of tricks that Slaney was an old hand at, along with Mrs. Hansen. Miss Best was going to be a young lady spirit that Mrs. Hansen and Slaney would conjure up out of some lights and mirrors they had. Then you and Bierce brought the coppers to that Argentine ship and Slaney had to run for it, being a fellow with warrants out."

I felt guilty to be pleased that Bierce had been taken in by pretty Mrs. Hansen.

"Said you thought the other lady had been drugged," he went on. "Done it herself, she said. Laudanum and whiskey."

I wondered about Miss Best and the Gent, who was a ladies' man like Reuben Slaney; as was Ambrose Bierce.

"So Slaney was Mrs. Hansen's accomplice. What about Slaney and Miss Best?"

My father rolled the cigar between his lips. He closed one eye thoughtfully, and shrugged.

Mrs. Hansen had been caught in some kind of mediumistic trickery in Buffalo, New York, which had cost her her reputation in the East. So she had come west, and had in fact been headed to Argentina, where her reputation was unknown. Had Slaney been her accomplice in Buffalo?

"Thank you for this information," I said. "Bierce will be grateful. I'd like you to meet him sometime."

He brought the cigar out of his teeth and regarded it, squinting. "You know, son, I don't disapprove of much. I have taken life and times the way I found them. But I do disapprove of your pal Bierce. I disapprove of Ambrose Bierce because he disapproves of just about damn-all everything. Disapproves of women, disapproves of the railroad, disapproves of the Republican Party. And the Democratic too, as far as I can make out. Doesn't disapprove of drink; I suppose that is a chit for him."

"There are some things that ought to be disapproved of," I said.

"That is surely true, son. But when you disapprove of something a ton that only ought to be disapproved a hundredweight, then you have disapproved too much, the way I see it."

I did not wish to join an argument over Bierce, who was difficult to defend.

My father seemed relieved, also. My mother was fine, she had a new set of teeth. But he didn't want to talk about her, he wanted to talk about his friends in the legislature. I listened to character studies and actions, in all of which my father's wisdom was established.

And again he recited his poem, which seemed to me to indicate that he was sick of his SP and legislature pals:

> I've labored long and hard for bread
> For honor and for riches
> But on my corns too long you've tread,
> You fine-haired sons of bitches.

I asked him where the poem came from.

"Why, from Black Bart," he said, laughing. "That grand poe-ate!"

I knew vaguely of the stage robber Black Bart, but my

father was pleased to tell his story. Black Bart had appeared in the late seventies, wearing a sack with eyeholes and flourishing a double-barrelled shotgun to halt the Russian River stage. His command was to become a familiar one over the next six years in northern California. "Throw down the box!"

When they recovered the empty Wells Fargo box, within it was a poem, with which the bandit had replaced the gold freight. That poem, which my father loved to recite, was signed with the name "Black Bart, the PO 8."—which accounted for my father's peculiar pronunciation of "poet."

———

Captain Pusey wore his nine-button blue uniform and carried his cap under his arm. He had a small round pink mouth like a kitten's button, set in the midst of white whiskers. He gave the platform rocker a good working over getting himself settled.

"Now, Mr. Redmond," he said, gripping his big, white-haired, gnarly-knuckled hands on the arms of the chair. "What I want to know is, how is Mr. Silas Underwood connected to all this Hay-wy-yan business?"

"Money lent to the monarchy," I said.

"Pals with the king, was he?"

"Was."

"He is a fellow throws some weight in the City here, no doubt about that. State, country too.

"I will be frank with you, Redmond. I am interested in the other Hawaiian judge fellow recently deceased. Tell you why. He was a bosom friend to Mr. Marshall Smith, the State Supreme Court Justice, that knew him from Harvard College, and wants to know what happened to his friend and why. That's why."

It was encouraging that the disappearance of Mrs. Charles Perry had not come up again.

Pusey gazed at me steadily. "Who killed that old *kanaka* judge, Redmond?"

"Lapidus Kanekoa," I said.

———

Later in the afternoon a sous-chef in a white cap from Foulard's showed up carrying a steaming pot of clams, with half a loaf of bread under his arm. He sat in the platform rocker with his gloved hands knitted over his belly and watched me gobble clams and chunks of bread soaked in clam broth, Bierce's delicacies.

Bierce himself arrived within an hour.

I asked if he had solved the Judge Akua murder.

He waved a hand airily. "Rose Hansen will solve it with the help of her spirit friend."

I gaped at him.

"We will have a séance with all present," he said. He looked pleased with himself.

"Tonight?"

"This very night."

I mentioned the scene aboard the *Guillermo Fierro*, which had taken on a different complexion.

"Yes," Bierce responded. "Rose will present the solution to the murder of Judge Akua, and I intend to save her from the Svengali who has dogged her life, and sock Pusey right in the solar plexus."

He did not expound on any of this. I sat on the bed and re-called Rose Hansen asking me if I wanted to contact my wife. It did seem that Bierce at least had her interests at heart.

I said, "Is Mrs. Hansen's Miles going to speak to the shade of Judge Akua, who will reveal the murderer?"

"Not exactly," Bierce said, looking superior.

"Isn't this the kind of manipulation that she got in trouble for before?"

"This is in the cause of justice."

I told him what I had learned from Charles Perry, from my father and from Pusey, but he did not seem much interested. He was in one of his moods where I recognized that his stance of insufferable superiority stemmed from apprehension.

"Where will this dramatic event take place?" I asked.

"At the Underwood establishment on Van Ness. It was with some difficulty that I arranged this with Aaron Underwood, in view of his wife's illness."

"Is she still alive?"

"In extremis, however."

"Is equipment necessary for the séance?"

"There is Mrs. Hansen's cabinet, a table and some other items. It is important that she has her familiar appurtenances, you see. She has an assistant who deals with these things."

"Fishing poles and lights and mirrors?" I said.

He scowled as though I had insulted her. "She is not so crass, Tom."

"So I will be a free man today?"

"Later," Bierce said, rising, and suddenly seemed in a hurry to get out of my cell in the Dupont Street jail.

CHAPTER 29

WRATH, n. Anger of a superior quality and degree, appropriate to exalted characters and momentous occasions; as, "the wrath of God," "the day of wrath," etc. Amongst the ancients the wrath of kings was deemed sacred, for it could usually command the agency of some god for its fit manifestations, as could also that of a priest.

— The Devil's Dictionary

TUESDAY, JANUARY 27, 1891

I was released into Bierce's custody.

I told him of the meaning of PO–8 on our way to the Underwood mansion on Van Ness Avenue, with rain crackling on the canopy of our hack.

"EC–4 must be Engine Company Number Four in some aspect thereof," Bierce said. "So we have all the elements except the type of vessel indicated by those raised arms."

"Not a sidewheel steamer," I said. "Nor a steam yacht."

"Or not a vessel at all," Bierce said.

———

Under the porte cochere at the Underwood mansion, we were greeted by the stout, maroon-tunic Hawaiian butler and directed to wait in the entryway, where we gazed up at the portrait of the old tycoon while Aaron Underwood was summoned. Bierce nervously switched a step or two one way and then another, as though the eyes of the portrait of Uncle Sugar bore down on him with weight.

Aaron appeared, wearing a solemn expression, a rangy worried-looking man whose wife was dying.

"I must tell you, Mr. Bierce, that I am not enthusiastic, under the present circumstances, for this séance you have planned."

"I am distressed to hear of your wife's illness, Mr. Underwood, but arrangements have been made that I believe will disclose the murderer of Judge Akua."

With a sigh Underwood capitulated, and directed us toward the parlor.

Gray light through high windows revealed a number of people assembled in the room; Haunani in a handsome black and gray dress, with light hair piled high, and her face turned toward me, which always seemed pleased at what she saw. She stood beside Walter's chair where Walter's arms and hands wove and twitched above his white face—welcome in his father's house at last with his mother on her deathbed in the hospital.

Haunani wore a thin gold chain displaying a brilliant stone that gleamed against her flesh.

The Reverend Prout, in his scarecrow black suit, hunched in a chair beside the fire on the hearth.

Walter stammered out my name, and Bierce strode across the polished parquet to greet Prout. I went to join Haunani and Walter. His hand clutched for mine.

"Have . . . you . . . heard, Tom? My . . . mother . . . is *very* ill!"

I said I was sorry and left my hand in his. Haunani smiled at me. Aaron stood uncertainly by. He colored when I said, "Interesting and informative dinner aboard the *Hally*."

"So you have decided to contact the astral plane in order to solve the murder of Judge Akua," Prout said to Bierce. Even seated beside the fire, he huddled in his chair as though chilled.

Bierce slapped his hands together in a hearty fashion. "We have some time before Mrs. Hansen arrives with the paraphernalia of her profession."

"Captain Pusey will attend?" Aaron asked.

"He will be here," Bierce said. "And Mrs. Pleasant. Will your father join us, Mr. Underwood?"

Aaron's face twitched with irritation. "It is impossible to say how an invitation will strike him."

Haunani's eyes met mine.

"And Mr. Perry?"

"He will attend," Aaron said.

"I believe Mr. Regan will be here," Bierce said.

"I am very surprised to find myself taking part in a spiritualist demonstration," Prout said, with his drawn-down carp's mouth.

Bierce spun on his heel to examine the room, a finger touched to his chin like a theatrical producer.

There was a disturbance in the entryway, and a clatter of footsteps.

Silas Underwood strode in, taller than anyone in the room, white-haired and white-bearded, hands swinging at his sides, black suited like his missionary forebears. With him was his factotum Barley, with his center-parted hair and anxious expression.

"Who are these people, Arnie?" the sugar tycoon demanded. He thrust his unsmiling mouth at Aaron.

"You know Mr. Prout. And Mr. Bierce and Mr. Redmond, of course."

Uncle Sugar glared at me. He glared at his son. He almost

shouted, "I have had an absolutely damnable day amongst your lawyer cronies! Will you stop at nothing in your efforts to deny me, sir?"

"No one is trying to deny you, Father," Aaron said with some spirit.

"I say you are trying to deny me!" Underwood shouted. "You and your damned sheep-faced shyster!"

"Calm yourself, Father."

Bierce watched this exchange with interest.

It did not appear that we would be awarded the vowel drill laugh today.

Barley took hold of Silas's arm and made placating sounds.

Silas jerked away and paced in front of his son. He took a step toward him as though to walk right over Aaron, but halted when his son did not retreat. Aaron folded his arms on his chest.

Haunani watched with her hands half-raised as though in protest against violence.

"You are my son!" Underwood boomed.

"And proud to be your son!"

"You will obey my wishes!"

"I will not obey your wishes when you are wrong, Father. You are cheating people who invested in your good name! I will deny you when you act unjustly and illegally."

"I will cut you off with a penny, and throw you out on the street as well, despite your carping pettifogger, sir!"

"You cannot do that, Father. You made that arrangement yourself."

Underwood stalked around his son with a queer kind of strut, Aaron turning a step, and then another, to face him. Barley stood anxiously watching with his hands clasped beneath his chin.

Perhaps Aaron had braced himself for encounters like this in the past only to fail, but I understood that Haunani's presence had given him his *huahua*s.

Her face was screwed up in anxiety. Her necklace gleamed in the light from the wall sconces.

"Silas, this is unseemly," Prout said from his chair.

"A son's disobedience is unseemly, Jonathan," Underwood said in a lower voice. "Loyalty is his first duty." He glared at me again.

I managed to grin back at him.

Haunani gripped Walter's hand. Bierce teetered on his heels, watching the show.

"I will replace you with Horace Wilton!" Underwood proclaimed, taking another step around Aaron, who turned always to face him. "You have occupied your position only on my sufferance. I will have loyalty and obedience!"

"You will not replace me with Horace Wilton or anyone," Aaron said.

"You are incapable of controlling a major modern corporation! You are incapable of anything other than passing my instructions along. No one will take your orders except scoundrel lawyers who will have to be paid out of funds you do not command. You are self-destroyed, sir! You are nothing at all without my favor, and if you think otherwise you will soon be disabused of it!"

Circling, he went on: "You have always disappointed me. You have all the worst traits of your mother's side of the family. You have always been a trial and a poor excuse. You are a joke in Honolulu, sir! You married a sorry excuse for a woman, an invalid crank and scold. You—"

"She is dying, Father," Aaron interrupted, with dignity.

I was beginning to admire him in his low-key defiance.

"She has been dead for years!" Silas Underwood sneered.

"You have only just discovered the fact. She has given you nothing but one defective offspring—"

"Don't you say *that!"* Haunani cried out.

Silas Underwood swung toward her. "You will keep out of this, Missy!"

"You will not say that, Uncle Silas!"

Walter moaned, *"Nani—"*

Silas Underwood took two steps toward her. I placed myself between them and looked him in his eyes, which were pale blue and flat, and transparent as water. He was insane, as Haunani had said. Barley approached, moving his hands in a placating way. Silas swung away from him.

"Nani," he said. "I will say I am sorry. But this disloyal, ungrateful, thankless scoundrel is worth no one's concern. He can give you nothing, for he will have nothing. He cannot give you strong *keikes.* He—"

"Stop this!" Haunani said.

"Nani—"

Haunani gripped Walter's hands and held them against her breast. Her face was fierce.

Aaron said, "Father, will you sit down, so we can have a civilized conversation—"

"I will not take orders from you, sir!" Underwood said. "I have had enough of you and your bullying lawyer today to last me to kingdom come."

He began pacing again, now in a broader circle. Barley retreated, to seat himself beyond Prout.

Bierce said, "The crowned figure on your china is not a Hawaiian tortoise, as you proclaimed, Mr. Underwood. It is the Island of Maui. It is well known that you are building a regal dwelling there. I believe it is your intention to become king of Maui."

Underwood halted to face him.

"The Kingdom of Hawaii owes you a great deal of money," Bierce continued. "It is your intention to settle that loan by possessing the Island of Maui, of which you already own a considerable portion. I believe it is also your intention to strengthen your claim to the island by a union with a descendant of the last king of Maui before it was conquered along with the other islands of the archipelago by King Kamehameha."

"Must we listen to the meanderings of this busybody?" Silas Underwood enquired in a normal tone of voice.

"Whom you ordered abducted by your henchmen, one of whom is dead because of it. Is it not true?"

"I do not respond to asininity," Silas Underwood said.

Walter's face was hectic red with emotion, cheeks streaked with tears.

"Let me explain in less melodramatic terms," Silas Underwood said, drawing himself up to his full height. His sneer of a grin reestablished itself as he thrust his beard out like a shovel. His Saint Nick white hair gleamed in the light.

"I have considerable possessions in the Hawaiian Islands," he said in a reasonable tone of voice. He began his pacing again. "Those Islands are beholden to me, as is my son. Like my son, they think they can rebel against whatever power and monies I have accumulated by hard work and judicious investment. Perhaps the queen can obtain a loan from London bankers, but it will cost her dearly.

"I approach the end of my life. It has been a full and a good and decent and successful life, although I regret that I have only one offspring, who is ungrateful and a fool, but at least the resemblance of a human being—"

Haunani threw something at him. He clutched his cheek with an exclamation.

"See here, Miss!" Barley cried, springing forward from his chair.

Haunani's face was pale with fury. Her neck was bleeding. She had jerked her necklace loose and hurled it into Underwood's face.

"There are things you will not say!"

"Will you bear me children who will continue my name?" Underwood shouted at her. His cheek was marked with a thin curved line of blood where her necklace had struck him.

"I will not!"

"Nani . . ." Walter was crying. She stepped back to clasp his hands against her waist. The connection of the blood on her beautiful neck and on Underwood's gray cheek speared my heart. He loomed before her with his arms raised like the Telegraph Hill semaphore. This time it was Aaron who stepped between them. There was silence.

Walter said clearly, "Nani . . . will . . . you . . . be . . . my . . . *mother?*"

Haunani jerked her hands away from his and pressed them to her cheeks. I ached for her. Then I felt a crush of shock for, hands still to her face, she was nodding. *Nodding!*

On Aaron's face was the expression of the lookout of the Santa Maria who had just seen the first smudge of the New World on the horizon.

Haunani whispered, *"Yes, I will!"*

The butler appeared in the doorway. "There is a woman and a man here, Mr. Underwood. "They have brought a large cabinet."

CHAPTER 30

*YESTERDAY, n. The infancy of youth, the youth of manhood, the entire
past of age.*

— *The Devil's Dictionary*

TUESDAY, JANUARY 27, 1891

Rose Hansen's assistant was a tall East Indian in a red and
gold burnoose and a snowy turban with a gemstone affixed
above his dark forehead. His eyes, with their startling whites,
glanced from face to face as he bowed to the assembled, hands
locked together at his waist where there was a broad sash.

After a consultation with Bierce, Mrs. Hansen wandered
around the room on an erratic course with her vulnerable,
sidling gait. The light was beginning to fail.

The butler and the East Indian moved the cabinet, which
seemed not so heavy as it appeared, into a space past the fireplace. A stool and a small table were installed in it, while the
assistant, bobbing and clasping his hands between actions,
placed nearby an equipment box painted with gold medal-
lions.

Mrs. Hansen appeared distracted, circling as though
searching for something. She wore a long gray gown that covered her torso to the throat but left her white arms bare, with a

curious impression of nakedness. Her arms were often in motion, her hands weaving through gestures that must be related to inner thoughts.

Charles Perry arrived, wearing a dark suit and a red cravat. He made a gesture toward me with one hand flapped up and hitchings of his eyebrows that I was unable to interpret. Edward Berowne came shortly after. He conferred with Haunani near Walter Underwood's wheeled chair, and, I assumed, was being informed of her decision to marry Aaron Underwood.

Silas Underwood disappeared with his man Barley, and, after a time, reappeared without him, his face etched with bitterness, his shock of white hair stiff as a brush, his beard jutted like a bowsprit. He carried one big hand in the other as though it were a parcel. It was as though the muscles of his cheeks struggled to regain his ugly grin, but failed.

Captain Pusey arrived with a stout policeman I had seen often on Market Street, who carried his baton and his helmet. Mr. Regan appeared in their wake. Mammy Pleasant was the last to arrive, in her cloak and poke bonnet, carrying her handbasket. She stood apart from the others, studying them in turn. Bierce engaged her briefly in conversation.

The guests, or maybe they were suspects, stood about the parlor in conversational couples and threesomes. Bierce moved from one grouping to another, conferring here with Captain Pusey, there with Aaron Underwood. The chaplain watched all this from his chair beside of the fireplace. His scalp gleamed through the pale hairs brushed across it.

Charles Perry sidled up to me. "Marianne is in New York. I sent a telegraph to her friend there, who reported back to me. There have been fraudulent statements and charges made."

"Thank you," I said.

252 · Oakley Hall

He saluted and moved on. I squinted at Captain Pusey, who had observed our exchange.

The East Indian assistant had taken up a pose beside one of the curtained windows, watching the assembled with a severity that increased the tension in the room. Mrs. Hansen passed close by him in her perambulations, but they did not acknowledge each other. This waiting was like a pause before a game with a rival team to whom you couldn't bear to lose. I realized that we were waiting for darkness.

The gray light through the high windows had certainly dimmed. The charges and inferences that Bierce had begun and not completed hung like a cloud over the room.

"Good evening, Thomas," Berowne said, coming up to me. He was, as usual, impeccably dressed. His gray vest fit him like skin. His pearl cuff links glinted as he presented me with a hand to shake. His big affable face was solemn.

"Are you enjoying your adventures among the Islanders, my dear chap?"

I nodded, fashioning an expression of irony.

"I must say I object to b-b-being dragooned into this experiment," he said with a wrinkled forehead. "What can Amb-brose b-b-be thinking of?"

I didn't see that I had to defend Bierce, who was watching the movement in the room with his I'm-Ambrose-Bierce-and-you're-not expression of superiority that did not enhance his personal charm.

"I am ap-p-palled at Haunani's decision!" Berowne said to me.

He wandered off to join Aaron and the government person, Regan, who had a foursquare style of standing with his shoulders back and his boots braced apart, as though watching a polo match.

I thought Berowne was probably congratulating Aaron Underwood on the decision that he had just told me appalled him.

Silas Underwood lumbered toward me. He was a head taller than I, with a long body and bandy legs, so that he resembled an erect bear in his expensive black suiting.

Hands in his trouser pockets, he stuck his beard out at me.

"I understand that you are employed by the *Chronicle* newspaper, Redmond."

"Yes, sir."

"I will do my best to persuade Mr. De Young to terminate your employment."

"I'm sure your best is very good, Mr. Underwood."

"You killed Lap Kanekoa like a dog!"

"I killed a person who was trying to abduct Miss Brown."

"That is a mistaken conception that I have impressed upon Captain Pusey."

"I'm sure you have made a deep impression on Captain Pusey," I said.

He gazed at me with a pucker of genuine humor softening his iron trap of a grimace. "Tell me, Redmond, what is this silly business here tonight?"

"It is an effort to enlist the astral plane to uncover the murderer of the royal counsellor, Judge Andrew Akua."

"Tell me if I am wrong, sir. Did not your Mr. Bierce assure me that this was a police matter and he had nothing to do with it?"

"I do remember some conversation on the subject."

"Akua was as disputatious an old lobster as it has ever been my misfortune to encounter," Underwood said. "Tell me, who *cares*?"

"I understand that a justice of the California Supreme

Court cares, who was a friend of Judge Akua's at Harvard. He has spurred Captain Pusey's efforts."

"Ah!" he said. He squinted across the room at Bierce, who was now in conversation with Pusey and the patrolman.

"High opinion of himself, Bierce," he said.

"Yes, sir," I said.

The dark-faced assistant was placing chairs in a semicircle facing the cabinet.

Silas Underwood was watching his son. Head up, shoulders squared, Aaron looked younger as he crossed the parquet to Haunani, his smile matching hers, her two hands raised to touch his raised hands. I could almost feel whatever flash of electricity passed between those meeting hands.

The gratifying grate of sound I heard was Silas Underwood grinding his yellow old teeth.

The light was dimmer still, with it a sense of anticipation, maybe dread. Underwood had moved to corral his son, so I went to join Haunani. We sat on the window seat together in the gathering darkness.

Her hands gripped mine in her lap. I could feel the warmth of her coursing through my hand, my wrists, my arms, which Aaron must also have felt. "He has always cared for me," she said in a low voice. "And I have realized I have always cared for him."

"He is too old for you," I said, and knew it was cruel to say it.

"Only twenty-one years," she said, smiling. "It is what the feminist ladies call the material necessity, Tom."

The material necessity was the requirement that a lady marry someone who would support her wardrobe in the style to which she was accustomed.

When I tried to consider my feelings rationally I couldn't

perceive where my anger was directed, as though, sighting along a rifle barrel, all I could see of my target was hot pink mist.

"They have been so generous to me," Haunani continued, gripping my hands. "I was raised as a member of the family. A generation younger than Aaron, and half a generation older than Walter. I have known Cousin Aaron all my life."

"Yes," I said.

"A young man may be free to marry for love, Tom," she went on. "A young woman is not so free. Some day it may be that a single woman can say yes because that is her desire, as a married woman may say no because it is not her desire. But that is not yet.

"I have said yes to you because I wanted to say yes, Tom," she said.

I turned my face down. I shame.

I said I hoped she would be very happy. "I will never forget you," I said.

She rose. Her knuckles were white where she gripped the fabric of her skirt swinging away from me. That sweet angle of her cheek and chin in profile would stay with me always.

She whispered something in Hawaiian, like a blessing, and left me.

Men had seated themselves in the chairs before the cabinet, and now in the semidarkness Mrs. Hansen made her way to her closet and installed herself upon the stool there, hands on the table. Her assistant stood by the decorated box, fingers knitted together before him. Bierce beckoned.

I seated myself beside him. Haunani and Aaron sat together, with Walter's wheeled chair drawn up beside her. Charles Perry sat with Berowne, Regan with Silas Underwood, Pusey with the big patrolman, Mammy Pleasant apart, with her handbasket in her lap. Darkness closed down.

Rose Hansen perched on her stool with her hands flattened on the table, her face turned down. There was no saucer of milk this time. All around me intent profiles watched her. I thought this long wait cleverly devised.

"Miles?" Mrs. Hansen said in a low voice, at last.

There was a gasp.

The table rose, tilting, pushing Mrs. Hansen's hands upward until the tabletop was level with her chin. It wavered there a long moment before slowly descending, halting with its three legs two inches above the floor. Then it came to rest.

"Miles?"

A hoarse, wordless response raised the hairs at the back of my neck.

"Miles?"

"I AM HERE."

Mrs. Hansen said in a conversational tone, "A spirit has passed over, Miles. He was a respected man, a Hawaiian man, a judge, a counsellor to the Hawaiian king, a much-loved man. There was violence. Can this spirit be contacted? Will you seek him on the other side?"

There was another pause. I had to think to relax my clenched fists.

"THE SPIRIT IS HERE."

There was a gasp, and immediately another.

A ghostly face, turned up toward Mrs. Hansen's, floated before her, flat as a platter, eyes, nose, lips, in a greenish light. It was a manifestation.

"Will you enquire how he came to pass over?"

The conversational silence again.

"The guilty person is here," Mrs. Hansen commented.

And now Miles spoke, not from her lips, which did not move, nor from the lips of the manifestation; slow, slightly harsh, slightly British:

"TWO BROTHERS AND A SISTER. THE SISTER HAS A LOVER WHO CANNOT BE ACCEPTED BECAUSE OF THE COLOR OF HIS SKIN. SHE CARRIES HIS CHILD. THE BROTH-ERS CONSPIRE TO KILL THE LOVER. THE SISTER KNOWS IT WAS DONE. HER HEART IS BROKEN. THE CHILD OF MISCE-GENATION IS BORN. THE MOTHER WASTES AWAY IN HER GRIEF."

The words came in a flat and uninflected manner, each word a separate sound, the sentences unconnected, a sense of doom spoken. But Mrs. Hansen's lips had not moved. I remembered the photograph that Haunani had showed me, of her father, her uncle, her aunt, and Daniel Akua.

Who must be her father, then.

I could hear the shaky suspiration of breath around me, as though this little band of auditors breathed in perfect synchrony.

Miles's voice continued: "THE FATHER GRIEVES FOR HIS DEAD SON. HE IS A CHRISTIAN MAN. HIS CHRISTIAN GOD TELLS HIM HE MUST FORGIVE. HIS LIFE IS ONE OF TRYING TO UNDERSTAND AND FORGIVE. THE YEARS PASS. THE ONE BROTHER DIES. THE CHILD BECOMES A BEAUTIFUL YOUNG WOMAN. THE OTHER BROTHER HAS GRAND PROSPECTS. HE MUST PROTECT THOSE PROSPECTS. BUT THE OLD FATHER DISCOVERS WHAT HAS HAPPENED. THE DISCOVERY THREATENS THE BROTHER OF THE GRAND PROSPECTS. HIS CRIME IS TO BE REVEALED. HE—"

"Stop!" a voice said, and Miles stopped.

Haunani was standing, quivering like a knife plunged into a plank.

"Light!" Bierce said.

The manifestation disappeared with illumination. Mrs. Hansen slumped over her table. The lights revealed Edward Berowne also on his feet. Others rose, some remaining seated.

"That is the solution to Miss Brown's patrimony," Bierce said, as though we might not have understood. "Judge Akua's son was her father, the Browns' sister her mother."

Haunani stood facing Edward Berowne with a face contorted with grief and fury.

"Uncle, is it true?"

"My dear, Amb-b-brose has contrived this contemptible business for reasons I cannot imagine. Amb-b-brose, what the devil are you after?"

"Your guilt, Edward."

"You cannot p-p-prove anything!"

"I can prove everything!" Bierce said.

"You killed Andrew Akua!" Haunani cried. "And my father!"

"William killed your father," Berowne said.

She started toward him, fierce-faced, and I moved to intercept her. For the last time I held her warm body and her strong arms in my arms, and trapped in my hands the fists with which she would have assaulted the murderer her uncle.

"Uncle!" Haunani cried.

"Now you know who you are!" I whispered to her. *"Now you know!"*

Her arms went slack and she slumped against me. I turned her gently to face Aaron Underwood, who had come up. She moved to him.

Bierce was pointing a long arm at the East Indian attendant, who stood at attention beside the decorated equipment box.

"That man is the criminal Reuben Slaney! Do your duty, Captain!"

Mrs. Hansen cried out hoarsely. The tall patrolman surged

to his feet and started toward her assistant, who managed to push a chair in front of him. He fell over it, shaking the floor.

In one lithe motion Slaney spun around and loped out the far door.

When he had disentangled himself, the red-faced patrolman lumbered after him.

CHAPTER 31

TENACITY, n. A certain quality of the human hand in its relation to the coin of the realm. It attains its highest development in the hand of authority and is considered a serviceable equipment for a career in politics.
— *The Devil's Dictionary*

TUESDAY, JANUARY 27, 1891

"The movement of the table is a simple matter," Bierce said to those of us who remained: Pusey; Perry; Regan; Silas Underwood; Mammy Pleasant, seated alone near Mrs. Hansen's cabinet; Edward Berowne; and me. Aaron Underwood had removed Haunani in her grief to another part of the house, Walter had been wheeled away by Mrs. Mulberry.

It was very like Bierce to lecture us on the subject of Rose Hansen's manipulations while Berowne still stood on the far side of the room with a stone face of denial.

The tall patrolman, who had returned unsuccessful from his pursuit of Reuben Slaney, stood beside him. The Reverend Prout had pulled up a chair on the other side of Berowne. Regan stood with his back to them.

Beyond the cabinet, Mrs. Hansen reclined on the window seat, her waxen face pointed to the ceiling and hands folded on her chest like a dead saint's. The parlor blazed and hissed with gaslight.

"There is a tack in the tabletop with a gap of a sixteenth of an inch below the head," Bierce went on. "Mrs. Hansen wears a ring with a corresponding slot cut into it. When she slides the slot in her ring over the head of the tack a connection is made that allows her to raise the table. Although it appears to be rising against her hand."

"Hocus-pocus!" Pusey said.

Mrs. Hansen ignored them, setting her jaw.

Silas Underwood sat watching her, hunched in his chair with his long arms dangling between his legs.

"You claimed my wife was not on that train," Charley Perry said to Captain Pusey.

Pusey nodded.

"May I ask—"

"Let us hear Mr. Bierce out, if you please, Mr. Perry."

"You have betrayed me, Ambrose!" Mrs. Hansen cried out suddenly, in a cracking voice.

"I have exposed your exploiter."

"I trusted you!"

"He is a criminal!"

She pursed her lips and squeezed her eyes more tightly closed.

"You must believe the worst of that fellow, Missus," Captain Pusey said. He did not, however, appear much disturbed that Slaney had not been recaptured.

Mrs. Hansen sniffed powerfully.

"The main mechanism here is this magician's box called a Pepper's Ghost," Bierce went on. "I presume one would call it a Pepper's Ghost *Box*. It projects an image in a beam of light. Would you bring it here, Tom?"

I carried the heavy, decorated box over to the table. There was a door on the top, and a smaller door on the side, whose flap hung open, revealing a lens surrounded by a knurled brass ring. Bierce opened the top to show a black-painted interior, a slanting plate of glass carrying a transparency, and a dead candle in a holder.

"With the light of the candle behind it, the lens will project the image onto the glass to a previously calculated distance and alignment."

He applied a lighted match to the innards of the box. Immediately the green, flattened face appeared afloat in the atmosphere beyond the cabinet, hardly visible now in the concentration of light.

"This is a trick that mediums use to produce manifestations. It is commonly employed. It figured in a fraud that was discovered in Buffalo, which led to an end of Mrs. Hansen's career as a medium, and to Slaney's arrest and imprisonment for confidence crimes. Slaney has entered and reentered Mrs. Hansen's life like a bad penny. When I insisted on this trick in order to expose Edward Berowne, I was certain that she would get in touch with her former assistant for his expert manipulations. She did so."

"Conniver!" Mrs. Hansen said.

Bierce's face twitched with a complicated expression which I thought showed irritation that no one had flattered him for his cleverness of killing two bad pennies with one stone. There was a third to go.

Bierce removed a transparency from the slanted glass in the box, and substituted a sheet of paper for it. He made some adjustment with the lens and the siting of the box itself. Dim lines and figures appeared on the wall beside the fireplace. It was the drawing Bierce had made from the Jongleurs original, which Captain Pusey had retained. I could just make out the handwritten "Jongleurs," EC–4, PO–8, the signalling arms of the semaphore. The words "many pastries" were barely legible.

"Confirm this fact, Edward," Bierce said. "In the past you employed a rather well-known cook . . . who was proud of his cakes, pies, Sally Lunn?"

Berowne made no response.

"I had hoped to save you embarrassment," Bierce said. "I will proceed to reveal your persecutor."

Berowne stared at the letters and figures with a set jaw. He dampened his lips with his tongue.

Mrs. Hansen sat upright and pushed at her hair, which had become flattened on one side. Her pale, pretty-frog's face was expressionless as she gazed above the cabinet at this new manifestation.

Bierce said, "Jongleurs was the name of the plantation on the Island of Maui owned by the brothers Brown. It referred to poetical and personal activities that were a part of the life there. The first Jongleurs referred to young people at play. Young Daniel Akua, son of the royal counsellor who was then a minister to England and in England at this time, fell in love with the Brown brothers' sister Julia. She became with child by him. A miscegenous union was intolerable to Edward and his older brother William, and an accident was contrived in which the lover was drowned.

"The sister gave birth to the half-breed child. She herself died shortly thereafter.

"Judge Akua, although he did not then know all that had happened, was able to forgive. He said as much to Tom Redmond and to me. However, another person in this room, who knew the facts, when he thought he was on his deathbed, confessed them to Judge Akua. Judge Akua was then prepared to make a public accusation, and reveal her actual parentage to

Miss Haunani Brown, who had been kept in darkness all her life until this moment. This public disclosure was intolerable to the one who would suffer from it."

I glanced at Chaplain Prout, whose head was bowed in his chair, hands covering his face.

"Some of this is speculation, you understand," Bierce went on. "The original of this spectral menu, which you see illuminated by the light from the box, was printed on the hand press upon which poems were often printed. I believe it was presented by Lydia Kukui, the king's handmaiden, to Judge Akua. She had obtained it from her friend the fire marshal at the Palace Hotel, who knew of the history of Engine Company Number Four.

"You see the word Jongleurs on this menu. This second Jongleurs association was a very different one. There is a kind of friendship, known as Greek, which Oscar Wilde has recently professed for certain young men of his acquaintance. An older man shares his wisdom and experience with a younger man, or men, who revere the older in return. This kind of Greek friendship was the idea of the second Jongleurs.

"A group of young men from Engine Company Number Four congregated at a house on Telegraph Hill, where they were given their fill of cakes and drink, and had social intercourse in the Greek manner I have described. I have no means of knowing what else transpired among them.

"The revelation of the recurrence was deeply disturbing to Judge Akua who, as I say, had been trying to forgive and forget.

"The EC–4 characters are intertwined with the PO–8, poeate, for poet, which stands for Edward Berowne. This was derived humorously from the signature on a well-known poem of the outlaw Black Bart. The semaphore arms above them, which at first it was thought must refer to some type of vessel, actually only symbolize Edward's cottage on Telegraph Hill where meetings were held, *beneath* those semaphore arms."

"This is *all* b-b-barefaced speculation!" Berowne spat out.

Bierce bowed to him, and indicated Captain Pusey.

"Captain Pusey was well aware of it."

"You *devil*!" Berowne cried in a stifled voice. "You assured me——"

Pusey pushed a flattened hand at him to silence him.

"Captain Pusey has collected blackmail for many years," Bierce said. "How many years, Edward?"

Berowne stood silent.

"That is a damned lie!" Pusey burst out.

"It is a damned truth, and as such it will appear in 'Prattle' on Sunday, Captain!"

And he continued: "Mrs. Pleasant was also aware of the activities of Edward Berowne and the group of young firemen who partook of his hospitality. The Jongleurs were not as secret as they wished to be, is that not true, Mrs. Pleasant?"

"That is so, Mr. Bierce," she said in her harsh voice. "Some of those fellows made jokes about Mr. Berowne while they accepted his hospitality, but none of them wanted it known what they were doing. There were menu cards like that printed. Some people knew of it."

The enigmatic letters and numbers trembled on the wall.

"In the present state of his honors, his prospects and expectations, Edward could not afford to have the existence of this peculiar club made public," Bierce went on. "Nor of the fact that miscegenation and murder had taken place on the Island of Maui twenty-one years ago——"

"Enough!" Berowne said hoarsely. "I do not wish to hear any more of this, Amb-b-brose!" He stood with his shoulders back in a defiant stance, the center of attention who had of late demanded to be that, although his honors and expectations lay in ruins around him. It was as though the others here were embarrassed to speak to him, or even to look at him in the revelation of his motivations and his secrets.

Bierce bent to blow out the candle, and the letters and figures on the wall disappeared.

"Damned blackguard!" Pusey said, sunken in his chair.

"Conniver!" Rose Hansen said again.

"I have rid your life of an incubus that preyed upon you, my dear!"

"Calm yourself, madam!" Mr. Regan said. "Mr. Bierce has only done what had to be done."

"Men always do what has to be done, and always it is at a woman's expense!"

"Mrs. Hansen has the grievances of a divorced woman," Bierce said.

"Divorce laws were meant to free women from abusive husbands," Mrs. Hansen said. "They are themselves another abuse. And now I have been abused again."

She swiped a hand at the corner of her lips, where moisture glistened.

It was interesting to me that everyone contrived to ignore Edward Berowne in his guilt, as though the ignoring was to be a part of his punishment. He blinked at those around him with his big naked face red with humiliation.

"Edward Berowne beat Judge Akua's head in with a poker," I said. It was as though I felt impelled to bring him back to the foreground where he so wished to be.

High-shouldered and big-bellied, his white fists clenched into knots, he glared at me. No one else met my eyes.

Silas moved over to seat himself facing Rose Hansen. The ugly grin was back on his face.

"My old friend Commodore Vanderbilt employed a medium to advise him in financial matters," he said.

"Yes, Tenny C. Claflin," Mrs. Hansen replied. "I have shared a platform with her. She is a handsome, intelligent, and lively young woman."

"Served as more than his advisor, as I understand it."

"I am aware of that rumor, sir."

"Tell me, madam, has your spirit guide been able to assist you with prognostications about the future? Financially, I mean."

"Sometimes when I have consulted Miles he has been able to divulge what is to come," she said. "It is a matter of knowing the proper questions to ask."

"Queen Liliuokalani uses a medium in the formulation of her policies, as is well known," Perry said. He stood with his back to Edward Berowne.

Barley bustled out of the depths of the house with a bottle of medicine and a teaspoon. "Time for a little restorative, Mr. Underwood!" He measured purple liquid into the spoon and proffered it to Silas Underwood, who imbibed it with a birdlike swell of his lips.

"Thank you, Barley."

The patrolman lumbered over to the Edward Berowne. "I believe Mr. Bierce has made his case, sir."

"Almighty God B-B-Bierce!" Berowne said hoarsely.

Pusey had not moved, but finally he rose from his chair, pale-faced, and, with the patrolman, escorted Berowne from the room.

Bierce had made his triple play.

———

But in a hack rattling away from Aaron Underwood's mansion, beside me in the darkness, he said, "I see that you and I must take the advice of Aristotle, that pleasures should be considered as they depart, not as they come."

He referred to Rose Hansen, and to Haunani Brown.

I said, "How did you figure Edward Berowne?"

"My old principle: why now?" he said, settling back in the tufted leather seat. "Judge Akua had just come to town. There was his old acquaintance with Edward on Maui. There was the tragedy of the judge's son, there were the continuing mysteries about your young lady's parentage, and there were Southern attitudes about the color of skin. There was the matter of the Jongleurs. And there was the all-important fact that Edward had fame and fortune to lose. Everything pointed to him."

After a time he said sourly, "One is compelled to view one's performance with an appraising eye. I believe I overstepped myself." He sighed, and said, "My urge for melodrama has given Slaney temporary freedom."

I was feeling downcast myself, an eye on a future whose horizon was crowded with the banked clouds of loneliness.

"I sought to perform what I considered a great favor for Rose Hansen," Bierce continued. His voice was chilly. "She has been a Trilby to that fellow's Svengali. Why can she not realize it? He ruined her in Buffalo. He would have used her shamelessly in the Argentine. Rose complains of her abuse. What did she think was in store for her and Miss Best? Slaney is totally unprincipled."

"Pusey will run him down," I said.

"I don't believe we can expect much of Pusey in the future," he said with satisfaction.

"You have the admiration of tonight's assembled, all but three," I said. "Miss Brown will be exceedingly grateful."

"As you are aware, not so with Mrs. Hansen." He sighed.

Nor Captain Pusey.

I was ashamedly pleased that Bierce had not only overstepped himself in his cleverness, but had had to admit it.

"Your large young lady has found her true niche," he said

with an edge to his voice, as though he knew that I had been thinking disloyal thoughts.

"So it appears," I said.

"I think I will shed the ties of city pent," he went on, after a silence. "I hanker for the scent of pines, the calm of the countryside. I will remove myself from these busy marts of men to the healthier air of the country."

"Give up 'Prattle'? "

"Oh, no, no, no, no! Give up the one grand enterprise of my existence?" His voice was jagged with sarcasm. "The country, Tom! Sunol, Auburn, Calistoga! The scent of pines, the wisdom of simple country folk, the feel of grand space!

"Where the woodbine twineth," he said. "And the whang-doodle whineth."

———

When I was let off at Sacramento Street, the dark cloud I had anticipated enveloped me. I bought a bouquet of violets from the corner flower stand to take to my next-door neighbor.

She opened the door wide at my knock, and, regarding my bouquet, pressed her hands grandly to her bosom. She had not donned her wig but wore instead a kind of stocking cap pulled down on her forehead. In her frilly white wrapper she looked as big around as the steam engine of the *Haleakala*.

"Oh, I thank you, young sir! What is the occasion of these lovely blooms, may I ask?"

"They are in gratitude for the beautiful songs that I hear through my walls, which I have not heard lately."

"Ah!" She made the gesture to her vast bosom again. I had not realized how short she was. Her head nestled into her shoulders with no apparent neck.

She took the bouquet from me as though they were rare and exotic blossoms.

I asked her to take supper with me at Malvolio's in the

Montgomery Block. I would give her a good dinner at an expensive restaurant.

———

In the warm bustle of Malvolio's, amongst the bowing waiters in their black suitings and black bow ties, the white napery, glittering silverware, the guests in their finery, Signora Sotopietro was splendid in her voluminous gray velvet gown with the rose-embroidered shawl over her shoulders, my violets pinned to her bosom, and her wig slightly crooked. She leaned on my arm with laboring steps as we were ushered to a table by the Montgomery Street window.

A crusty loaf of bread was brought, butter, cut-glass bowls of olives, celery, radishes, and tiny hot pickles. Elsewhere steaming platters of linguines and taglierinis were borne between the tables.

I ordered champagne.

At every favor Signora Sotopietro bridled and clucked, before accepting it as her due.

Minestrone was brought in a white cauldron, fussed over, uncovered, served with a porcelain dipper. My guest regarded the process with her hands pressed to her bosom in her characteristic pose.

Salads were followed by a huge platter of tagliarini, with a tomato sauce thickened with chopped garlic, mushrooms and bits of bacon. She was more adept than I at twisting the strands of pasta with the fork grasped in the palm of her hand, enthusiastically raising her fat arms in the exercise.

The tagliarini, washed down with Valpolicella, was followed by a platter of veal scallopini, followed by glass cups of spumoni. Signora Sotopietro dissolved a spoonful of ice cream in her coffee, while I poured coffee on my spumoni, inciting her comments and chuckles.

Conversation consisted of tales of grand triumphs on the opera stages in Milan, Paris, New York and San Francisco.

I watched a week's salary disappear down her golden throat.

Glasses of red-glowing port arrived at the table, unordered. They were followed by Malvolio himself, tall and whip-thin, with a deeply lined old face like his cut-glass bowls, bowing to Signora Sotopietro.

"*Madama diva!*" he addressed her, with a dramatic bow. "Will you not favor us with an aria? All would be grateful." He gestured. "My little *ristorante* would be so honored. I would be honored!"

Sweeping bows, flourishes of a linen napkin as white as skim milk. Signora Sotopietro did not have to be urged twice. She rose to general applause, including my own. Four waiters stood in a line alongside the kitchen door battering their palms together.

At first the fact that she was standing might not have been obvious, she was so short, so stout with her thick bare arms, and her hands placed to her bosom. She had straightened her wig. She bobbed her head to the applause, to the bravos.

That young and vibrant voice whispered from her lips. She raised her chin higher, the volume increased. Her voice soared. The sweetness increased with the volume.

It was, of course, "Caro Nome."

Her voice did not dissolve into coughing. She finished her aria to the room crackling with the applause of the happy guests of Malvolio, who had witnessed an event of their lives.

I listened to Gilda's sad song with the familiar tears scratching at my eyes, but this time, at last, they did not overflow.

EPILOGUE

STORY, n. A narrative, commonly untrue. The truth of the stories here following has, however, not been successfully impeached.
  — The Devil's Dictionary

1

The *Examiner* for February 16 brought the news from Honolulu of the reception of the dead king by his subjects.

The *Charleston* required six days for the crossing, and laid off Oahu for the night so that the cruiser could be draped in black for its arrival in Honolulu Harbor, like an ill-omened ship out of Greek myth:

GRIEF IN HAWAII.

MERRIMENT CHANGED IN AN INSTANT TO MOURNING BY THE APPARITION OF DEATH.

The Islanders Could Not at First Comprehend the Charleston's Sad Mission.

Impressive Demonstration Over the Body of the
Late Monarch Kalakaua.

*The Widowed Queen
Rends Her Garments in a
Paroxysm of Anguish.*

THE SCENES GRAPHICALLY DESCRIBED.

Belamy had described, graphically, the anguish of King
Kalakaua's widow, Queen Kapiolani, in sentences Bierce
might have found excessive:

"The dowager queen has a frightful expression: eyes bloodshot,
cheeks furrowed with dark lines, mouth and lips drawn down as if by
paralysis—the general look of a madwoman. Only an hour before she
had rent her garments in twain and torn them from her body; but now
clothed in a black gown she enters on the arm of Prime Minister
Cummins. She does not walk erect, but bends toward the ground,
swaying this way and that, swinging her head toward the people on
either side with the ghastly smile of hysteria. The people cry out and
she answers them fiercely.

Her eyes are gleaming now, and, dragging her hand from Cummins, she totters toward the king's bier, casting herself at the foot of
the coffin and clasping it between her outstretched arms. . . ."

Gee-whiz writing for the *Examiner*'s front page!

2

At his trial Berowne was always nattily dressed and well-
groomed, thinning hair parted perfectly on the dome of his
head, waistcoat buttoned over his belly, trousers well pressed,

shoes shined to a starlike gleam, a cheerful countenance rising above his high collar. He maintained his innocence. His lawyer was James Faulks, very society sure of himself, with dundreary whiskers and large dramatic gestures. But the case did not go well. When it became evident that it was lost, Edward Berowne hanged himself in his cell with his belt.

3

Ambrose Bierce took the train into San Francisco from Sunol, where he was rusticating after an attack of asthma, and where he had spent an unpleasant day with the young California novelist Gertrude Atherton, to testify at the trial.

4

Captain Pusey was not prosecuted after he was denounced by Bierce in "Prattle." He took an extended leave of absence, purportedly to visit relatives in England, and returned to San Francisco to occupy his old post when the Union Labor Party came to power.

5

Haunani and Aaron Underwood were married in Honolulu, thirteen months after the death of the first Mrs. Underwood. Haunani promptly produced a half-brother for Walter, John Daniel, of whom I am the godfather. After Silas's death Haunani and Aaron, Walter and John Daniel returned to Honolulu to the big house, *Hale Nuuanu*. A year later she had a second child, a girl, Catherine. I never saw her again after the christening of John Daniel, but learned that, over the years in Honolulu, she had gained considerable weight, and became, in someone's phrase, "majestic."

6

Rose Blessing Hansen resided with old Silas Underwood in his half-unfinished or half-finished palace on his immense acreage on the Island of Maui until his death, upon which, as I heard of it, she was left well provided for. She then disappeared from the islands, and neither Bierce nor I heard of her whereabouts thereafter.

Bierce was convinced that those whereabouts may well have included Reuben Slaney, who was never apprehended.

7

Princess Leileiha was sent to the leper colony on Molokai. She was accompanied by Alexander Honomoku, who cared for her until her death twelve years later. He never contracted the disease.

8

Liliuokalani was not queen of Hawaii for long. The haole merchants took arms and declared a republic. The U.S. minister, John L. Stevens, did not hesitate to order ashore the bluejackets of the USS *Boston*, 162 strong, armed with rifles and double ammunition belts, purportedly to safeguard American nationals. The queen had no choice but to capitulate.

———

Annexation was argued in Honolulu and Washington.

The Reverend Sereno Bishop, a Honolulu minister and the Hawaiian correspondent for the United Press, set to work to blacken the queen's reputation. Liliuokalani was declared to have been under the influence of *kahunas*, native sorcerers and her notorious medium. She had sacrificed to the goddess Pele and encouraged the dancing of the lascivious native dance, the hula. She and her brother Kalakaua were not even true royalty, but the offspring of a chiefess of low rank and her paramour, a Negro bootblack named John Blossom.

9

And westward the course of empire made its way. In the Spanish-American War, to pursue the conquest of the Philippines, the navy required a coaling station midway to the mainland United States, and Pearl Harbor was a necessity.

Hawaii became a territory of the United States of America in 1898.

For more from Oakley Hall, look for the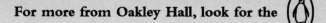

Ambrose Bierce and the Queen of Spades

Turn-of-the-century San Francisco's celebrated newspaperman and misanthrope, Ambrose Bierce, makes his detective debut in this savvy historical thriller. When the Morton Street Slasher murders prostitutes near Union Square, he marks each victim with a playing card. Ambrose immediately suspects his sworn enemies, the corrupt Southern Pacific Railway tycoons. With the aid of his young protégé, Tom Redmond, Ambrose "Bitter" Bierce sets out to uncover the sordid mystery, and unravels a sinister web of corruption in this suspenseful and smart detective novel.   *ISBN 0-14-028860-0*

"If you like historical mysteries with some literary meat on their bones, Oakley Hall's *Ambrose Bierce and the Queen of Spades* should hit the spot. The veteran novelist conjures up a wonderfully yeasty San Francisco . . . the dialogue and detail are sung with perfect pitch."   —*Chicago Tribune*

"Like Henry James and Mark Twain, Oakley Hall is a master craftsman of the story."   —Amy Tan

"Oakley Hall is a novelist who never seems to make a wrong move. . . . He is a writer to read again and again."
           —Richard Ford

"I loved this new mystery, with Oakley Hall's unique brand of riveting storytelling, historical scholarship, parody, suspense, and fun."   —Diane Johnson

"Superlative entertainment . . . a beautifully paced thriller that must have Wilkie Collins spinning in his grave with envy."
           —*Kirkus Reviews*